New York Orphan

Orphan

Rosemary J. Kind

Printed in the United Kingdom

First Printing, 2017 Alfie Dog Limited

The author can be contacted at: rjkind@alfiedog.com

Cover image: Katie Stewart, Magic Owl Design, http://www.magicowldesign.com/

Cover image of Peck Slip - Art and Picture Collection, The New York Public Library. "Peck Slip, N.Y., 1850." *The New York Public Library Digital Collections*. 1857. http://digitalcollections.nypl.org/items/510d47e0-cd9e-a3d9-e040-e00a18064a99

ISBN 978-1-909894-35-8

Published by
Alfie Dog Limited
Schilde Lodge, Tholthorpe,
North Yorkshire, YO61 1SN
Tel: 0207 193 33 90

DEDICATION

This book is dedicated to the hundreds of thousands of children, then and now, living on the streets and hoping for a better tomorrow.

Other books by Rosemary J. Kind

Alfie's Diary

Alfie's Woods

From Story Idea to Reader

Lovers Take up Less Space

Pet Dogs Democratic Party Manifesto

Poems for Life

The Appearance of Truth

The Lifetracer

ACKNOWLEDGMENTS

This book would not have happened without the help of a number of people. First and foremost I need to thank Rev. Ruth Duck for mentioning Charles Loring Brace and the Orphan Trains and setting the whole process in motion. I can only apologise that I didn't listen to another word you said after that, because I was too busy plotting a story that took shape before my eyes.

My research would have been incomplete without the help of: Amanda Wahlmeier, former curator of the Orphan Train Museum in Concordia; John Shontz, Project Coordinator, Orphan Train Rail; Gerard Taylor Wallace, for treading the streets of New York with me and bringing them to life; Steve Areseneau of the Dowagiac Museum and Connie Black of Kusciusko History.

I am indebted to a wonderful panel of beta readers for their encouragement, questions and corrections: Henry Mitchell, Lori Mohr, Roger Noons, Brenda Kind and David Cairns. Also my thanks to my writing buddies, without whom my writing would be much the poorer: Patsy, Suzy, Sheila and Lynne.

Thanks go to Dr Sheila Glaseby for her proofreading of the final book and her far greater knowledge as to which of my over-enthusiastic use of commas to remove, and to Katie Stewart, of Magic Owl Designs, who has brought the story to life in the cover far better than I could ever have dreamed of. Thanks to Adrienne Mansfield for helping me with marketing plans and being an ever-present support and sounding-board.

Finally and particularly to Alan Kind and Chris Platt, not only for your beta reading but for your overwhelming belief and support in this book – thank you.

INTRODUCTION

Whilst this novel is a work of fiction, and all the characters have been invented purely for the story, it is based heavily on facts. In certain places extensive licence has had to be taken and the dates of some of the songs noted are unknown and may have been slightly later than the period. In the light of the humanitarian crisis resulting from millions of immigrants seeking refuge from war and famine in Europe, the Orphan Train Movement, started by Charles Loring Brace, took tens of thousands of children off the streets of New York and relocated them into families across America.

The adoptees were largely expected to work on farms, with the understanding that they should receive schooling in the winter. Some put the number of children as high as 200,000 over the course of the programme, which lasted well into the early 20th century and covered other East Coast cities as well as New York. For many, the programme turned out to be a wonderful opportunity, whilst for others it brought little more than slavery. The train journey that Tom and Daniel take on leaving New York is based on accounts of that first train from New York, although again all the characters have been changed and my account is a fictional one.

If you read the early chapters and doubt that life could have been as grim as that for them on the streets, then I regret to tell you it most certainly was, and much research has gone into trying to make their lives authentic. There are incredibly strong parallels to the current migrant crisis, and at that time America absorbed millions of incoming European migrants.

I hope you enjoy reading this book as much as I have enjoyed writing it. I have included at the back the many works of reference referred to, and they are worthy of a closer look.

NOTE:
The characters are all fictitious and any resemblance they may have to children who rode the Orphan Trains and the families they were placed with is entirely coincidental. This book is not intended to suggest that the events portrayed happened to any of the children who rode the trains which are alluded to, or with the families with whom they were placed.

PROLOGUE

"And then I prayed I yet might see
our fetters rent in twain,
and Ireland long a province,
be a nation once again."
Thomas Davis from about 1840

"That ain't how ya do it." Tom snatched the blade away from Daniel's trembling, grubby white hand. Even in the oppressive shadow of the alley, amongst the putrid remains of carcasses waiting for their bones to be picked clean and boiled, the edge of the metal caught the light. During an hour of sweat and toil, each boy had taken his turn to break through the dullness of the blunted knife, trying to sharpen it against the brickwork of the warehouse tenement. The outer edge of the blade remained marked with the murky pattern of pig, dog and human blood. The rich, red flow dried much the same, once it left a lifeless body.

Tom took rough hold of his own forearm. His penetrating green eyes caught Daniel's gaze and urged him to look down. With his lips clenched, in one sweeping movement, Tom dragged the blade hard across his tautened skin, drawing blood at the first skim. "See."

Daniel took the heavy-handled knife and, biting his bottom lip, with his eyes screwed tight, he plucked at his arm, a staccato tune of timidity.

3

Tom shook his mane of fiery red hair and laughed. "Don't be so soft. You're no better than Molly would be. If you don't hurry up I'll have to do mine again."

Daniel looked into his friend's sallow face, searching each freckle for the strength and courage to match his actions. Then he took a deep breath and scored his arm. A trickle of blood flowed across the blade into the dirt. He broke into a grin as he wiped away a tear with the back of his other hand and held his arm out to Tom. They linked forearms, the blood running together onto their ragged, stained clothing.

"Forever, blood brothers," said Tom, clasping Daniel's hand in his.

Daniel sniffed. His shaky voice cracked as he echoed, "Forever, blood brothers." Then, as Tom released his hand, Daniel dragged his tatty sleeve across his face, sniffing into the harsh material.

Tom slid the knife back down the inside of his boot. "Best be getting back to work then."

Daniel shrugged as he had seen his own father do in times of high emotion.

"You ought to cover your arm before you start singing. Nice folks ain't going to give money to a child who don't look so angelic." Tom was ready for business without a moment's pause.

Daniel rolled the sleeves of his shirt to their full length, leaving the frayed ends to cover the congealing scar, and prepared himself to go out into the street and draw a crowd through his songs of home.

CHAPTER 1

Fare thee well my own true love
And farewell for a while.
I'm going away, but I'll come again
If I go ten thousand miles.
Traditional

Daniel Flynn looked around at the magnificent warehouses, grown tall around the dock. They must have been higher than the trees around Lough Leane, higher than he could have imagined until he saw them. Whilst they displayed a majesty all their own, they shared none of the sweet meadow smell. Daniel found the noise and bustle oppressive. He swallowed hard. He had no idea what to do. He was seven years old and arriving in a strange land, alone. He shuddered. He was used to the single-storey, tumbledown cottages scattered around the lanes, not these huge buildings of brick and timber, piled ramshackle as far as his eyes could see.

"You fetid lumps of bog rot. Go back to where you came from." A man in plaid trousers and a bright, well-tailored jacket, with an accent as alien as the buildings, hurled insults at the hundreds of starving Irish families descending from the ship.

Shoulders dropped, Daniel drew his rag-wrapped belongings closer to the tiny frame of his beleaguered body. He walked a few faltering steps before looking back at the open expanse of rigging against the cloudless sky. The view belied the cramped conditions he'd suffered below deck. Then, with his head bowed, he moved forward onto the quay. Through the gaps in the planking he could see excrement floating on the surface of the water, while the stench of rotting life filled the air. He was immune to the smell. Rot had dogged his life so far. You'd go a long way to find a worse odour than the fields of rotting potatoes, black-stalked and grey-slimed, decayed with blight, which marked the early years of his life. After that it was disease which filled the air. He thought setting sail for America would mean fresh sea air to breathe, but he reckoned without conditions on board ship. Seven weeks of waste, sea-sickness and death had left him wishing he were back amongst the yellow-flowered fields of Killarney, where he had loved to wander, escaping from the decay.

A dark-suited man with a neat-trimmed but extensive beard approached him. "Bread, soup and make sure your mammy and daddy vote for Kelly."

Daniel readily took the offered food, hoping his luck was starting to change.

"Move along, young man."

"Please, sir, I ain't got no mammy and daddy no more." Daniel looked up with pleading eyes into the kindly face, but the politician transferred his insincere benevolence to the next person coming off the boat, and the next, onward down the line of hungry, destitute countrymen from Cork and Kerry.

It wasn't supposed to be this way. He was accustomed to the hunger. God knew, he'd felt it long enough. He savoured the soup as he dipped the bread and drank the sops. He ate quickly, eyes darting around lest someone should take it from him.

Compared to the last few weeks, the food was fit for a king. He imagined his Uncle Seamus wagering that not many kings ventured onto the wharf. Uncle Seamus would have wagered on the date of his own wake, if he'd had anything left to wager with. For a moment Daniel almost smiled, until he remembered how far away his uncle was now.

They'd left the dockside of Cork a hopeful family, having journeyed from their native Killarney. 'Desperate to find a better life', that's what his da had said. 'A land of opportunity' was what the great Michael Flynn told his wife and son. Their landlord helped with the passage. He was a generous man whose land could no longer support them. 'Now don't you go forgetting the goodness of Mr O'Connor there, Daniel. Don't you go forgetting.' His da was insistent they show what gratitude they could, when so many of their neighbours were left to the mercy of the poor house, forced to give up what little land they had in their desperate need of alms.

With both his parents despatched to watery graves, New York was now an opportunity Daniel Flynn faced alone. Weakened by years of famine, his ma and da hadn't the strength to overcome seasickness and the diseases on board ship. Within five days of each other, they died, while he watched in helpless horror. First his mother and then his broken-hearted father, lost without his childhood sweetheart, were taken from him, leaving Daniel with no one to rely on but himself. Back home there'd have been family to take him in, but not here. It would have been a starving family, but it was family nonetheless. On board ship it was every man, woman and child for themselves, and with barely enough to feed their own families no one was going to give preference to someone else's boy.

He took a deep breath, blinking back the tears, and did the only thing he'd been able to sustain himself with over the last days and nights, singing the ballads of home that his father had sung. He sat on a wooden crate, closed his eyes and sang, imagining his da might be there to hear him and wishing it were so.

"By Kilmore's woody highland,
wandering dark and drear,
A voice of joy came o'er me,
more holy to mine ear..."

Daniel's nasal intonation mimicked his father to perfection, but he possessed no more idea of where Kilmore was than of the layout of New York. As he sang the beautiful words of his homeland, he clung to his small bundle of belongings, barely aware of the crowd gathering around him or the halfpennies and pennies being thrown at his feet. For a few precious moments Daniel could believe he was back in Ireland with his family, with his father singing and his Uncle Patrick's fingers dancing their own jig across the strings of his fiddle.

It was only when the suited figure's voice broke over the music to move the crowd along that Daniel once more became aware of his surroundings and of a scruffy figure, lanky for his young age, scooping up the coins in front of him. Daniel sized him up; probably a year or two more than he was, but with a streetwise edge which to Daniel made him seem older.

"Ain't you going to stop me? I'm easy to spot with this mop." The boy laughed, pointing to his flame-red corkscrew curls, defying control under his weather-beaten hat.

"Stop you what?" Daniel asked, wide-eyed.

"Nicking your money."

"What money? I don't have any money."

"You're good, you are. 'What money? I don't have any money.' I likes that. Folks liked your singing. I guess it reminded them of home. What others do you know?"

"All the ones me da used to sing."

"I'm Tom," said the boy, holding the coins out in his hand to Daniel, "and these I believe are yours."

Daniel blinked, taking the coins from Tom's hand and looking at their strangeness. He closed his fist around the money and held tight. "Tom?"

"Thomas H. Reilly, pickpocket extraordinaire, at your service." Tom stood, took a sweeping bow and then opened his hand to reveal a pocket watch, a locket and a pair of gold cufflinks. "That little crowd you drew proved quite good pickings. It don't cost me much to let you have the coins they threw. We should do it again sometime, maybe not on the waterfront where we're likely to be seen, though. Where are you staying?"

Daniel bit his lip and shrugged. "I dunno. I don't rightly know anything, except I'm Daniel Flynn from Killarney." He smiled as he thrust his hand out to shake Tom's hand and waited while Tom put his treasure store back into his trouser pocket before he could reciprocate. A feeling of relief flooded through Daniel; for the first time in three weeks he didn't feel completely alone.

"You'd best come with me," Tom said, offering to take Daniel's bundle.

"It's fine." Daniel clutched his belongings.

"I ain't going to nick it. Anyways, come and meet me ma. Where we live, it ain't much, but it's a roof. Though you gets wet when it rains. It's not as bad as some." He walked on across the cobbled street. "That there's Ol' Tinker. He's one from the old country. He ain't so bad."

Tom grabbed Daniel's arm and pulled him behind a barrel at the front of an alleyway. He pointed to a man with a curled moustache, dressed well in bright suiting and carrying a cane. "We owes him," he whispered. "He's our landlord, or leastways the one who collects the rent. May as well be the same thing for the difference it makes to us. If Ma says you can stay, maybe them coins could help us pay."

Daniel stared at the man passing the alley, his head held high, a handkerchief clasped over his nose with his left hand, leaving the extensive grey whiskers curling out at the side. Daniel nodded to Tom, holding out the coins whose value meant little without the security of a family.

"Not yet. We'll talk to Ma." They moved away from the barrel and onwards along Pearl Street. Further along Tom hesitated, shot darting glances over his shoulders and then guided Daniel through a narrow doorway into a rickety warehouse, piled high with wooden crates.

It took a moment for his eyes to adjust to the gloom, as Tom led him to an uneven staircase with as many gaps as remaining steps to negotiate in order to reach the floor above without incident. Dan opened his mouth, but Tom held his finger to his lips. Daniel nodded. Tom placed a hand on his shoulder, preventing him moving forward along the landing, and Daniel nodded again.

Tom walked on into the darkness of the building, almost dancing with an experienced step around the rotten planking. Once he was out of sight, Daniel strained his ears to hear what was happening. There was the sound of a nervous cough and then silence. After a few moments he could hear a number of metal objects, including a chain, being laid down. Daniel presumed it was the afternoon's pickings. No words passed. He heard the items being drawn across a table top and then once more there was nothing. Moments later Tom returned, walking straight past Daniel, his jaw thrust forward in defiance. Tom headed down the staircase and Daniel struggled to follow him. As he disappeared into the street, Daniel ran to catch him up.

"They was gold, to be sure they was."

"The cufflinks?" Daniel asked, not knowing what else to say.

"I knows gold when I sees it. I should do by now." Tom spat in the gutter. "And them was gold. You should 'ave seen the bloke wearing 'em." He stopped and leaned back against a wooden strut supporting the overhanging awning to a saloon bar, and let out a deep sigh.

A scrawny, flea-ridden dog ran past, sniffing them as it went.

"It's different if you're in the gangs. You gets better prices then, but that ain't for us, we're no Daybreak Boys. Pickpocketing's one thing, but I don't fancy killing no one." He kicked the toe of his oversized boot in the dirt. "We've got each other now. You and me, we'll be all right." Tom punched Daniel's arm. "I'll race you to the corner."

Daniel felt the warm thrill of acceptance as he picked up speed to catch Tom, but Tom's longer legs made it easier for him to get away. Daniel didn't see Tom stop suddenly in front of him and he went careering into his friend, landing them both in a tangled heap on the dirt.

A small girl carrying a jug came and stood over them. "Now what are you doing down there, Thomas Reilly?"

Daniel couldn't help but laugh to hear a girl so obviously younger than he was tearing a strip off his new friend.

"Hey, Molly, we've got a visitor."

The girl looked at Daniel for the first time and her face broke into a smile. "So if I know our Thomas, he'll be blaming you for rolling around in the dirt."

"It was my fault." Daniel wanted to hold the gaze of this girl for as long as he could. He smiled back, admiring her long brown curls pinned back under a once-white cloth bonnet.

Tom brushed the dirt off his hands as he got up. "This here's me kid sister, Molly. She's all right for a girl." He laughed and gave her an affectionate jostle.

"Careful, mind. Don't make me spill the grog. What'll Mammy say?"

"She's a chip off the old block, is our Molly." Tom put a hand down to pull Daniel up from where he was still sitting, gaping at Molly.

They walked another few yards along the road, ducking under the lines of drying rags which criss-crossed the alleyway, until Tom nodded as he approached a tumbledown shed. It was little more than a frame of wood, leaning against the side of a stable. A horse whinnied from the other side of the boarding and then pawed the ground with its hoof. Straw scattered from the stable doorway into the street.

"This is it, then." Tom stood back with a flourish, allowing Molly to pass through the entrance. A pot was stewing on the fire and the smell of damp filthy rags filled the air.

Daniel blinked as his eyes adjusted from the brightness of the day to the muted grey of the shadowy hut, lacking, as it did, any discernible window. The wooden boarding leaked occasional strands of broken sunlight as surely as it must have failed to exclude the wind and rain. A single candle flickered on the shelf, ineffective in its spluttering attempt to cast light. Embers beneath the pot cast an orange halo around the charred hearth and packed earth floor, while as much smoke escaped into the room as was drawn up the makeshift chimney. Daniel was grateful the wood smoke was more gentle on his nose and throat than the biting of the peat they had burned in the hearth at home.

A rasping cough made him look around at a woman sitting on straw matting in the far corner. In this light, her delicate features, drained of colour, made her look more like a rag doll or a corpse, indistinct from the piles of bones littering the alley.

Molly placed the jug on the floor and rushed over to her mother. "It's ok, Mammy, I'm here now." Molly couldn't have been more than six years old. She pulled the blanket around her mother's shoulders and sat beside her, taking hold of the woman's frail hand, which clutched a rosary of rough wooden beads.

"You've been praying, Mammy." Molly's voice was almost a question.

Her mother tightened her hold on the beads in answer.

"I don't know why you bother with that thing. Much good it's done us." Tom shrugged and scuffed his boot across the dirt floor. "We have a visitor. Can he stay a while? He's no other place to go and he can be useful to us."

Tom's mother beckoned Daniel forward and as she went to speak a retching, rasping, blood-riddled cough overwhelmed her.

"His name's Daniel, Mammy. Tom says he sings like an angel."

Mary Reilly wiped her mouth on the shawl and smiled. The smile gave an echo of Molly; a beauty and gentleness which made Daniel's heart miss a beat as he thought of his own lost mother. He wondered at the tragedy that had reduced Mary Reilly to this. He wanted to help, wanted to say he'd take care of her, and at the same time longed to be just a child again, wrapped in her arms and mourning for his own dear mammy, for whom there'd been no chance to grieve. He wanted to promise to be good, if only she'd let him stay, but he found no words, only a shyness and a longing.

"We've got money for the rent." Tom nodded to Daniel, who understood he should empty his pockets, relieved to be offering a contribution so soon. Tom took some coins from his own pocket. "I'll be here to pay when he calls later."

For a moment Mary Reilly looked younger and less drawn as she leaned back against the boarding and closed her eyes. Molly wrapped the darned and patched blanket across her mother's chest and moved over to bolster the fire. As she passed Daniel she cast him a coy look. "Sing us a song while I work?"

Daniel felt awkward, but Tom nudged him and he felt obliged to sing.

"As I was a walking one morning in May,
I saw a sweet couple together at play…"

His eyes were closed and in his head he could feel the warmth of late spring sunshine in the fields of Kerry. There were yellow flowers dotted across the landscape and a bird sat in the hedgerow accompanying his song. He didn't want to open his eyes and see the dim interior of the shack, or breathe in the stench of this New York alley. He longed for the past, a broken, hungry past, but one in which there

14

was hope of better times. A new and better world. A land of opportunity. No one had said the opportunity would mean being orphaned and penniless. No one mentioned survival through gathering rags and bones at best and begging and stealing at worst. This new world felt like fool's gold at the end of the rainbow, but whatever else, it was his opportunity and the only one he was going to get. If he could sing for his supper, so much the better.

"O, the one was a fair maid so sweet and so fair,
And the other was a soldier and a brave grenadier..."

He opened his eyes to see Molly stirring the pot, her head on one side, smiling, listening to the song. Daniel kept his eyes open and began to sing for her, as though she were the only person there. She reminded him of an angel version of the older sister he'd had, before the hunger separated them forever. He wanted to spend his whole life singing for her, and he would have carried on to the end of the song if Mary Reilly hadn't coughed so deep the whole shack seemed to vibrate with her.

Molly rushed over to her mother. "Come closer to the fire, Mammy. The stew's almost ready."

Tom moved to the other side of his mother and between him and Molly they lifted her and guided her towards the fireside. Tom made her comfortable while Molly ladled a thin broth into a bowl and then, tearing a chunk from a leaden loaf, took it to her mother.

"Yous'll have to share." Molly looked apologetic as she spooned broth into a bowl and handed it to Daniel. He held it towards Tom, who shook his head and urged Daniel to eat first. Molly sat by the fireside, humming *The Nightingale* that Daniel had been singing minutes before. She waited patiently for her mother to eat, before taking the bowl and finishing what was left in the bottom.

Daniel finished his share and passed the dish back to Molly. She ladled out another helping and was about to pass it to Tom when a shadow passed across the doorway and a cane tapped on the ground outside. Tom started to his feet as though a bolt of lightning had shot through him and rushed to the doorway.

"Is your mother still with us, boy?"

"My mother's well enough, thank you, sir."

The man laughed as though Tom had said the funniest thing he'd heard all day. Daniel tensed at the sound.

"It's all there," said Tom, handing over a pile of change. "Three shillings."

"You'll let me know if circumstances change."

Daniel could imagine the curl of the lip which accompanied the statement. He balled his fists in ineffectual rage as he listened from inside.

"Good day." And with that, the shadow moved away and Daniel saw Tom's shoulders relax.

Molly went over to her brother and put a hand on his arm. "Come and eat your broth."

In a voice of steel Tom answered, "Give it to Mammy, she needs it more." Then he went out into the evening. Daniel hesitated, not knowing what to do.

"Go after him, please, Daniel. No good will come of his being out there now."

Daniel nodded to Molly and left in search of Tom.

Outside, the autumn sunlight filtered through the dust-speckled air. Pigs foraged for scraps in the open street. The sound of their snorting and snuffling was comforting. Daniel had no idea where Tom would head amongst the debris-strewn alleys or saloons spilling their drunken life into the street. He passed a basket of calves' heads, with portions of jowl in every stage of putrefaction, the air around them thick with flies. He walked a little way, jostled first by the drinking crowd and then pushed aside by a youth swaggering down the street as though, despite his rags, he owned the place.

At the end of the block, the buildings clambered over the tentacle-like roots of a massive tree, its shape and leaves quite different to the ones he knew back home. Leaning against the trunk, with his knees pulled up to his body, sat Tom. Daniel felt awkward approaching him. He didn't know what to say. He went and sat beside him and began stripping the bark from a twig he found lying on the ground.

"We'll be thrown out when she dies." Tom drew the back of his sleeve across his face.

"She'll get better." Daniel spoke more in hope than certainty.

"You've lived in Ireland all your life and you're still an optimist? Welcome to reality. Folks don't get better, they die. Or they leave you. Don't you want to know where me da is? That drunken eejit. He works the railroads some place. Said he'd send money back for us. Said he'd send for us to join him. He's out there drinking hisself silly, while Mammy lies here dying."

Daniel felt a flood of anger, not at Tom's absent father but at his self-pity. "You don't think I knows what it's like? I'd lost everything." His nostrils flared as he spoke. "I found you and Molly, that's my hope. I ain't got no one but yous." Feeling the overwhelming urge to cry, but desperate not to show his weakness, he instead punched Tom's arm.

Tom punched him back and before long they were sprawling in the dust, each trying to pummel their frustration out on the other, until they eventually fell laughing in a heap. They were hardly more filthy and tattered than when they began.

"You an' me, we ain't got much, but we got each other," said Tom, slapping Daniel's back.

Daniel watched a cloud of dust rise from the rough material. They'd barely caught their breath when the youth Daniel had seen earlier walked towards them. He stopped some distance in front of Tom. "Who's your friend?"

"What's it to you, Patrick Mahoney?" Tiny dots of perspiration formed on Tom's forehead and he held his body very still. Daniel could feel the tension and, without understanding the danger, his breathing became shallower.

"Come now, little Tommy." Patrick's voice hung heavy with sarcasm. Taking a knife from his pocket he picked at his nails with the blade and said, "You don't want to be talking like that to one of the Roach Guard, now do you?"

Tom stared unblinking back at Patrick, and Daniel admired his courage.

"From what I heard, you'll be begging us to join you before long," said Tom, swallowing hard.

"And what would we be wanting with you?" Patrick stepped nearer, the blade of the knife angled towards Tom.

Tom got up from where he was sitting and walked towards Patrick, clenching his small fists as he did. "I'll tell me ma Patrick Mahoney senior sends his regards."

Daniel watched as the colour drained from Patrick's face and his knife hand sank down towards his side.

"I'm watching you, Tommy Reilly," he said, with none of the bravado left in his voice. Then he sloped off towards the other side of the street.

"What was that about his da?" Daniel asked as Tom sat down again and let out a deep breath.

"Just business," said Tom, picking up a long stick off the ground. "What you needs to know is this whole city is split up between the gangs. If we want to work on a patch, we either has to join them or pay them. We pays them. The Roach Guard's Irish, but that don't make 'em all right. It means they'll take our money so as we can work on their patch." He began to draw with the stick in the dust. "We's here." He marked a cross. "These roads here, they belongs to the Roach Guard. Here…" he moved the stick further across the ground, "this belongs to the Bowery Boys and here…" he drew a big circle, "don't go near here."

"Why?" asked Daniel, trying to remember the map as best he could.

"They're the Daybreak Boys. Rumour has it they'll kill you soon as look at you."

Daniel's mouth fell open. He was silent a moment, then said, "Do you make all your money by thieving?"

"Mostly," said Tom, rubbing the stick across the ground to erase the drawing. "We collect rags and bones too, but picking pockets is easier. I leave Molly to look for rags. Ma stays home and boils them up. When she was well, Ma used to…" Tom left the sentence unfinished. "We'll be getting back," he said, coughing to clear his throat and scrambling to his feet. "We needs you in good voice for the morning. We'll have dues to pay if we don't want to see Patrick's knife any closer than that."

CHAPTER 2

"The first Nowell the Angel did say
Was to three poor Shepherds in fields as they lay;
In fields where they lay keeping their sheep,
In a cold winter's night that was so deep.
Nowell, Nowell, Nowell, Nowell,
Born is the King of Israel."
Traditional

"And what are you doing there, young Daniel Flynn?"

Daniel threw his head back and laughed, caught unawares by Molly. "Well, I was seeing if I could cover your snowy footsteps with some of my own, before they disappear, don't you know?"

"Well if you'd been any longer, you'd have not seen mine at all. Get yourself in here out of the cold and show us what you've got." Molly was standing hands on hips in the doorway, looking for all the world twenty years older than she was.

"How's Mammy?" He shook snow off his hat before going through the doorway. It was more a matter of respect than practicality, with the leaky nature of the shack, but the snow was providing a layer of insulation and, for all the cold, it was drier and less breezy than normal.

"Mammy's fine," came the reply as the gaunt figure of Mammy peered out into the gloomy day.

"Now, you be getting yourself back to the fireside,

Mammy," Molly chided, drawing a grin from Daniel. "And where's that brother of mine?"

On cue, Tom came tearing around the corner and straight into the shack ahead of Daniel.

"It's rich picking this Christmas, to be sure it is." He dropped a pile of coins by the hearth. "Daniel sang like a real cherub." Tom made a comical beatific smile making them all laugh.

Daniel felt his cheeks colour as Mammy laid a hand on his arm and mouthed, "Thank you."

"And tomorrow, for our grand finale, we're going Uptown for Daniel to sing to all those rich folks with more money than everyone round here put together." They laughed again as Tom walked a few mincing steps the length of the shack, twirling an imaginary cane, then held his arm out for Molly to join him.

Joining in the fun, Daniel began to sing and Molly and Tom began to dance a reel, round the small interior, while Mammy clapped them on.

Eventually, Mammy stopped laughing to cough and clear her throat. While her coughing fits had subsided, it was still an effort to do much more than sit, but that didn't prevent odd moments of lightness among them.

"Going Uptown… you boys be careful, I can't afford to lose either of you."

"Och, don't you be worrying yourself, Mammy. We's fine. The luck o' the Irish, don't you know?" Tom slapped Daniel on the back and gave his ragged grin.

"Sing for us a carol now, Daniel," Mammy said.

When Mammy spoke to him, Daniel's heart melted. He was proud that his contributions helped pay the keep. As each day passed, Mammy seemed a little stronger and Daniel poured his heart into his singing, clinging to his hope of a brighter tomorrow.

"God rest you merry, gentlemen
Let nothing you dismay,
For Jesus Christ our Saviour
Was born upon this day…"

As he sang, Daniel watched Mammy sit gently down by the fire, her face so like a seraph's in the firelight that Daniel almost wondered if she were really there.

"I says we goes direct. It's too far to go the long way."

Daniel swallowed hard. "But yous said not to mess with the gangs, and that way…"

"Ah, chicken. We'll be right. You see. We're no Roach Guard or nothing."

"But you said Bowery weren't safe."

"Nah, but we're just gentlemen, out for a stroll up Mulberry Street." Tom put on a swagger as he walked north, leaving Daniel trailing behind, dragging what was left of his heels as he walked.

Tom turned back to him, grinning as ever. "C'mon you – we've got miles to go."

Daniel picked up speed and, despite or probably because of his nerves, started singing as he walked. It took them over an hour in the snow to trudge their way to Madison.

"The stage is yours, sir." Tom swept a low bow. "And if you sees a bobbie, hope you can run faster. I'll see you back at the corner of Union Square, unless they catch you first." He ducked into an alley and was soon lost to sight.

Daniel straightened his shirt as he looked around him. He spat on his shirt cuff and pointlessly tried to use the grimy rag to make his face look cleaner. Then he sat himself down on a low wall, as experience had taught him, the innocent child lost in his own world, and began to sing. If he were singing to himself, it stood to reason that it wasn't begging. If people stopped and threw money, that was up to them. He didn't put his hat down to ask for it. He hoped that way the police wouldn't chase him off quite so soon. As to what Tom was doing in the meantime, he didn't like to think. To his mind that was the dangerous stuff. It was only a problem for him if they realised he was an accomplice.

"I saw three ships come sailing in
On Christmas day, on Christmas day..."

Daniel sang with his eyes closed. There was still snow on the ground, although it wasn't fresh. He hoped he'd find any coins that were thrown around him before he went. He could sense a few people stopping to listen and, as the carol ended, looked up briefly, his eyes blinking slightly as though surprised to see them there. Then, without faltering, he began again.

"Hark, the herald Angels sing,
Glory to the New-born King..."

He worked his way through two more carols before stopping and taking his hat off, the sign to Tom that he was finishing so they could move to a new location. As the small crowd drifted away, Tom disappeared into the background and Daniel gathered up the pennies around him. He smiled; the Christmas spirit was alive and well.

"Rich pickings?" Daniel sauntered up to where Tom

was waiting two blocks away.

"The best." Tom's grin was unnaturally broad.

"Where to now?"

"We'll find a corner of Union Square."

"And where'll we run to if the boys in blue come our way?" Daniel couldn't help thinking that maybe they should quit while they were ahead. Pray as he might, luck never seemed to last for long.

"Top of Mulberry Street. That'll be right."

"Are you crazy? Why don't we go back now?"

"And what's Molly going to say to you when you were too scared to do any more?"

Daniel felt himself blush. Tom always knew the ways to get to him. "Just one more then. After that we go back and we don't walk through the Bowery Boys' turf."

Tom laughed and ran ahead, clucking and flapping imaginary elbow wings, leaving Daniel running to catch up, slipping and sliding on the icy snow.

Union Square was busy as Daniel found himself a place to sit. He could feel the cold and damp through his trousers from the stone beneath, and shivered. Taking a deep breath and closing his eyes, he started to sing, this time *Silent Night*, before repeating some of the carols he'd sung earlier. He was singing *I Saw Three Ships* and had opened his eyes to look for them when he saw a policeman watching from the street corner, rocking back and forth on the balls of his feet. He couldn't decide if he was listening for the pleasure or about to intervene. Daniel removed his hat, but no sooner had he seen Tom darting from the back of the crowd than he saw the policeman following. He paused, uncertain what to do. He didn't want to leave the money, and if the bobbie had gone after Tom then he wouldn't be there to stop Daniel. He kept his breathing even to finish the song, despite his quickening heart rate, and then got up, blinking innocently at the crowd, who immediately began to disperse.

As soon as the coast was clear, he collected the money that could be reached without looking too conspicuous. As no one seemed interested in him anymore, he started picking up some of the pieces which had fallen further away.

He walked away at a steady pace and tried not to look as terrified as he was feeling, all the time crossing his fingers, hoping that the policemen hadn't caught Tom. As he looked ahead he thought it was the policeman he could see in the distance, so he ducked into an alley to wait for him to pass. As he did, Daniel smiled to himself. Not only was there no sign of Tom, but it looked for all the world as though the policeman had fallen headlong in the snow. His trousers were wet and there was a patch of ice sticking to his jacket.

Tom was imbued with the luck o' the Irish all right. If he hadn't been living in New York so long, Daniel would have sworn his friend had kissed the Blarney Stone. There was almost no situation he couldn't talk himself out of, or so it seemed to Daniel.

As he approached Mulberry, he saw Tom leaning against a wall, whistling, appearing not to have a care in the world. Daniel was about to shout to him when he saw half a dozen Bowery Boys come out of the neighbouring alley and move to surround Tom. Daniel crossed himself and sent up a prayer, desperately pleading with the Virgin Mary to help him save his friend. There were more than enough of the gang to attack him as well. He needed a way to distract them so they could both run. As he walked a few steps forward to where they were menacing Tom, he felt some of the coins in his pocket. If he didn't rescue Tom, money wasn't going to be much use to any of them. He swallowed hard, then took a fistful of coins and with a breaking voice shouted, "Hey!"

The six lads turned as one, focussing on Daniel. They were all older; fifteen or sixteen maybe, and swaggered as though they owned the world, rather than a run-down block or two.

Daniel's voice croaked, "Look, it's raining money!" With that, he threw the coins in the air so they came down scattering around the lads. As the Bowery Boys turned their attention to the ground, he indicated to Tom and raced as fast as he could down Mulberry Street. He knew Tom had understood when, in only a block or so, his longer strides had outpaced Daniel and left him behind.

"Wait..." Daniel could feel his lungs burning. Then the unthinkable happened; he slipped on the ice and went sprawling in the snow at the side of the road.

Tom glanced over his shoulder, seeing his friend in trouble, and relief flooded Daniel. Then, to his horror, he saw Tom turn his head forwards and keep running, leaving him to the mercy of the Bowery Boys, who, despite the money collection, were not far behind.

There was no time to hide or to run anywhere now. Daniel closed his eyes and curled himself tightly into a ball.

Time moved slowly as he waited for the first foot to strike. He felt a boot prod at him, rolling him a few inches before he fell back to his starting position.

"Think you can stop us with a few coins, do you?" The boot moved to his chin, trying to force his head away from his chest, but Daniel resisted. He could smell the wet, filthy leather beneath his nose and despite its being no worse than many of the smells around him, he felt himself gag.

"You're on our land."

Daniel swallowed hard. Even in his terror he thought of the irony of the struggles for land which had tracked his short life.

"Gonna speak?"

Daniel gave a minimal shake of his head from beneath where his arms encircled it in protection.

Then it came, an agonising thud to his thigh, and there was absolutely nothing he could do but pray. His lips moved silently over his clenched teeth. "Holy Mary, Mother of God, pray for us sinners now and at the hour of our death..." His muscles were taut, steeled against the next blow... but it didn't come. Instead he heard an Irish accent shouting from a little way away.

"Will you leave him be? He's only a kid. Pick on someone your own size."

He heard boots shuffling to change position and unscrewed his eyes enough to see through his lashes, as a line of the Roach Guard were squaring up, facing the Bowery Boys.

He recognised some of the Guard, including Patrick Mahoney with a large piece of wood in his hand which he was tapping against his other palm in a menacing gesture.

"Go home, lad, this ain't goin' to be pretty," called the one standing at the front of the Roach Guard. "Get out while you can still walk."

Daniel uncurled his body and gingerly edged away from the action to the side of the street. He used the wall to haul himself up to standing and started to limp along Mulberry back towards Five Points. He was flooded by exhaustion and for the first time in two months he felt lonely. When he'd needed him, Tom had run and left him to the mercy of the gang. Daniel frowned in confusion as he thought over what had happened. Was it possible that Tom hadn't seen him fall? He knew the answer even as he posed the question. Tom had abandoned him and saved his own skin.

The walk back felt a long one, but worse than that, he didn't know where to go. He'd thought he belonged, but that meant looking out for each other, as he had done for Tom. Now he wasn't so sure. There was an icy chill in the air as he slumped down on the old tree roots. He'd still got a few coins in his pocket and could maybe buy food and shelter for the night whilst he worked out where to go next. He longed to be back with Mammy, with Molly chiding him for how little he was bringing back. He longed for his own parents, but they were little use to him now.

"You got nothing better to do than sit here feeling sorry for yourself?" It was Tom.

Daniel didn't reply. He felt uncharacteristic anger welling inside him and balled his fists.

"You know I'd seen Patrick standing there on the opposite corner. No one was going to hurt you when the Roach Guard were around. Besides, Molly would have killed us if I'd lost the day's pickings through your stupidity."

Daniel felt his control loosen. "My stupidity? My stupidity, to be sure. How d'you work that one out?" He was on his feet now, squaring up to Tom. It wasn't a time to think about the fact that he was a good two inches shorter and with no more muscle than a swallow. He punched Tom as hard as he could with his right fist and then stood back a pace, shaking his head, surprised at what he'd done.

Tom stared at him, clutching his lip, then broke into a broad disarming grin. "You wouldn't be wanting to do that again, now would you? Besides, Molly's cooked a special stew with real meat in it for once."

Daniel slumped down on the roots again and Tom landed beside him. "How did you know Patrick would protect me?"

"We pays the Roach Guard protection money, don't we?"

"But there's more than that, isn't there?"

"To be sure there is." Then, as though it were the most natural thing in the world, he added, "I think Molly's his sister... but she don't know that."

Daniel blinked and shook his head, almost as though he was expecting that last sentence to fall back out of his thoughts. "But Molly was born in Ireland, same as you and me."

"Have you got straw for brains? Where d'you think Patrick Mahoney came from? Have you heard how he talks? They was from the same village as us back in Ireland. Mammy's known Patrick Mahoney for years. I overheard her arguing with Da before he went away to work on the railways. He sounded real bitter and said she could always get that low life Mahoney to take care of her again."

Daniel fell silent. He wanted to believe that Tom had known it would be all right, but a deep nagging feeling told him otherwise. As for Molly having a different da, so what? He'd thought of Tom as a brother, and they didn't share either parent.

"Did you get much for today's pickings?" He looked up and studied Tom's face.

"Not been yet." He grinned. "Let's take 'em now and then tomorrow maybe we can swear blood brothers and you'll believe I didn't run out on you."

Daniel's shoulders relaxed a little and he nodded. He

wanted to believe that he'd still got a home and a family to go to. He thought of Molly and the special stew and smiled. "Blood brothers, to be sure." For a moment he could have been back in the beautiful surroundings of Killarney. He shrugged in that way of his father's again and smiled, and brushed his eyes with his shirt sleeve. "Blood brothers."

CHAPTER 3

"I've been a wild rover for many's the year,
And I spent all me money on whiskey and beer.
And now I'm returning with gold in great store,
And I never will play the wild rover no more."
Traditional, circa 1830

To Daniel, Mammy's smile was warmer than the late spring sunshine.

"Won't you sing us a reel, Daniel?" She remained weak, though her voice was much clearer now. The gentle lilting accent washed over him, bringing comfort whenever he heard it.

He often sang for her as she boiled the rags that Molly brought back from her searches. He would practise the songs he was to sing in the afternoons, occasionally learning a new one by standing outside the bars listening. The time had passed when, closing his eyes, he sang for his da. Now it was Mammy and Molly he was singing for. He'd die for them if they needed him to; the least he could do was sing for them.

Other times he'd help Molly grubbing through the dirt in search of more rags, which Mammy prepared for the collectors to take to the paper mills. The streets were littered with waste from neighbouring households. What else was there to do with it? It was no worse picking through the rubbish than living among it as they did. At least it was honest work and he was paying his own way, and more besides. The times Daniel went rag collecting, Tom stayed behind, always one of them there by Mammy's side, as Daniel was now.

Mammy began a fit of coughing and Daniel went to her. Molly hated being away from her mother, but Daniel promised to do his best when Mammy shooed Molly out of the shack to search for that day's rags.

As the coughing subsided and the shack quieted, Mammy spoke softly. "I'd not be here now if the Good Lord hadn't sent you to us. You surely are a gift from God, Daniel Flynn."

Daniel felt his cheeks warm as the strength of her words melted around him. He watched Mammy sit a minute with her rough wooden rosary, running it between her fingers as she took strength from her Lord.

Later that evening, when he and Tom returned from his singing, they were all sitting around the fire. The chill had gone from the air, but the fire still shed a welcome light across the tiny room. They kept it alight as best they could, which was easier than starting again if they lost the flame. Molly was sitting close to her mother and Mammy was stroking her hair.

"I remember the days when you was a baby and we was still back in Ireland…"

As Mammy told stories of the old times, Daniel wished fervently they were his history too and that he had been part of their world. Instead, his own stories were fading and it was hard to remember the sound of his own ma's voice. His memories of her were merging into images of Mammy and he was hardly sure of the truth of his own family now.

"Tell us about life before the blight," he begged her.

"Tell us about the fields and mountains."

"But you tell it so much better in your songs. They're beautiful because the land is so bonny and they're mournful because of the sadness it's brought." She looked into the fire, distant and with a gentle frown. Shaking herself, she got up. "I'll tell no more tonight. I need my sleep, even if the three of you don't."

"I'm away out." Tom kicked forward from the wall he'd been leaning against. "Are yous coming, Daniel?"

Daniel gently shook his head. As Mammy lay down, Molly joined her and Daniel sat alone, staring into the fire. A tear slipped down his cheek as he tried to remember. However hard he tried, he could find no more to hold onto that was real than the songs, and even with those he couldn't recall which he'd known before and which he'd learned since arriving in New York.

Daniel was still discovering the new pattern to the seasons. Nothing seemed much like he was used to. The winter had been colder and the spring sunnier and now there was heat unlike anything he'd experienced, except as he recalled on the hottest days back home. As the temperature had risen, so too had the stench of the streets, and fresh air was a thing of the past. He thought he was used to the vile smell of the putrid remains, but now he gagged as he passed the worst of the rotting carcasses, remnants of animals too diseased to be eaten. Tom seemed immune to it, already used to the changes the heat brought. Most of the time they made a good team and their system hadn't failed them yet. Tom wasn't greedy in his picking of pockets, enough to make the day worthwhile but not so much as to get them caught. With his unruly mop of red corkscrews, he'd have been an easy target if the chase were on.

"Now, you're not going to go all useless on me, being sick and all?" Tom slapped his back as they passed yet another pile of decomposing remains and Daniel swallowed repeatedly to stop himself vomiting. "It'll do that voice of yours no good at all, to be sure it won't. Anyways, we gotta run. I told Mammy I'd be there to pay the rent. I don't like her seeing Mr Clyde with none of us there."

Tom broke into a run and Daniel joined him. They had only a couple of blocks to go. As they approached they could see Mr Clyde, already at the doorway, about to call Mammy outside. Tom sped up, Daniel puffing behind him.

"Good afternoon, madam." He rapped his cane on the ground to demand attention.

"And a good afternoon to you, sir."

Daniel's stomach turned, seeing Mammy wasting a smile on Mr Clyde.

"Your rent, Madam."

How could one man inject so much venom into every word? Daniel watched Mammy turn to go inside and saw Mr Clyde duck his head to follow. Tom barged past the man, almost knocking him from his feet.

"You stays out there. We'll get your money." Tom's face was scarlet and the rage was plain to see.

"Get away, vermin." Mr Clyde struck Tom across the legs with his cane. Then, towering over him, "You'll pay for that. I will personally see that you do. No one pushes me around. Remember that, boy. No one!" A snake could not have hissed more effectively as he shoved Tom aside and held his hand out to Mammy, an evil smile playing across his lips. Wrapping his hand around the coins, he lifted his cane so the ball was under Tom's chin, almost lifting him from the floor. "I'll see you next month."

Tom kicked the ground and spat into the dirt.

"Now what did you want to go doing that for?" Mammy asked in the gentlest tones.

"He's scum." Tom spat again.

"But it doesn't cost you to be civil. I haven't brought you up to be as bad as he is, Thomas Reilly. You remember that. Ah, you're your father's boy all right. To be sure you are."

"And what father would that be?" Tom turned away.

"Thomas Reilly, come back here this minute. That's no way to talk to your mammy."

She went to the doorway. Daniel realised she was in time to see Tom's back receding. Molly looked at Daniel and gave a slight nod. He should go after Tom and see he didn't go looking for trouble, as he usually did when he was angry. Daniel sighed. Last time he'd come back with a black eye, but at least he'd brought Tom back safe and calm.

As the days grew hotter, Daniel longed for the cool sea breeze he knew back home and even wondered if he wouldn't prefer the smell of rotting potatoes to the sewage-strewn streets of New York. He'd watched some of the men go off to work on digging the new sewers in other parts of the city, but sewers were a luxury that wouldn't be wasted on the likes of them.

Molly and Tom had gone to get the grog and Daniel was enjoying the cooler evening sunshine. He could see them now, Molly, jug in hand, leaving the nearby bar and making their way back. He pushed away from the tree that was giving him shade and ran to join them. Tom hung back to walk with him and they were a few paces behind Molly as she entered the shack.

"Mammy!"

They quickened their pace, hearing the terror in her

voice. In the gloom Daniel could see Mammy doubled over in the corner of the shack, vomiting violently.

Molly's hands were shaking as she poured a little of the drink into a cup. When the retching stopped, Molly reached to wipe Mammy's sweating and vomit-covered face. She tried to offer up the cup to her, but before she could even sip, Mammy was retching again.

"Go and get help," Molly called to the boys.

"And what doctor is going to come out for the likes of us?" Tom's face was ashen despite the bravado in his voice.

"Then get Ol' Tinker. Now!"

Daniel ran from the shack with Tom hot on his heels. He ran as though the Bowery Boys were behind him and his life depended on it. Daniel knew what the sickness meant and it sent panic through him. Ol' Tinker had remedies for many ailments, but surely even he couldn't help with cholera.

As they approached the warehouse that Ol' Tinker called home, he was sitting outside as he so often did.

"And what's got you boys all of a racing?"

"Molly says..." Tom panted heavily, "we're to fetch you... It's Mammy. She's real sick."

Ol' Tinker nodded sagely and vigorously scratched his ear. "Oh, she did now, did she? I doesn't come for nothing."

Daniel frantically dipped his hand in his pocket and brought out some coins. "How much?"

Ol' Tinker pushed himself up without answering and simply exhaled a long puff on his pipe in apparent contemplation. "She's a good woman, your mammy. You go back and I'll be right behind you, that I will." He turned and went through a wooden door into the warehouse behind.

Daniel put the money back in his pocket and shrugged.

"I guess we'll go back then."

"You go. I'm going for a walk." Tom headed in the direction of the port.

"But…" There was no point; the way Tom's chin was jutting out, Daniel could see his determination. He turned to run back the way he'd come. By the time he got there, Mammy was shivering despite the heat. Molly was trying to wrap a blanket around her but, trying to hold a cup to her lips as well, she was struggling.

"Here, let me." Daniel took the blanket and wrapped it around Mammy's shoulders, while Molly held the drink. It seemed that no sooner had she sipped than she was vomiting again.

"She's got terrible bad diarrhoea as well," Molly whispered to him.

Daniel hadn't needed telling. He could smell the state of the shack and was close to being sick himself.

The doorway darkened and Ol' Tinker was there.

"Oh, thank God." Molly went over to greet him.

"Give her this…" He thrust a bottle in her direction. "… Every time she wants a drink. I can't make no promises, but it may work, God help her." He didn't stay for payment, but turned and immediately walked away.

Molly's shoulders slumped, but she took the bottle to Mammy and tried to encourage her to sip from it. She vomited again almost as soon as it touched her lips and then fell back onto the matting, moaning. Molly carefully drew the blankets around Mammy, picked up the wooden rosary and, sitting close to Mammy's side, started working her way around the beads.

There was no sign of Tom as Mammy fell into a fitful sleep, waking at intervals to retch. Each time, Molly was ready with the bottle to encourage her to drink, but each time she was sick as soon as she did. Daniel sat quietly, watching over the women, praying his own silent prayers and letting the tears course down his cheeks unchecked. Eventually he must have drifted off, because he was woken by the sound of Molly howling, "Mammy!"

As he opened his eyes he was aware of Molly, first gently, then more vigorously, shaking Mammy. Then she fell upon her mother's lifeless body in great heaving sobs. "Oh, Mammy, Mammy, Mammy…"

Daniel gasped and closed his eyes a moment, wondering what he should do. Should he comfort Molly or find Tom? Tom would come back when he was good and ready, so he went over and put his arm tenderly around Molly. She looked up at him in the gloom, her eyes searching his face, confusion written large. They fell into each other's arms and both gave in to the tears, letting forth great sobs of anguish, Molly for her Mammy and Daniel for both the mothers he'd lost. The loss of his own parents fell upon him and for the first time he started to mourn.

Daniel had no sense of how long they remained like that, but after a while he became aware they were being watched. He looked up and saw Tom standing in the doorway, frozen rigid, with the light of the early sun behind him.

When he spoke, it was quietly at first but then getting louder. "No, no, no, NOOO!" He fell to his knees, to where the other two still embraced, and they opened their arms to include him. "I should have been here. I could have helped. I could have stopped it."

"Tom," said Molly in a cracked whisper, "there was nothing you could have done. There was nothing anyone could have done."

"Ol' Tinker?" Tom made to get up.

Molly arrested him with her hand. "He came. He tried to help."

"And how much of our money did he take for that?" Tom's temper was flaring.

"You'll not find someone to blame now, Thomas Reilly. He charged us nothing. Mammy's at peace now. She's with Jesus."

"Oh, shut up about your damned Jesus." Tom picked up the rosary and hurled it at the far wall. "What's God ever done for us?"

Neither Daniel nor Molly replied.

CHAPTER 4

Yes, when this flesh and heart shall fail,
And mortal life shall cease;
I shall possess, within the veil,
A life of joy and peace.
John Newton, 1779

"She looks so peaceful." The outward signs of Tom's anger left him as he knelt close to his mother's body. Daniel knew the temper would be back, but for the moment there was no one to direct it towards and that left Tom a small orphaned boy, the same as he was.

They sat in silence for a while, each lost in private confusion.

"It's not as though I've not seen death before, so I have, but never so close. I don't know what I thought it would look like," Molly said. "It's as though it's not her. She's gone somewhere. My real mammy is some place else."

Daniel understood what she meant. He'd thought the same thing when he'd seen the bodies of his own parents as they were hauled over the side of the boat into the Atlantic Ocean. The unreality had made that part easier.

"What do we do now?" The courage and bravado was gone and Molly looked to her brother for an answer.

Tom shrugged. "Same as yesterday, I guess. Except you'll have to do the boiling." He wiped his cuff across his face and sniffed.

"I meant…" Molly fidgeted with the rosary beads. "I meant with…" She took a deep breath. "With Mammy," she said finally, as though in a hurry now to get the words out.

Daniel looked at Tom and watched as he suddenly changed. His back straightened and he looked more serious than Daniel had seen him before.

"We can't tell. For as long as possible, no one must know." He stood up, looking inches taller than he had a moment previously.

"But what about…?" Daniel couldn't bring himself to say 'her body'. He looked across at Mammy, then up at where Tom was standing.

"Cover her with blankets for now. We can't tell anyone. There's no one to trust. We needs this room to live in. If Mr Clyde finds out, we're done for. At least we can stay until next rent day if he doesn't know."

Daniel suspected that Tom was right, but the thought of living with a decomposing corpse wasn't something he fancied, not in such close proximity. It was bad enough to find corpses of animals near to their door, but biding with one would be an altogether different matter. For a start, the flies would come and then there was the smell, but more important to Daniel was the gut-wrenching emotion of keeping their loss so close. "What about Ol' Tinker?"

Tom's jaw jutted as he nodded slightly. "I'll sort it. I'm going out. Don't say anything to anyone, d'ya hear?"

Molly got up, biting her lip and sniffing. "I'll be gathering rags then," she said, her shaking hand reaching for the basket. "And you, Daniel Flynn, you can…" Her eyes darted from the corner where Mammy lay to the empty fireplace. "You can…"

"It's ok, Molly." He laid his hand gently on her arm. "I'll

stay here a while. I need to practise my songs."

Molly nodded, visibly biting harder on her bottom lip. Daniel wanted to hold her in his arms again and let her cry it all out, but there was no room for wallowing in grief, not if they wanted a roof over their heads and food on the table. She pursed her lips and followed Tom out into the street.

Daniel busied himself trying to clear the worst of the soiled straw from the floor into the street. The hours passed and he wondered if he should be out looking for an audience, but it didn't feel right to leave Mammy's body unattended. He set to preparing the fire for supper and a pot to boil the rags that Molly would surely bring. As he did so, he sang quietly, a gentle lullaby prayer for Mammy and all the adults he'd been close to in his short life.

Evening was starting to fall when Molly returned. "Am I ever pleased to see you, Daniel Flynn," she said, stumbling into the shack under a pile of rags.

He smiled at the sight of his friend weighed down with the collection. It seemed she had been venting her grief by working harder than ever.

"I've a stew on, if you're hungry," he said as she let go of the pile in the corner of the room.

"I'm not sure I am." She glanced over towards the corner where Mammy lay and shrugged. "I guess I need food in me, but I can't say I feels much like eating it." She gave a crooked smile below the confusion of her eyes.

"Molly, she wouldn't want you to starve. She'd be wanting you to grow up into a fine daughter, so she would."

"That I know…" Molly didn't have time to finish before there were scuffling feet outside the door.

Daniel stood rigid, holding his breath.

"We'll be here waiting," were the words he heard.

It was only recognising Tom's voice that made him breathe easily again.

"And who will we be 'here' to, Thomas Reilly?" For a moment the fight was back in her voice and Molly ladled a bowl of stew, passing it to her returning brother.

"Ol' Tinker. He's going to help. He says we should go to the Potter's Field tonight and take Mammy. He says they'll find her there tomorrow and know what to do with her."

"And how are we going to get her all that way, brother of mine? She's hardly going to be walking, now is she?"

"Ol' Tinker's going to bring a cart. He ain't bringing it here. We'll have to meet him. We can disguise what we're carrying with the rags."

Molly's lip trembled and she balled her fists. Before Daniel knew what was happening she was pounding them ineffectively against Tom's chest. "You'll not take my Mammy wrapped in worse rags than the ones she lived in."

"Shhh." There was urgency in Tom's response and he grabbed her wrists as he turned and looked over his shoulder towards the doorway. "Will you listen to yourself, Molly Reilly? Do you want to be sleeping on the streets? She's gone now and no amount of finery is going to bring her back to us."

"You're hurting me, Tom. Let go of my wrists."

"Then will you quieten yourself down and think a minute?"

In the midst of the fight, the stew had slopped onto the floor where the bowl had fallen. Thankfully the bowl had not broken and Daniel quietly ladled another portion of the thin watery mixture and handed it to Tom. The other bowl he filled and passed to Molly. He'd eat when one or other of them finished. The waning sunlight glistened off a silent tear that rolled down Molly's cheek as she stared into the bowl of soup. Tom turned his back and stood against the doorway looking out, casting a shadow over his sister. Daniel went to her and put his arm around her shoulder. He was conscious it was still only a child's arm and, despite her small stature, it was too short to circle her completely as Mammy would have done. He wanted to screw his fists tight and beat them against something to release the frustration, but there was little point.

They sat silently, waiting for night to fall, Tom constantly watching for the signal they should start Mammy's final journey. Daniel could feel his eyelids heavy after the long day and night and so began to sing to help keep himself awake. For the first time Molly joined in, providing a beautiful melody to his lilting intonation. He wanted to stop and listen to her and hold the sound of her voice in his heart forever, but as he was thinking on the calm it brought him, Tom suddenly got up.

"Ok, yous two. It's time."

Daniel took a deep breath and went with Tom to the corner of the room. Tom had brought the rags that Molly had dropped over with him, and proceeded to bundle them around the awkwardness of Mammy's corpse. Tom spoke almost tenderly to his sister when he said, "You can stay here if you want, Molly. We'll manage, won't we, Daniel?"

Daniel nodded, but Molly shook her head. "I want to be with Mammy to the last. And besides, I don't think I wants to be here on my own."

Tom said nothing, but finished wrapping the rags, then he and Daniel lifted the feather-light weight of Mammy, only made substantial by the day's collection, and started to shuffle toward the doorway.

They only had two blocks to walk before finding Ol'

Tinker, but they were the longest that Daniel ever remembered. Even a relatively small weight becomes heavy when covered in rags and held for a length of time. Daniel's arms were aflame with pain from the strain of it. With the stiffness of the body it was hard to get a comfortable hold and he was grateful for the sight of the barrow. The walk after that was long and quiet. It took them most of the night to take a route which Ol' Tinker hoped would keep them out of trouble. The first silver strands of morning were appearing when, with heavy hearts, they eventually left their load by the burial ground for those with nowhere left to go.

Daniel saw Tom trying to press money into Ol' Tinker's hand as they turned to move away, but the old man shook his head. "She was a good woman." Without saying more he took up the barrow and walked away into the morning.

Daniel felt his loss starting to overwhelm him again at the sound of these few words. If it had not been for Tom ushering them back the way they'd come he would have broken down completely.

There was little conversation as they went back, just the regular sound of their feet tramping, made louder by the flapping of the sole of Tom's left boot with every step.

CHAPTER 5

But the sea is wide and I cannot cross over
And neither have I the wings to fly
I wish I could meet a handsome boatsman
To ferry me over, to my love and die.
Carrickfergus

Daniel slept fitfully through the rest of the day. He woke with a start several times, from the noises of the street during the hours of light. There'd be no singing, no wake celebrating a life well lived, no fiddlers and no cheer. The sound of Molly's sobbing was all that punctuated the quiet, sombre mood. Tom had gone out into the day as soon as they'd returned. He said nothing of where he was going and neither Daniel nor Molly asked. Each of them needed to grieve in their own way and for Daniel it was an overwhelming bone-weary tiredness that descended.

When he roused himself sometime well after noon, Molly was at the pot boiling rags, weeping as she pounded the cloths with a long stick to move them round in the murky water. She made to wipe her eyes when she saw he was looking, but he stayed her arm. "It's ok."

"Now don't let Tom be hearing you saying that." Her lips turned up slightly in a smile, but there was no sign of the rest of Molly's face joining in and the sadness in her eyes was unabated. "Don't you go thinking you can be lying about here all day when I've got work to be doing."

Now Daniel did smile and he thanked God for this feisty companion who was so like Mammy had been while she was well.

"I'll be needing more rags for boiling, Daniel Flynn. You can either stay here and mind the fire or you can do the collecting, but you can't stay here and only watch." She paused, as though there was more to say but she was holding back.

He waited to see if words would come, but when they didn't he kissed her cheek as he made toward the door. "Yes, ma'am." He saluted her before he went out into the glare of the sunshine.

Pickings seemed slim as Daniel tramped the streets. He wondered where Molly found the bundles she had returned with the previous day and guessed she'd walked further than they'd realised. Much as he knew the need, his heart wasn't in it.

He turned the corner of Bayard and, blinking at the sight ahead of him, quickly dropped back into the shadows. Tom was leaning against a wall, talking to Patrick Mahoney. It was not like the day when Patrick was threatening them; this time, the two were in conversation. That couldn't be good. To be sure, they were going to need more protection now than ever before, but Tom wouldn't join up with the gang without telling him.

He and Tom were a team. More than that, blood-brothers – Tom swore they were. He stood in the alley, breathing heavily and wondering what it meant. He'd faced Tom's rages before and wasn't ready to confront him. Should he mention it to Molly, or was it safer to say nothing? Daniel's heart raced as he watched, waiting for them to move on before coming out of his hiding place.

He could feel the cold sweat trickling down his back as

he returned the way he'd come, making certain that Tom hadn't seen him. He'd wait for Tom to give the word. Maybe he still planned to include Daniel. He wouldn't go back on their promises now, would he?

Daniel sighed as he returned to the shack with so few rags that their carrying was easy.

"Reckon you're better at singing than searching for cloth," Molly said, taking the few items from him and placing them in the far corner of the room.

Daniel said nothing but sat with his head in his hands, wondering what to do.

Days passed and Tom didn't speak of Patrick Mahoney or the Roach Guard. Many a time he'd excuse himself and disappear for a few hours, but Daniel had more sense than to ask where he was going. He felt Tom's absence keenly and his singing was more mournful than ever. Pickings weren't so good, going out singing on his own, and Tom rarely seemed to have much to add to the family coffers.

At night, Daniel lay wondering what Tom was doing with his time. If it were anything profitable, then he and Molly weren't sharing the gains. He neither had the courage to follow Tom nor the willingness to leave Molly on her own of an evening, so he waited, hoping Tom might take him into his counsel.

Daniel and Molly spent many hours together, searching for rags or boiling them. They kept each other company and sometimes she would go with him when he sang, to help pick up the coins, but not to pick pockets as her brother would have done. They'd set aside the money for the rent. They would give no cause for their landlord to look further, but nevertheless Daniel dreaded the day of his calling and hoped more than anything that Tom would be there. They knew the day, but not the hour. They sat waiting for the tapping of the cane that preceded the odious man.

For all Tom's absence through the recent days, he was ready and waiting. He was at the doorway before any chance of a head stooping to look inside.

"Ah, don't you sweat yourself. We've got your money." Tom stood, legs apart and arms folded, dwarfed by the shadow of Mr Clyde.

From the corner where he was crouching, Daniel could see a tremor run down Tom's legs. Daniel clutched Molly's hand and felt the drip of her tears on his bare arm.

"And your mammy? I need to speak with your mammy." The voice sounded as though it carried all the coarse gravel and detritus of the streets.

Tom stood firm, biting his lip.

Daniel wondered what Tom could say in answer to that. If he said she was out, Mr Clyde would only come back later. Surely he was left with no choice.

Tom stared at the ground. His shoulders dropped as he said, "She's passed."

Daniel felt Molly shiver and drew her closer to him.

"But the agreement's with your mammy."

Daniel could hear the sneer even though he couldn't see Mr Clyde's face.

"Then the agreement's in heaven." Tom spat on the floor by the landlord's feet.

"You'll not be staying then." Mr Clyde prodded Tom with his cane.

Tom balled his fists but managed not to step back. "I've got your money and plenty more where that came from. What do you want, blood?"

"No mammy, no room. 4 o'clock. Be gone or I'll drive you out." The landlord raised his cane to support the threat, then turned on his heel and strode from the doorway.

"What'll we do now?" Molly whimpered, her small frame shaking against Daniel.

"We're not going!" Tom looked fearsome, considering he was only a year older than Daniel. "We're staying here."

Daniel knew not to get involved in arguments between brother and sister. He never forgot that he wasn't family, only a lodger dependent on their kindness.

"What'll we take with us?" Molly went over to the pot by the fire. "We can't carry this, we've nowhere to take it."

Tom took her by the shoulders. "We're staying, d'you hear me?"

Molly continued as though Tom hadn't spoken. "We'll need our blankets. We can wrap things in them."

"We're not going," Tom shouted, and suddenly slapped her across the face with the back of his hand.

Molly reeled away from him, landing in a heap against the wall, and let go to uncontrollable sobbing. Daniel gasped. Tom turned on his heel and went out into the street.

Checking that Tom was out of sight, Daniel went to Molly and wrapped his arms around her. He had no words. No way to express his shock at what Tom had done, or his fear of what lay ahead of them. Like Molly, he thought they should prepare to leave, but now his courage failed and he dared not. His fear of how Tom might react was greater than that of the landlord. He needed Tom more. Besides, what did they have that they could take, save the clothes they stood up in and the thin moth-eaten wrappings they called blankets? They couldn't boil rags on the streets. At best they could collect them for someone else and hope to receive small payment for their labours.

Quietly, Daniel prepared for leaving, whilst staying in the shack awaiting Tom's return. Surely he would come back before the appointed hour? Tom wouldn't leave him and Molly to face Mr Clyde alone, would he?

Molly was quiet now, sitting waiting by the hearth as though the loss of it was already being keenly felt.

When Tom did come back he was in the company of Patrick Mahoney. Daniel sent up a silent prayer of thanks. Perhaps he had been too swift to judge his companion. Maybe his dealings with the Roach Guard were a good thing after all. Tom and the older boy stood in the doorway, waiting. Patrick didn't come inside, but stood where the sun glinted off the blade he was making no effort to hide. Daniel could see two others of the Guard standing a little distance away, and for a moment allowed himself to relax.

When the hour came, the landlord was not alone either. Two rougher men, both armed with clubs, stood alongside.

Tom stepped forward, his face defiant. "This is our home, we'll not be moving." He stood proud, despite his ten years.

The landlord stepped forward to meet him, lifting Tom's chin with the end of his cane to force the boy to look up at him. "You've got five minutes to be out of my sight."

Patrick pulled Tom aside and moved to stand in front of the landlord, his arms crossed but the knife blade still visible and ready. "And what if yous was to rent it to me? You knows me father. Let me take it on."

For reasons he couldn't understand, a chill ran through Daniel as he waited for the reply.

"And what would you be wanting with a place to live at your age? Be gone."

"I'll pay good money."

"You'll pay what I ask or you'll not rent one of my houses."

Patrick seemed to Daniel to be winning. The landlord

was at least still talking to him.

"How much do you want?"

The landlord turned to walk away, inclining his head to his henchmen as he did.

"Wait!" Patrick went after him and made a show of putting his knife away. Daniel could not hear them talking from where he was, but from the body language it looked as though the landlord was relenting. He held a hand up to stay the other two and within a minute there was a grinning sneer across Patrick's victorious face and the men were called away.

Daniel felt Molly's body sag against his own with relief, but he wasn't ready for celebration just then. They'd struggled to meet the rent before, but any increase, as well as any extra share that Patrick demanded, was going to be impossible.

Tom swaggered into the doorway as though he now owned the place. "It's a good job one of us hasn't been sitting around these last days," he said looking in on Daniel and Molly.

Before he had time to come through the doorway, Patrick's hand was on his shoulder and wheeling him round to face the other way. "And where d'you think you're going, Thomas Reilly?"

Daniel could see the flashes of light on the blade that Patrick brought up under Tom's chin.

"I thought…" Tom suddenly sounded pitiful.

Patrick spat on the ground. "Then you thought wrong. This is my place now and yous all have to leave. Your mammy's not here to call on now and me da won't be bothered by the likes of you without her say so… Ready, boys?" Patrick clicked his fingers to call the other Roach Guard boys across. "This gentleman was just leaving… and his young friends."

Daniel didn't intend to stop for what was going to happen next. He took Molly's hand and pulled her up. He could feel her shaking. He grabbed the carefully folded blankets he'd left ready for them and started pulling her towards the door.

One of the Roach Guard had pinned Tom against the side of the building and had nicked his face with the edge of his blade as a foretaste of what was to come.

Patrick stepped aside for Daniel and Molly to pass and, as he did so, Molly pulled away.

"Wait." She went back into the shack but Patrick blocked Daniel's way to stop him following.

Daniel felt more alert than he had ever felt. Patrick had started to follow Molly into the shack. Daniel was terrified of what he was going to do to her. He could see the blood trickling down Tom's cheek. He couldn't move from where he was. Daniel's way was now blocked by the other Roach Guard member who was accompanying Patrick. He heard Molly scream and his heart raced. He did the only thing he could think of. "She's your sister! Leave her be."

Suddenly, Patrick was back out of the doorway, knife raised. "What did you just say?"

Daniel's voice was barely audible as he tried to form the words. It wobbled as he spoke. "She's your sister." If he died now, at least it would have been to save Molly.

Patrick slashed his face with the knife. Daniel could feel the searing pain from his cheekbone to his chin. Then Molly was there, clenching her little fists and clutching her mother's rosary, the one possession she'd thought it worth going back for. She kicked at Patrick's shin. Despite the fact that Daniel thought the relationship was news to her, she stood firm. "Go ask your father, Patrick Mahoney, and do

Daniel no more harm. What of it if I am your sister? I wouldn't call you family if you was the last man alive." She turned on the two holding Daniel and Tom hostage. "And you two should be ashamed of yourselves, picking on small boys."

Daniel saw Tom physically sag under the label of 'small boy'.

"Go fight the Bowery Boys or someone else your own size and leave us alone."

Her feisty nature would have been funny in other situations, but with his cheek dripping blood and his throat as dry as it was, Daniel felt no inclination to laugh. Instead he sent up a silent prayer of thanks that Mammy's spirit lived on in her daughter, whoever her father was.

Molly stood, hands on hips, tapping her foot in a meaningful way. Patrick and his cronies stepped aside and allowed the three children to step away from the shack. They moved off quietly. Molly, her head held high and her back straight, led the way, her taut white knuckles grasping the rosary tightly to her side. When they reached the big old tree's roots, they sank to the ground beneath it. None of them spoke for some time.

It was Molly who eventually broke the silence. "What d'you want to go getting yourself involved with the likes of Patrick Mahoney for, Thomas Reilly?"

Tommy shrugged but said nothing.

Then in a quiet voice Molly asked, "Is it true?"

Tommy nodded.

"But I was born back in Ireland, before Da went away."

Tommy nodded again. "Ma knew the Mahoneys before we came here. You're Patrick's sister. That's why I thought he'd help, but I reckon he didn't know."

Daniel thought that, after months of being the man of

the house, Tom once again seemed the boy he really was, lost in a confusing world, much like he and Molly were. Daniel almost felt sorry for him, but the betrayal of the last few weeks still made that hard.

Molly sighed and fell back into silence.

For a brief moment Daniel felt lucky to know that both of his parents had cared for him. He might be an orphan, but at least neither of his parents had left or disowned him.

He remembered the bundle he was carrying and opened it up. "Yous will need these," he said, thrusting a blanket towards each of them. "I brought these too." He held up the two wooden bowls. "We might find something to go in them sometime." He forced a smile. "We need to sleep somewhere." He prodded the grass-covered roots. "I guess it's not perfect, but it will do until we find somewhere else. Maybe tomorrow we can find something better." He took a few small coins from his pocket. "We could maybe get ourselves some bread and some ale."

Molly looked up at her brother. "What happened to the rent money, Tommy? We've still got that."

Tom cast his gaze down to the ground, picked up a stick and started prodding at the soil.

"Tommy?" Molly spoke very gently to her brother, but Daniel feared he knew the answer to the question. The money had been taken by Patrick Mahoney.

Tom said nothing, just shook his head, and Daniel saw a tear splash down onto the earth, before Tom used the stick to rub out any trace.

The summer night was warm but they huddled together, the three of them, below the embrace of the tree. Daniel slept little and from the movement of the others he guessed they were restless too. They didn't speak. Daniel was lost in thoughts of the money Tom had so easily been conned out of. In some ways, he minded that less for the thought that Tom was back amongst them once again, and he hoped things would be back to how they used to be, if that were possible.

At first light, Daniel rubbed his eyes and felt the aches from the hard ground poking at his arms and legs. At least in the shack there'd been straw on the ground. They'd taken it little by little from the neighbouring stables when it spilled out into the road, grateful for whatever the horses cast out.

Molly had finally fallen asleep and he didn't want to wake her so he stayed where he was, breathing softly and thinking about the day ahead. It would be hard to sing sweetly after so little sleep, but he'd try his best. It was their only income now, that and Tom's thieving. Maybe they could find work selling newspapers or blacking shoes. He'd seen others doing it. They'd probably need some money to even get started, and they needed to eat as well. He wanted to help take care of Molly, even though he still wasn't quite nine years old.

As the street became busy, Molly stirred. Daniel sat up and folded his blanket. Tom was already sitting, his back leaning against the tree, picking pieces of bark off a stick. He looked at the two of them and looked away, as though waiting for their reproach, but they said nothing.

Daniel took the last of the coins from his pocket. "I'll get us some bread." He walked away along the street, still clutching his blanket, to join the queue at the bakery for whatever he could afford. They could drink water from the well if they could find someone with a pail to draw it for them.

Once they'd finished eating it was Molly who got up. "I'll see you boys here this afternoon. I'm going to look for rags and see if I can sell them."

Daniel admired her courage. It gave him more strength for the day ahead. "I'm going to sing for our supper." He forced a grin. "Maybe someone will want to hear me."

"You've a lovely voice, Daniel Flynn, and I'd listen to you all day if I didn't have things to do." With that, the brave little soul scooped her blanket beneath her arm and marched toward the streets she normally searched for rags.

Tom was clearly downcast. Daniel reckoned it wasn't the time to chivvy him along.

"I'll see yous later," Tom said.

Daniel had a suspicion Tom was going to remonstrate with Patrick Mahoney, but doubted it would get him anywhere. Left alone, Daniel started to walk further up into town, skirting the areas policed by the gangs and constantly watching for trouble. He found a corner to sing near Bryant Park, but mournful, heart-rending songs were all he had a care for and with crowds of people enjoying the warm summer sunshine there were few who stopped to hear his pitiful sound. He made a few coins, which he pocketed gratefully, but after only an hour or so it was time to move on.

He began to walk, without aim or intent, and found himself close to the place they'd left Mammy so recently. He walked along the edge of the ground, not knowing why but feeling that for now there was no other place he wanted to be. He'd only walked a short distance along the perimeter of the Potter's Field when he saw a figure he thought he recognised slumped on the ground, head in hands and shoulders heaving.

He was uncertain if his approach would be welcome, but went up to Tom nonetheless and sat beside him. "I've missed you." His simple statement said everything he was feeling. He didn't know what else to say to Tom.

Tom looked up, his cheeks stained with tears. "It's all my fault. I just thought…"

"I'm guessing you didn't get any money back from Patrick Mahoney."

Tom shook his head.

"You could go asking his father…"

"And say what? It's time to look out for the girl you disowned while our Mammy was alive?" Tom rubbed his sleeve across his face and grinned. "It might work, but somehow I don't think so." Then he punched Daniel's arm and sent him sprawling and, as good as any apology, Daniel knew they were friends again.

CHAPTER 6

She was lovely and fair as the rose of the summer,
Yet 'twas not her beauty alone that won me;
Oh no, 'twas the truth in her eyes ever dawning,
That made me love Mary, the Rose of Tralee.
Edward Mordaunt Spencer, 1846 approx.

"And what am I supposed to be doing with this now?" Tom held out the silver pocket watch on the palm of his hand.

Daniel gaped at the beauty of it. "Won't anyone buy it from yous?"

"I can hardly stand on the corner shouting to any gentleman who passes, and we've no dealings with the Roach Guard no more. I'd wear it if I weren't likely to have meself caught as a result." Tom swaggered a pace or two, twirling the chain, causing Daniel and Molly to laugh despite everything.

"No one'll buy the rags I'm finding either." Molly slumped down in the doorway. It had been hard to find one which wasn't already filled with sleeping tenants. By night it had become their shelter.

They soon learned the peril of staying too long in the morning, when, on the second day, a boot landed firmly in Daniel's ribs, kicking him down the steps into the street. It meant four days of no singing, and their already meagre resources were stretched to breaking point.

"Can't you turn your hand to stealing food for us

instead?" Molly looked seriously at her brother.

"That's not so easy as picking pockets. There's always somebody watching. I gets us a little when I can." He grinned as he thrust a small chunk of bread towards them and they broke it hungrily.

"I'll try to sing tomorrow," Daniel said, wincing as he reached forward. "If we don't get more to eat soon, I'll not be singing again."

The following day, Tom and Molly sat close by as Daniel held his arms around his pummelled body, his voice quavering when breathing too deeply sent a ripple of pain through his ribs. Molly was quick to collect any coins that were thrown, before they could be lost to the gutter or kicked by a passing shoe. That night they ate like lords, compared to the four nights of no food, and it brought them more joy than a banquet could have brought to a king.

Over the next days, although they could ill afford to, and their stomachs growled in consequence, they kept just a little money back, saving for tools so Tom could shine shoes. They'd decided that would be a better option then selling newspapers; as Tom had put it: "I don't trust words I can't read and understand."

For his singing, Daniel always found a corner where he could sit with the still-crusted scar on his face turned away. No one wanted to throw coins to an angel who'd been in a street fight, even if it had been to defend Molly.

"Shoe shine." Tom grinned and bowed as Molly and Daniel applauded when he was ready to go out in search of custom. He polished what remained of his own boots until they as near shone as possible. Daniel hoped that no one would judge Tom by the holes in the uppers, or the places the stitching had given up completely.

"I'll try tomorrow, once I've got enough money for

some black," said Daniel, eager to be part of the new venture. He'd rather do that than sing about a land and a time that now seemed so far away.

Tom wasn't sure yet where he'd pitch himself. They knew from Daniel's singing where crowds of people could be found, but had little idea if they were the right places for shining shoes.

Once Tom had gone, Molly went with Daniel to find a pitch for singing. She had nothing else to do and besides, Daniel was glad of her company.

Tom had worked long hours to earn the money he brought back. He was in a vile mood from being polite, however rude his customers were. Daniel wanted to ask him for every detail, but thought better of it.

It was early the next morning when Daniel set off in search of polish and his own pitch. He reckoned he'd do best around where the men of business worked so he found himself a spot ready in the hope of trade.

"Shoe shine," he shouted as men passed. He'd been there about twenty minutes and already had his first customer. He sang softly to himself as he worked, earning a small tip on top of the charge. There was a lull in activity in the street so no point in shouting; instead he sat quietly, humming a tune with his eyes closed.

It was the punch to his face that brought him back to the world. "What you doing on my pitch?" The child facing him was no taller than he was, but seemed to be twice as wide. Before Daniel could gather himself, another punch landed him in the gutter and he put his hand to his misshapen and bleeding nose. As soon as he was able, he pulled himself up, grabbed his shoe black and cloth and, holding the cloth to his bleeding nose, he ran.

He had no idea where the others would be now. They

hadn't expected to meet up until much later in the day and the steps they slept on would be in use. He thought of going to check in case they were there, but his head was spinning and he needed to rest first. He found a nearby well and waited for someone to draw water before asking if he might have a little to wash some of the blood away. Then he sank down to the ground in despair. There'd be no singing in public for him for a while and without it, he couldn't see how they could survive. Tom had at least found a pitch that no one else was using, but he guessed the reason for that was because the pickings were so poor. They could barely all eat on what Tom was earning.

It was early afternoon when he found the others and was delighted to be back with Molly so she could tend his wounds.

"We'll have you sorted in no time." Molly's hands were gentle as she wiped away the worst of the remaining blood.

Her cheerful optimism made Daniel smile, despite knowing it wasn't going to be as simple as that.

"At least you've still got the shoe black, so you have. Although the cloth's not looking so good, Daniel Flynn." She held up the blood-covered shoe rag accusingly, but she was grinning as she spoke. "Now," she said, "how much money do we have?"

Daniel looked at Tom, but as a curious frown spread across his face, the pain of his wounds stopped him short. "Ow."

"Now you stay still there, or I can't be cleaning you up. I said, how much money do we have?"

Looking straight ahead, Daniel reached into his pocket and withdrew his coins. Tom did the same.

"Right," said Molly. "I want no arguments from either of you. Tommy will have dinner as he needs to work tomorrow. You and me, we'll share a small crust to stop the pangs being too bad, but the rest ye'll give to me."

Daniel knew better than to ask what Molly was planning. He trusted her completely and he knew she'd have a reason. He also thought the money was probably safer with Molly than anywhere else. Tom sullenly nodded his agreement and handed his coins to Molly, who dropped them with Daniel's into her apron.

"You'll do," she said to Daniel, taking the rag away. "I'm going to be gone for some time. While I'm away I'll try to find you a better rag for the shoes." She looked at Tom, one eyebrow raised, as though challenging them to ask where she was going, but Tom only grunted.

It was several hours before she came back, and as she approached she broke into a wide smile. "Now will you look at yourself? Those eyes are already the colour of the shoeblack and with that scar to go with it you look quite the little ruffian."

Daniel could feel the swelling of his face and wondered how bad it looked. He wasn't going to be welcome in polite company any time soon, but as he had no other company than Tom and Molly, that wasn't so much of a problem.

Molly was carrying a small ragged bundle, from which she withdrew a cloth for Tom. She curtsied as she presented him with it and then mischievously said, "Or should that have been a bow?"

Again, Tom didn't respond. Daniel was confused and was none the wiser as Molly took a dirty old cap and breeches out of the bundle.

"They're hardly less worn than my dress and apron, but they'll serve the purpose." She changed out of her dress and into the breeches, then pushed her hair up inside the cap so that she looked for all the world like the boys. "Will

I do?"

"And what should we call you, mister?" asked Daniel, realising she was meaning to look like a boy.

"Ah, now there's a good question. What do you think, Tom?"

"I guess 'Michael' would do it," Tom said, and Daniel was glad to see him almost break into a smile before punching his sister on the arm as though she were a boy.

"Hey, now don't you be hurting my poor arms. I'm going to be needing those for what I'm doing."

"And what would that be?" Tom asked.

"Never you mind. You'll find out soon enough."

It was before dawn next morning when Molly thrust her blanket at Daniel and whispered, "Look after this for me. I'll see yous later." Then she put Mammy's rosary around her neck inside her shirt, made sure it was hidden, twisted her hair up inside the cap so it was completely covered and walked away down the street.

Daniel's nose was still throbbing and he could sleep no more. He spent the morning sitting waiting and wondering what Molly was doing, while Tom went off to black shoes. He was hungry, but with no food left from the night before and no money, there was little he could do. With a broken nose and two black eyes he couldn't even sing for his breakfast, and he kept his head down to avoid attracting yet more trouble. He levered a piece of bark off a nearby tree and chewed it in an attempt to convince his body it was getting food.

When Molly returned she looked triumphant. Tom had come back some while earlier, more dispirited than the day before.

"Oh, boys, you're never going to be believing all I've got to tell you."

"Then there's no point telling us." Tom laid out the coins he'd collected, barely enough to cover bread for the three of them.

"Now don't you be worrying about that, Thomas Reilly. I've money for all three of us, but better than that…"

Daniel looked in wonder at her radiant face, eager to hear what was obviously important news. Even Tom looked up from his slouched and defeated attitude.

"… I've got us somewhere to sleep for the night and we've enough to get a small amount of food on the way."

"Molly, what have you done?" Tom looked thunderous.

"Don't you be assuming I've done anything wrong now, Tommy. You know that I wouldn't do anything the good Lord and Mammy wouldn't agree to."

"Apart from the thieving," Tom spat back at her.

Molly stood, hands on hips. "I didn't tell you before so you wouldn't say a girl shouldn't be doing this. I know you want to protect me, but as it turns out I'm pretty fair at doing that for meself."

Molly's mood was so infectious that Tom began to relent.

"So what have you been doing?" Daniel wanted to hear how this fine girl had managed so much when he and Tom had failed her.

"I've been selling newspapers, don't you know? Your brother Michael turned out to be quite good at it and sold every one he started with. He even went back and got some more to sell and when he sold those he got even more. Anyways, there's a hall with beds and I've made enough for all of us to sleep there and enough to buy a few papers to start tomorrow. But you have to call me Michael and we're all three brothers." She looked seriously first at Tom and then at Daniel.

In turn, they nodded.

"We're to go a little later. Oh, Tommy, what do you think? Maybe you could sell papers. And when your face ain't that ugly, so can you sell them too, Daniel."

"It's got to be better than this." Tom threw his blackened rag to the ground and held up his hands, the colour of shoe polish.

"I'm not so sure about that." Molly held up her newsprint-covered hands and grinned. "I think it might be much the same." She reached as though to an apron and then corrected herself and drew her money out of the breeches pocket. "We've not had so much since you were thieving, don't you know?"

Daniel couldn't help but wonder how the people at the lodgings were going to react when they saw his black eyes and scarred face. Short of covering them with shoeblack, there was nothing he could do to disguise them and besides, the swelling would still risk giving him away. He just had to hope that they wouldn't turn him away. The thought of being off the streets, even for one night, was a luxury. Sure, the temperatures were still warm enough, but he got little sleep for fear of being kicked from the steps again and was constantly alert to the noises of the world around them. He longed for a night and a day without fear of someone doing him more harm.

It was with trepidation that Daniel followed the others to Fulton Street. It was not far from where they were and took little time.

"But it's the newspaper's office," said Tom, looking up at the building that housed *The Sun*.

Molly smiled. "That it is, but there's a floor above with real beds." The pride in her voice almost made Daniel forget how frightened he was.

They followed Molly, or Michael as they would call her, up a narrow staircase on the left. Molly turned to them before they reached the top. "Oh and we'll be getting some learning while we're here as well." Then she turned around and continued up the flights.

Daniel wanted to pinch himself. A bed and a chance to learn something. He'd never dared to hope such a thing could happen. He remembered back to the little village school in Ireland, which seemed more of a dream than ever having been a reality.

They came to a door with lettering that Daniel found hard to make out. He remembered what some of them were, but he'd done no letters for a long time and not a great deal before that. Molly knocked, while the others waited behind her. The door was opened by a kindly gentleman.

"Excuse me, sir, I was told there might be a bed for me brothers and me." Molly used her best speaking voice and held out a shaking hand with the eighteen cents that would be needed for payment.

"Your name?"

"Michael, sir. Michael Reilly. And these are me brothers, Thomas and Daniel."

The boys were beckoned into the room and Daniel hoped the gloom might lessen any response to his injuries, but the man started slightly when he saw him and when he spoke again his tone was a little changed, with suspicion creeping in.

"We don't allow fighting and brawling in this establishment. If you get into any trouble you'll be asked to leave."

"Oh no, sir." Molly spoke quickly. "We'd never do anything like that. It wasn't Daniel's fault. He was attacked, sir, so he was."

The man nodded. "And what of your parents?"

It was Tom who spoke up this time, a slightly belligerent edge to his voice. "We've got no parents. It's just the three of us... sir."

"There's no need to take a tone with me, young man. Many of the children here are orphaned too. We do what we can. Now this gentleman will show you to your bunks and the location of the wash room." A stouter gentleman had joined them as they were talking. "And then, when you've got yourself cleaned up, you can come back through here to find yourselves a desk." He pointed to a hall laid out in neat rows.

They followed as requested, all the time with Daniel saying nothing but praying quietly that he'd be allowed to stay.

"Will you look at this?" Molly was prodding the straw mattress of the bed, after the gentleman had left them to get cleaned up before studying.

"Now don't you go getting too used to that, Mo... Michael." Tom grinned, having set aside all his earlier hesitation. "We'll not be affording this every night."

But as Tom sat on the edge of the bed it wasn't hard for Daniel to see he wished he could.

"Come along, boys." The stout gentleman was calling them through to the school room.

Daniel could feel the stares of some of the other boys and tried his best to stand tall, even though he wanted to hide.

"Now what would you be looking at?" Molly said defiantly to a boy much bigger than she was.

Daniel almost laughed as the boy, as rough from the streets as any he'd seen, promptly backed down. Molly followed it up by introducing them all. "Michael Reilly and these are me brothers, Daniel and Tom."

Somehow her bold approach disarmed all around her and Daniel had no difficulty understanding how she'd done so well selling papers that morning. No one would suspect that Michael was a girl.

It was a long time since Daniel had sat down to any learning and, as he was shown once again how to form his letters, they felt almost as alien as they had at his first trying back in Ireland. He was amazed as he looked across at Tom to see the eager concentration on his face and the look of real enthusiasm as he made steady progress. His efforts were held up by the Superintendent and Tom beamed with genuine pride. The letters were quite new to Molly. She'd been too young for any schooling before she left Ireland and she appeared even more lost than Daniel was feeling.

It was later that Daniel had a chance to shine, when the lessons in writing came to an end and a music lesson began. As the music teacher began to sing a song that Daniel knew, he felt the tiredness drain away and before long couldn't resist joining in. Despite his broken nose, the song was haunting, and before long he was singing a solo. Even without his eyes open Daniel knew from the silence of the room that both adults and boys were enraptured. Afterwards, it was as though no one could see his black eyes and scarred cheek; he was accepted into this place and thanked God for the fortune He'd shown them that day.

Molly went out to sell papers again the next morning and was gone before Daniel woke up. Tom left to shine shoes and Daniel went out in search of some place to spend the day. It was no fun wandering around on his own and his face only brought unwelcome attention. In the end he sat down by the wharf, looking out over the river and thinking about what life might be like across the water. He searched his memory for thoughts of Uncle Patrick and his fiddle, images frozen in time. He hoped the family in Ireland had fared better than those who'd travelled, but it was unlikely. He shook himself to stop the maudlin thoughts taking hold and instead turned his mind to thinking of a second night with a bed and the pluck of Molly to get them all there. His ma would have said she was a bonnie lass, but she was much more than that. She'd got pluck in a way he'd never known in a girl before, not that he'd known that many, apart from his sister. He stopped, aware once again that his thoughts were travelling back to the old times and knowing they were images he couldn't afford to dwell on. He tried to sing, not for anyone else but for himself, for comfort and to pass the time, but the pain of his face was too great and he fell silent again.

The day passed slowly and he was glad when it was finally time to find Tom and Molly and go for food before returning to their straw beds for a second evening. When they did, Tom talked of nothing but the difference reading and writing would make to his life.

"You see. We'll be rich one day. It ain't goin' to be like this forever."

Daniel smiled at his faith and ambition. He hoped Tom was right, but for his own part he was less convinced. He longed to sing, but the writing was much harder.

He expected the second night to be much as the first. However, when they went through the door he was surprised to find them greeted personally by the superintendent.

"Where are your parents?"

Daniel was confused. They'd gone over this the

previous day. Tom answered this time. "We ain't got none, sir."

"And how have you been living?"

"We got turned out on the street when Mammy died. We've done our best, sir."

Daniel was amazed at how polite Tom was being.

"And your father?"

"I dunno, sir. He left years ago. We don't know where he is."

"Then come with me, you three." And without another word he led them to a small room where a bath had been set up and a pile of clean clothes was waiting. "There's a train going tomorrow with places for you three to travel to find better lives. You'll take a bath and put on these fine clothes and be ready to leave at first light tomorrow." He went immediately, leaving them in the charge of another gentleman who was overseeing the bathing process.

Despite his wonder at the clothes which lay ready, without any apparent holes or frays, Daniel had a sudden horrible thought and looked at Molly. "No!" They looked at him and he could see the worry etched deep in Molly's face. She'd realised the problem too. Tom looked confused and went ahead with his bath first, without further comment.

Molly looked helplessly at Daniel, who shrugged in response. Without causing a scene, he could think of no way to get her out of the predicament. As Daniel followed into the bath, when Tom got out, he could still think of no solution. It would be obvious as soon as Molly undressed that she wasn't Michael. They got no further than her taking off her cap and shaking out her hair before the gentleman overseeing the baths stopped the process.

Daniel's heart sank as they were ushered in front of the

Superintendent again. He had no idea what reaction they were going to face. Surely girls could go wherever they were headed, too, couldn't they?

"Name?" He looked down on Molly, but there appeared to be no anger.

"Molly, sir, Molly Reilly."

"Parents?"

"That part was true, sir. We've got no parents."

The man nodded. "I'll arrange for you to be taken somewhere 'suitable' for your kind." He raised his eyebrows as he emphasised the words.

Daniel's heart sank. "But, sir, she's our sister and we need to stay together."

The man continued almost as though he hadn't heard Daniel speak. "You two go to the schoolroom. Miss, you come with me." He led Molly towards the door, and the look of horror on her face as she turned to Tom and Daniel was too much for Daniel to bear.

"Noooo…" He tried to cling to her, but his hands were forcibly removed as they dragged Molly away from him.

He'd lost all the people he'd ever loved in the world and now Molly was to be taken from him too. Whilst Tom turned and headed for the schoolroom, apparently unmoved by what was happening, Daniel could do nothing to stop the tears, and he stood and sobbed until the stout gentleman of the previous day bustled him off to join the others at the desks.

Daniel could not even begin to think about lessons. Every part of him was sick with fear that he'd never see his beloved Molly again; she who had come to mean so much to him, who had saved him from starvation and tended his wounds; she whose bravery had carried them this far. Even when it came to singing, Daniel remained silent.

As soon as they finished he went to the music teacher, hoping that the previous evening would have given the man a good opinion of him. "Excuse me, sir. Do you know where they've taken my… sister?"

"Not at all, boy. Now run along."

With this dismissal, Daniel felt as though life had ended. Tom seemed so far away, with pride in his new-found learning, and showed no care for where his sister had gone. Daniel felt more alone than he had done since arriving on the docks a year previously. More, even, than when he thought he'd lost Tom to the Roach Guard. Molly was gone and Tom was discovering a world that felt alien to Daniel. Whatever the morning held, it could feel no worse to him than the way life seemed now.

CHAPTER 7

I was wearing corduroy britches
Digging ditches, pulling switches, dodging hitches
I was workin' on the railway
Traditional

"Tom, I'm scared."

"Will you look at that? Daniel Flynn, scared of going on a train."

"It's not that. Where are we going?" Daniel stumbled after Tom as they were led off to join the rest of the group.

"Now how would I know that? To have a home of our own was all they said. To places where we'd have beds to sleep in every night and learning to do sometimes during the day. It's our chance, ain't it? There's nothing here."

"There's Molly." Daniel felt a lump in his throat as he said it.

"They'll send her too, you'll see."

"D'you think so? Oh, I hope you's right."

Tom laughed. "And how would I know that? I don't know where Molly is, but I know I've got a chance. A chance I'd never have if I stayed here. What's here for me? Blacking shoes, sleeping rough. Look at yourself with your broken nose. We ain't even part of a gang. What chance is there?"

To Daniel there was family, or what passed as that. He realised Tom's da had left and hadn't been back, and he wondered whether his leaving was what made Tom so hard. Maybe the death of a parent was kinder than being abandoned by them. He was quiet as they plodded on. His stomach churned and he felt awkward in the clothes he'd been given the night before, the collar buttoned and strange against his neck. He was trying to stay clean, as they'd been told to, but it wasn't as easy as it sounded when most of the time there was nowhere to sit but the floor.

There were a lot of other children waiting on the platform. They looked bigger than he was and he presumed they were older, but as they all stared at him he guessed it was his black eyes and scar that drew their gazes. They seemed to keep a little distance from him and he heard whispering and saw others pointing at him. A gentleman, some sort of priest by the look of what he was wearing, was going with them on the journey. The man seemed flustered as he tried to keep the children together and ready to board the train.

As they set off, many of the other boys seemed in high spirits. A train journey was new to all of them and even Daniel could imagine it would be exciting at another time. He sat quietly, staring out of the window, but registered little through the blur as he thought of Molly and wondered how long it would be until he saw her again. As the train travelled further from New York, he began to wonder if that time would ever come.

Tom punched his arm. "Will you look at that? I've not seen fields like those since I was in Ireland."

Another of the boys was shouting to the guardian, "Mister, what's that?"

"They're corn fields. That's how the cobs of corn grow."

"Where've all the buildings gone?"

Daniel presumed the boy had lived all his life in the

densely packed streets of New York and had never seen fields before. He, on the other hand, was relieved to see the back of the buildings. He just wished Molly were here to share it with them and couldn't understand how Tom could care so little about where his sister was.

The train rattled on and Daniel tried to console himself by singing quietly. Other boys were running around, enjoying what they saw as an adventure, but Daniel felt lost and alone, and as far from Tom as he'd ever been.

When the train finally stopped, Daniel thought they must have arrived and let his eyes close in relief and silent prayer. Instead, to his confusion, they were led away from the railway to a waiting boat, to cross a lake the size of which was unimaginable to him, with no shoreline visible on the other side. As they were led below deck, Daniel's breathing quickened as he remembered the last ship he'd been on and the outcome of that journey. His heart was racing and he could feel the sweat on his brow. He did the only thing he knew to ease his rising panic. He closed his eyes and sang the songs his father had sung. He ignored the pain of his battered face and sang as though his life depended on it.

After a while he became aware that the other Irish boys were beginning to join in and his was no longer a lone voice. He opened his eyes, looked around him and realised they were all focussing on him. He started to sing more loudly, and together they struck up quite a melody. He wondered if their earlier bravado was masking some of the same fears as he felt. Even Tom had joined in the song, something he'd never done before.

Suddenly there was a bustle and jostling and Daniel looked up, startled to know what was happening. The gentleman in charge was rounding them up. Daniel blinked, fearing he'd done wrong by starting the song. He realised he was shaking as he wondered what his punishment would be.

"Look lively, boys, and move towards the stairs."

Daniel frowned. Where were they going? He could feel the blood pounding in his ears as he followed the others up the passageway and was surprised to see they were being led into the saloon.

The priest was beaming. He looked around for Daniel and seemed about to pull him forward, but then, apparently having second thoughts, moved him to the middle of the group. "These ladies and gentlemen have asked that you sing again for them. Start us off, boy," he said, looking directly at Daniel, who had carefully hidden himself behind a taller boy.

Daniel felt his tension easing. He closed his eyes and, with his broken nose increasing the nasal sound, began to sing the same well-known Irish ballad he'd been singing below deck. Again, the others joined in and, as they ended, their audience applauded. He began another, but fewer voices joined him. As he'd sung for his supper for almost a year, Daniel felt no fear at having an audience and continued to sing, including a couple of solos. He wasn't singing to the people in front of him on the boat. He was singing to Molly, far away, back in New York.

After that, they slept a while having been given some of the spare berths on the boat rather than huddling in the steerage section as they were supposed to do. Daniel no longer felt so alone, as boys talked to him and accepted him as one of theirs. He was surprised to find that not all the children were orphaned as he and Tom were. A few had parents back in New York, who had sent them, hoping the children would find a better life than they could give.

Others were like him and Tom, homeless and without family. Some had been born in New York, but many, like them, had crossed the seas from Ireland. He thought he'd seen some of them around Five Points, but in the clothes they'd been provided with they all looked much the same as each other and he wasn't used to seeing his kind looking so clean.

Eventually the boat came to shore at a place called Albany. Their number was a little reduced as some of the adults on the boat had offered to take boys home with them. Despite Daniel's singing, no one wanted him or Tom.

It was a long wait for their next train and they were weary from the journey. Whilst not yet tatty, the clothes were already showing the signs of dirt that the boys found so hard to avoid. Crouching on the ground, for want of anywhere else to rest, probably wasn't helping.

When the wait was over, they were rounded up for their next train. Daniel was aware of heated voices and confusion. It seemed they were supposed to be in a carriage of their own, but instead the boys had to force their way into already full compartments. Tom was ahead of him and made it into the carriage before Daniel was stopped and redirected to a freight wagon at the end of the train. There were no windows and precious little light or ventilation. The boys tried to find space on the wagon's floor amongst whatever and whoever was already there, but in the darkness it was hard to find a vacant patch.

Later, the train rumbled into Buffalo and a now filthy Daniel was able to find Tom once again. He was uncertain how much time had passed since they left New York. It was Wednesday when they set off, he knew that. There were nights and days en route, but it wasn't clear how many. They waited once again, in Buffalo this time. Another boat was to take them across a similar expanse of water to the previous one, but even further away. Every mile increased the distance from Molly and took him to places where he felt as alien as he had first arriving in New York. The stench from the animals on the boat was hardly worse than anything he'd been used to, but that and the coarse filthy mattresses in the berths made the change of clothing seem pointless.

By the time the boat arrived in Detroit they were told it was Saturday night and yet the travelling was still not at an end. The novelty of the train had long since worn off for all of them, but they were bundled onto another, for what they were told would be the final leg of the journey.

Daniel did not know where Dowagiac was. All he knew was that they'd been travelling an awful long time and he was tired. Tired to the point that even lifting his legs to walk was almost too much. It was early morning and, not being expected until later, the children fanned out around the station and found places to sleep. As Daniel drifted off he was aware of an argument going on with the station master, but he was too tired to care and, curled up on the floor, was quickly asleep.

"Come on now, boys, wake up. Form an orderly line."

Daniel stirred himself from the depths of slumber. His limbs felt leaden and his mouth was dry and thick with dust. The sun was up and the morning advancing quickly as he went to the stream where others were swimming. He tried to wash the worst of the dirt from his face, before the gathering they were to attend. He'd never tried to swim and with the water so cold he didn't fancy starting now. His face was feeling less bruised than the previous days, but he couldn't judge what he might look like. He tried to see his reflection in the water, but with the ripples from the boys splashing it was impossible. He looked for Tom but couldn't see him, either swimming or on the bank.

Cleaned as best they could, the boys, in their by now ragged clothing, were ushered into the chapel and sat together to the side of the congregation. Daniel had only ever been to a Catholic service before and even that was a long time previous. He saw Tom further down the line and tried to catch his eye, but Tom didn't respond. Instead, Daniel spent the time looking around in awe at the women's hats and wondering why so many were crying when the priest talked about the lives the boys had led in New York. It was hard not to fidget but he was not alone, as other boys were shifting awkwardly and looking around. At least he recognised one of the songs, and for a few brief minutes was lost in the soul of the music.

It was later when the boys were called into the neighbouring hall. "Now stand nice and tall, no hands in pockets. Remember to look straight ahead and answer any questions you're asked."

There was sniggering from some of the boys, but Daniel felt lost and helpless. He wanted to stand near to Tom in the hope they'd find a home together, but Tom moved away when Daniel searched him out, leaving Daniel confused. He did his best to stand tall, but he was smaller than the older boys. He couldn't help feeling like the beasts he'd seen at a cattle market when he was younger, as the adults went around prodding and poking at the boys standing there.

"Name?"

"Daniel Flynn... Reilly, sir." For a minute he forgot he was supposed to be Tom's brother.

"Can't you even remember your name?"

"Yes, sir. Daniel, sir." He could feel his heart racing.

"That's me brother Thomas, sir." He leaned forward to point down the line, but Tom, his blood-brother and former confidant, was nowhere to be seen. Daniel swallowed hard.

"And how did you get the scar, you little ruffian?"

"It wasn't my fault, sir. It was when…" But the man hadn't stayed to hear the answer. He'd moved down the line and was testing the muscles of one of the remaining larger boys.

When the adults eventually left, a number of the boys went too. The supervisor took charge of those who remained and they were given bedding for the night.

"Excuse me, mister." Daniel approached him hesitantly.

"Yes, child?"

"Do you know where me brother went?"

The man looked down his records. "Yes, he's with a family out of town."

"Will I see him again?"

"Well, that depends."

However, he didn't tell Daniel what it depended on, and before he had the chance to ask anything further the man was called away. The boys were left in the care of the local helpers, who fed them and kept an eye on them for the night.

Daniel sat with his arms around his knees, listening to the bravado of the others.

"I didn't like the look of him so I made meself look smaller," one boy was saying.

"Na, you just know to be rude to them. They won't want yous then."

"What'll happen to the rest of us? Will we go back to New York?" The boy sounded hopeful, and for a moment the prospect lifted Daniel's spirits. If only he could go back and find Molly.

"No, child. There will be places found for all of you," said one of the ladies who were bustling around with drinks for the boys.

The following day more of the boys were taken off from the party, until only nine remained. Daniel could count those using his fingers, so he knew how many there were. He looked around at his company, the smallest and the weakest. The supervisor was back with them and rounding them up into a group.

"Off we go then, follow me."

They followed, all of them looking as defeated as Daniel felt. His heart missed a beat as they arrived back at the train station.

"Are we going to New York, mister?"

The supervisor laughed. "No, boy. I'm taking you as far as Chicago and then you're to get a train to Iowa, where you'll be met and housed."

Daniel had no idea where either Chicago or Iowa were, and from asking around, the others hadn't either. His only response was from one who thought 'it was terrible far.' He sighed deeply and settled in to sleep as much of the journey as he could. He longed for his family, for Molly, even for Tom. Biting his lip, he tried to stem the flow of tears.

Once on the train at Chicago, the supervisor made to leave them. "Now you all stay in the carriage and the guard will call you to alight at Iowa. I must be getting back. I've a long journey ahead."

"Sir?"

"Yes, boy, what is it?"

"Excuse me, sir, but if you're going back to New York, please tell Molly where I am." Daniel turned his hopeful face up to the man.

"And who is this Molly?"

"My sister, sir. Molly Reilly. They took her away from me. Tell her I'm thinking of her."

There was no chance for Daniel to know if the man said anything in return, as the whistle blew and the smoke billowing back across the train as it moved away blocked everything from view.

He was going to Iowa. He didn't know where that was, but he did know that once again they travelled many days and there was little chance of finding his way back to New York, or even to Tom in Dowagiac. It was time to look out for himself and remember all he'd learned across his nearly nine years of life. It was time to be Daniel Flynn, whatever that was going to mean in this strange world. He'd survived his arrival in New York and he could do it again. Quietly and to himself alone, he started to sing.

CHAPTER 8

Mellow the moonlight to shine is beginning
Close by the window young Eileen is spinning
Bent o'er the fire her blind grandmother sitting
Crooning and moaning and drowsily knitting.
John Francis Waller, 1809 - 1894

"Ah, here he is."

Daniel had been at the orphanage only a few weeks when he was led from the windowless, white-painted corridor into the office of the principal of the children's home.

"I think you'll find him a good worker." The principal addressed the man who was standing before his desk.

Daniel looked up briefly at the man he was ushered in front of, but was careful not to meet his eye. The man's moustache was long and well curled, but the face behind it was weather-beaten and ruddy. He looked down the worn tweed jacket to the trousers held by a heavy belt and to the well-worn and muddy boots. This was a working man, not a gentleman. Daniel kept his eyes cast down.

"Look at me, boy." The voice was harsh. "He doesn't look much more than a child."

"He's strong for his age."

As he'd done no hard labour since his arrival, Daniel felt as though the principal were selling him like any other commodity.

"I'm nine, sir," Daniel said, looking up for the first time.

"I didn't ask you. You speak when you're spoken to. Otherwise you keep your mouth shut. Do you understand me, boy?"

Daniel was unsure if he should answer, but gave a swift nod of his head.

The principal was fidgeting awkwardly.

"How did he get this scar? Is he trouble?"

"Er, no. He got that before he came here. An accident, I understand. He's been no trouble and he's a good worker."

There it was again – 'a good worker'. Daniel had an uneasy feeling. This didn't sound much like the life everyone had talked of. What about schooling? Was it just about working? At least here in the home he was getting some learning too, and working in the kitchen garden wasn't a difficult chore. It certainly couldn't be described as heavy labour. There were too few staff for supervision and he liked the freedom that afforded. He'd been independent of adult direction in New York and would not have welcomed it now.

"I'll take him, but if he's any trouble..." The sentence was left hanging and Daniel didn't want to think how it might have ended. He felt his shoulders fall slightly, but tried desperately not to show the disappointment he was feeling.

He collected his belongings: a small bundle which amounted to a copy of *Moby-Dick* he'd been given on arrival, as part of his lessons, and a second shirt. He was taken out to join the man, who he was now told was Mr Hawksworth. Daniel was directed to the back of the hay wagon, while Hawksworth got up front and took the reins. The man said nothing as he clicked his tongue and flicked the whip against the horses.

Daniel wasn't alone in the back of the wagon. Two lanky teenagers sneered at him as he climbed up. They were lounging against a couple of bales of hay and made no effort to move for Daniel's benefit. He was unsure what to say. The way they looked at him, he knew whatever he said was going to be wrong. He kept his mouth shut and tried to climb over their legs so he could find a place to sit, as the cart jolted away onto the dirt road. The older one raised his foot as Daniel passed, causing him to trip and fall face first into some loose hay.

"Well, will you look at that? The boy's clumsy."

Daniel righted himself and made no reply.

"What's your name, boy?" This time it was the younger one. Daniel guessed he was about seventeen, but it was hard to tell. He was kitted out in heavy work trousers, boots and a thick cotton shirt. None of it looked as though it fitted him terribly well and he doubted that this was their first owner.

"Daniel, Daniel Flynn."

"Well, Danny boy, you're not from these parts, are you? Round here, people are taught to respect their elders and betters and you need to apologise for kicking my leg."

Daniel swallowed hard. He knew he'd been tripped, but it was clear that now wasn't the time for an argument. He bit hard on his lip, then very quietly said, "I'm sorry."

"Now where are our manners? We ain't introduced ourselves, have we, Rick? I'm Jed and this is my brother Rick. He's called that on account of getting hisself stuck at the top of a hay rick when he was a nipper. Of course, when I says stuck, he may have been given a helping hand, but it ain't done you no harm, has it, Rick? He ain't the brightest, are you, brother?"

The younger one grinned and shook his head.

Daniel quickly worked out who he thought was the leader, but suspected the brothers were as dangerous as each other at the end of the day.

The farm was some distance out of the town and, without needing to ask, Daniel could see it was likely to be corn they were growing. The fields were tall either side of the dusty road, close on ready for harvesting. It didn't take much for him to work out why extra labour was being brought in.

They pulled up in the yard of the farm and Daniel clambered down from the wagon, after allowing time for Jed and Rick to leave before him. He hoped he wasn't going to be seeing so much of them.

Addressing Jed, Mr Hawksworth shouted, "Show this boy the bunkhouse and tell him what needs to be done."

Daniel realised the pair were not new to the farm, as he'd first thought. He wondered if they came in just for harvesting or stayed for more of the year.

Jed's grin filled Daniel with terror. "Well, that'll be my pleasure, Mr Hawksworth, sir." Then, throwing a bag about half Daniel's size in his direction, he added, "Bring that bag this way, Danny boy."

The bag was too heavy for Daniel to catch and he toppled in a heap with the bag on top of him. He looked up to find Rick glaring down at him.

"Now that was very clumsy, Danny boy." Rick's sentences were slow and drawn out. "That's no way to go treating my brother's bag. Now get up." Rick rather more than prodded Daniel with his heavy boot.

Before any further harm could come to him, Daniel scrambled to his feet and wrestled the bag into his arms, struggling across the yard under its weight.

His bunk consisted of a rough mattress and a small

cubby hole in which to put his belongings. The Newsboys' Home in New York had been more comfortable, but there was little point in thinking back. He'd long since learned that pining for the past was the road to misery. He placed his copy of *Moby-Dick* on the shelf, together with his shirt, and turned to find once again that Rick was standing over him. He'd been more worried about Jed, but was starting to change his mind.

"What are you doing with one of those darn books, Danny boy? Are you one of those children as learned them words?"

In truth, there were not many words in the book that Daniel could read, but he looked at the letters now and then so at least he didn't forget the ones he did know. He suspected that any at all were more than Rick might understand. He hadn't answered Rick's question when Rick grabbed him by the shirt and pulled him from the bunk.

"There's work to do now, boy, so you'd best be running along." Rick threw him in the direction of the door and Daniel pulled himself together as quickly as he could.

The work was hard, stripping the cobs from the stems. Struggling along the tightly grown lines of plants left his face and arms scratched and cut from the razor-sharp edges of the leaves. The corn was taller than he was by some way and no part of him escaped the savagery of the leaf edges. He needed a stick to pull some of the cobs down to his level, and God help him if Mr Hawksworth found he'd missed any as he went.

He started at first light and continued pretty near until dusk, eating the crust he was given for lunch as he worked. By the time he reached his bed, despite his discomfort, he was too exhausted not to fall asleep. It wasn't just the farm work, it was being called away from the field to do the fetching and carrying for Jed and Rick that took its toll. On the bright side, there was little time to be lonely or to feel sorry for himself. There were just the three of them in the bunkhouse. Mr Hawksworth said he was trying to bring in more men to share the work, but they never seemed to appear and, despite the words, Daniel doubted that much attempt had been made. He was under no illusion as to what was expected of him.

There was just the one night of the week that Daniel looked forward to and that was Saturday. Jed and Rick were paid on a Saturday and usually went into town to find something to spend it on. At one point, he'd found the courage to ask Mr Hawksworth if he too was being paid and had received a beating to his bare flesh with Mr Hawksworth's belt for this enquiry. He supposed that was answer enough, though not the one he had hoped for. It certainly made Daniel think twice about making any further enquiries of any sort.

One Saturday night, quite early in his stay, Daniel was sitting alone outside the bunkhouse in the early evening. His thoughts drifted to his dearest Molly and, trying desperately to picture her face, he began to sing.

Daniel was lost in a world which had held hope and warmth and, despite his resolution not to look back, the tears streamed down his face. He was aware of nothing and no one; just the song and the people he loved.

It was not until he reached the end of the song that a cough brought him back from his reverie. A woman was standing nearby holding a tray. He'd seen her before and knew she was Hawksworth's wife and that she kept house for the owner – not that the owner ever seemed to be there.

"I thought you might like this," she said in a gentle

tone, handing him a plate of pancakes with syrup. "The menfolk are out and I thought you might be lonesome out here."

He got to his feet and quickly wiped the tears from his face. "Why, thank you, ma'am." He took the plate gratefully.

"You can leave it by yonder trough when you're done. I'll collect it from there." She said no more, but turned and walked back to the house.

Daniel stared after her, wondering what Mr Hawksworth would say if he knew of his wife's kindness, and wishing she could stay a while.

Daniel didn't realise how hungry he was until he'd eaten his fill of pancakes and felt warmed and content, at least with regard to food, for the first time in as long as he could remember. Suddenly his thoughts turned to his life in Ireland, so long ago now. He remembered the struggle for food that plagued all his family and neighbours and the way they had never given up. He thought of his da and the fighting spirit which led him to search for a new life for his family, and Daniel made a decision. It was time to stand up for himself. Except for Mrs Hawksworth's act of kindness, no one else was going to help him, so he'd have to help himself. He wanted to learn to read and write. Not just know the shapes of the letters, but be able to put them together as Tom was able to do. There was no schooling for him and all he had was *Moby-Dick*. He knew its name because he'd been told when it was given to him, and many times he'd traced the letters on the cover with his finger.

He wondered how he could learn with no one to teach him. He was sure that neither Jed nor Rick could read and he could not have asked them if they could. He needed a plan.

Two weeks passed before he next saw Mrs Hawksworth. Again, it was a Saturday night and a calm stillness had settled on the house with the absence of the men. Whilst Daniel was delighted to see Mrs Hawksworth bringing pancakes and syrup, he could feel his palms clammy to the touch and as he went to speak his throat felt dry and voiceless.

"Ma'am," he stuttered, once he'd coughed and croaked his thanks for the food, "would you help me learn to read?" He let out the breath he'd been holding and drew out his copy of *Moby-Dick* from under his shirt. He looked up at her, pleading.

"Well, I'll be." Her eyes darted around the farmyard. "What'll the master say if he finds me teaching you, boy?"

He'd got past the most difficult part and his courage started to return to him. "Much the same as he'd say if he knew you were bringing me pancakes, ma'am. You've already showed how kind you are."

Mrs Hawksworth smiled. Her eyes darted around once more and then settled back on Daniel. "I dare say those boys won't be back a while yet. I'll bring a light down to the barn and help you for a little time. But youns mustn't say a word about it."

Daniel broke into a broad smile. "Yes, ma'am." His heart lifted as it hadn't done for many a day and he resolved to work as hard as any student could.

Daniel's lessons were not long or frequent, but he did work hard and Mrs Hawksworth was a good and willing teacher. Before long he was starting to read parts of the book on his own when she wasn't there, marking the difficult words that he needed help with by rubbing a little leaf juice on the page. There were not many hours with light enough to see the letters and no work to do, but at every chance he got, Daniel took out his book and made a little progress, even if only a sentence or two.

The harvesting was done now and the work should have been a little lighter for the winter. Jed and Rick worked less, but they set to making Daniel do more of their share and went into town more often. Daniel didn't really mind the work, but he dreaded their beatings when they were not happy with what he'd done, and the worst of those were the times they came back drunk. It was a high price to pay for more time on his own, but he took it as best he could.

The chores he did most willingly were the fetching and carrying for Mrs Hawksworth. Those he did with a light and cheerful heart and would sing quietly to himself as he worked.

"What have you got to sing about, Danny boy?" Jed pushed his shoulder hard as he passed, causing the milk in the pail to slop over the side. Daniel put the pail down quickly, to stop it losing more before he got it to the back door.

"Now look what you've done, you clumsy oaf. The boss ain't going to be too happy when he hears you've been spilling the milk." Rick kicked the pail with his boot, causing still more to slop out.

Daniel closed his eyes and took a deep breath. He could stand and fight or he could run, but how could a child fight against two grown men? He searched for inspiration and could think of none. He grabbed at the pail and tried to run from the barn to the back door before they could catch him, but as he did, he tripped and the rest of the milk was lost.

"Now will you just look at that?" Jed walked to stand over him. "The boy really is clumsy, tut tut tut. What's going to happen to poor Danny boy now?"

Daniel could hear the sneer in his voice and hated him. He hated him with a fury and passion he'd not felt about anyone before. Not even about the landlord who'd turned them over to the whim of Patrick Mahoney. Not even to Patrick for throwing them out on the streets. Hate was not a feeling Daniel normally bore, but it rose up in him now, and he felt the ineffectual rage of a child wronged once again by an adult.

"What's all this noise?"

Daniel scrambled to his feet as Mr Hawksworth approached. He looked at the empty pail lying in the dirt and at the slick of milk seeping into the ground. He looked round at Jed and Rick glaring at him, with just a hint of a smile playing across both their faces.

Daniel silently fumed. Then he looked up to Mr Hawksworth once again, but despite his balled fists, his courage failed him. "I… er… tripped, sir."

Hawksworth kicked the pail in Daniel's direction. "And who's going to pay for this?" He hissed the words at Daniel as he started removing his belt. "Who…" He took a step forward. "… Is going to…" He took another step toward Daniel. "… Pay?" He boomed the last word.

Daniel's eyes darted over to Mrs Hawksworth as she approached across the yard.

"Oh stop, stop. Lord have mercy, leave the boy."

"Keep out of this, woman. This is men's business. Get back up to the house." Hawksworth turned and whipped the belt in his wife's direction.

Daniel gasped as she flinched and he realised this wasn't the first time Hawksworth had taken his belt to her. No wonder she was always on edge when she helped him with his reading. She was as scared as he was.

Despite her obvious fear, Mrs Hawksworth was making

to remonstrate with her husband, but Daniel couldn't let her do that. He stepped forward. "It was my fault, sir."

"Stand your ground, Liza. Save you going too soft, you can watch what happens to the boy." Then, as Daniel bent over a bale of hay, Hawksworth struck him, blow after blow with the belt until his flesh was raw.

Daniel balled his fists again and bit hard into the straw to try to stop himself from crying out. He could feel the tears pricking his eyes and prayed for the beating to be over. Eventually it stopped, but he stayed where he was, bent over the bale, waiting to be left in peace. He wasn't even sure he was capable of moving. He heard heavy boot steps moving away from him in both directions. Even Jed and Rick said nothing at the finish of what they'd watched.

When he was sure he was alone, Daniel curled into a ball and sobbed. His back was burning with pain and he longed for the feeling to subside. He had no idea how long he'd been there. An hour, maybe more, passed before he was aware of a quiet presence beside him.

"Daniel."

He looked up to see Mrs Hawksworth smiling a weak but gentle smile at him. She held a bowl and a cloth.

"They's all gone into town. Let me tend your wounds." She darted little looks around as she spoke.

As she dabbed his back, Daniel flinched. "It wasn't me, ma'am."

"I knows it wasn't, Daniel. Mr Hawksworth knows it wasn't, too."

"But why did he beat me?"

"I don't know, Daniel." Her voice sounded far away. "Because he can." Then she carried on quietly with the work of cleaning him up and bringing a little relief to the pain. She gave him a small glass of whiskey to drink.

"This'll help."

He knew without her saying that he mustn't say a word about it, but she didn't need to fear. He'd made a decision. He wasn't going to stay to find when the next beating would be. He was going to head off to see if he could find a better life somewhere new. In his heart he wanted to go back to New York, but anywhere was better than where he was now.

A little while later, Mrs Hawksworth brought him out pancakes. He didn't set to and eat them as he would have liked, though he drank the syrup for the energy it would give. Instead, he carefully wrapped the dry pancakes in his spare shirt. Then, pushing his book in his pocket, he started walking away from the farm into the night. He knew not where he was going, or how far it might be, but at least the night was mild and dry. What he did know was that whilst walking was painful, pulling as it did on every last weal across his skin, he had to go while he had the chance. No place was home, but he reckoned that any place would be better than where he was right then.

CHAPTER 9

"William Dixon."

There was a long pause. "Yes, ma'am." It still took Tom a second or two to realise it was his name being called on the register. He wasn't sorry to lose the name Thomas Reilly; it had brought him nothing but trouble. When he was given the opportunity to change his name, he'd jumped at it. Thomas H. Reilly was consigned to history and, with it, all that Tom had been. His old life had been nothing at all like the life 'William' landed himself. There were almost no similarities either to life in Ireland or New York, except for the flame-red hair, and even that was not as unruly as his former mass of shaggy curls. His hair was one of the only indications of his true origin, but there were others with Irish ancestry who hadn't grown up on the streets and he fitted right in with the auburn hair of his new mother. He sat straight at his desk, listening to the rest of the register.

William took to studying easily and loved his days at school. He was focussed and determined, whatever he turned his mind to.

"Well done, Dixon." His teacher was walking up and down the aisles of desks, looking at the answers to the sums they were chalking on the tablets.

"Thank you, Miss."

He might have started his schooling rather later than the others, but he was catching up fast and his new family, as well as Miss Simpson, were proud of his achievements. He would never have imagined he could do so well at studying. He'd always been quick enough to know when he was being given a good deal on the goods he'd sold, but he hadn't linked that to any wider skills. There'd been little chance to see his own ability before coming to Dowagiac. Of course, there had been the village school in the days before New York, but he was too young then to make any real progress and it was hard to learn when he was hungry all the time. Now he was making up for lost time and had found a thirst for knowledge that would have surprised everyone he'd known. It was his meal ticket to a better life and nothing and no one was going to stand in his way – of that he was quite definite. Nothing!

The early days had been hard, with so many of the boys staying in the town. It was difficult to break out of the mould of being 'one of them', but after his experience with Patrick Mahoney and the Roach Guard he was going to be nobody's whipping boy again, not if there was anything he could do about it. One 'incident' in the playground was all it had taken for the others to know that William Dixon was not to be messed with. After that he was free to work hard without taunt or provocation.

His new father was a local lawyer and William set his heart on following the same profession. He wanted the wealth and the lifestyle that went with it, and he'd never shied away from hard work, whether it was picking pockets, shining shoes or studying.

"How did you get that scar, Will?" Jude McCaulay asked one day as they walked back from school together.

Jude was a local boy, born and bred, and associating with him had helped William not to be labelled with the other New Yorkers. It was another thing that set Will apart, although that was not the sole reason for him cultivating the friendship. The more Will built a new story of his life, the more even he believed it.

"That?" He'd rolled his sleeves up due to the warmth of the summer day, forgetting the scar on his forearm. He flinched as he looked at it; a momentary recollection of Daniel and Molly going through his mind before he pushed the thoughts away. "It's nothing. Just an accident a while back." That's what he told himself and, thankfully, Jude was happy with the answer.

He left Jude at the end of the road and went on to the house he shared with his new parents and the staff who worked for them. He couldn't help but smile as he walked up the driveway to the wood-boarded, colonial style house. Ma was sitting on the porch embroidering a tablecloth. Will put his bag on the decking, knelt down and kissed her cheek. He'd won the Dixons' hearts and was unafraid to turn on the charm.

"It's a beautiful day, Will. Your father thought you might like to take Bounty out for a ride."

"May I?" This was an unexpected surprise and he was almost breathless with excitement.

Bounty was a fine horse and he'd longed to take her out since he'd started learning to ride six months ago. In the past his father had said, 'Not until I'm happy she's safe in your hands.' Until now he'd only been allowed to ride Matilda. She was a good horse, but more steady than Bounty and without the glamour and spirit of the grey mare.

"Don't take her too far. Get Briggs to saddle her up." The woman rested her hand on his arm. "And be careful. It took us long enough to get a son; I've no wish to lose you now you're here. Thank the Lord the scarlet fever didn't take you and I'll be glad for no riding accident to do so either."

Will smiled. "No, ma'am."

A number of the children he'd been at school with had died in the scarlet fever epidemic and it had been a worrying time for everyone, but that had passed and Will felt invincible. Almost skipping with excitement, he took his bag into the house and went to change into his riding breeches.

He certainly was one of the lucky ones. There was no farm work to keep him from year-round schooling and few chores were expected of him around the home. He'd been legally adopted as 'the son the family had never had' within six months of his arrival and treated that way from the first day. He was a chameleon with an ear for language and accent. With a fine set of clothes and having learned to speak as his American family spoke, he effectively erased the whole of his beginnings. From time to time, there were still tortured nights, with sleep punctuated by pictures of Mammy in the barrow as they wheeled her to the Potter's Field. On those nights, as he cried out, Mrs Dixon would sit with him until he was calm. She never asked him to tell her of his former life and he never volunteered the information. He just strove to be the son they wanted and to enjoy for himself the privileges that brought. He liked acting a part and the longer he acted the more natural the part became. There were days he could almost believe he had been born to the life he now lived.

Riding Bounty had been Will's goal. He had taken riding seriously. He wanted to be the best at everything. He'd been the best pickpocket in New York, at least in his own mind. Now he was going to be the best rider, the best scholar, the best lawyer and, if necessary to get the things he wanted, the best son. Will held Bounty's head as Briggs saddled her for the ride.

His heart beat with excited apprehension as he climbed onto her back.

"Where shall we go, girl?" he whispered in her ear. She shook her head and snorted in answer. He could feel the power of her readiness ripple back through her flanks as he took the reins.

His was a moot question. He'd been rehearsing this moment in his mind for weeks. He longed to ride along the ridge, with the wind blowing through Bounty's mane as they galloped. He started a gentle walk away from the stable, concentrating hard until he had the measure of her. It felt good to be up so high. Bounty stood probably two hands taller than Matilda. She whinnied and tossed her head gently with pleasure as he asked her to go faster. It wasn't long before Will and Bounty were streaking along in sheer pleasure. He couldn't remember feeling a rush like this since the times of danger on the streets of New York, and much as he tried to forget those days existed, he missed the excitement and the feeling of alertness they had brought. It was about life on the edge, the balance between safety and tragedy and never quite knowing which side of the line you'd come down on.

He threw his head back and laughed into the wind, fuelled by adrenalin and filled with as much pleasure as he had ever experienced. Not for him scrabbling around in the dirt for rags, or digging fields. He was free and, as the wind whipped around him, he felt all-powerful.

He brought Bounty to a halt on the ridge. They were both out of breath. He looked down over the surrounding farmland and laughed as he thought of the other boys. Who would suspect him of sharing their background now, with his fine clothes and manners? Even his hair colour just made him seem like part of the family. It had been one of the reasons they'd picked him out of the line. That and the fact he already knew his letters and was so hungry for learning.

He could feel the sweat on Bounty's flank as they started to trot back along the path towards the house. Yes, sir, this was the life he wanted to live. Maybe one day he could be mayor of this place he called home. Will Dixon was going to be someone.

He left Bounty with Briggs to be washed down and made comfortable and went back to the house.

Pa was waiting for him. "By the look of that grin you've been out on Bounty."

"Yes, sir," said Will, grinning even more broadly. "Thank you, sir, she's a wonderful horse."

"She sure is, son. She sure is."

"Well, look at you with all that colour in your face. You look the picture of health," Ma said as she passed through the hall where they were standing. "Now get yourself cleaned up for dinner and come and tell us all about it."

Will went to his room to wash and change. A pitcher of warm water was waiting for him on the stand and his clothes had been laid out ready.

The table was set for dinner when he came down and he was just in time to take his place. He'd learnt very early that lateness was not tolerated and had made sure he was on time unless there was an unavoidable reason. He spoke little through dinner. He was hungry from his ride and was happy to listen to Pa relating the day's events. Occasionally he'd be asked what he thought on some weighty matter. He would consider carefully and reply with what he thought Pa wanted to hear.

It was towards the end of dinner when Ma spoke directly to him. Having asked for an account of the ride, she said, "We received a letter today, Will, from the Children's Aid Society. They want to know how you're doing. Pa will write back this evening and he'd like you to write a letter to be sent with it…" She hesitated. "Someone called Molly has contacted them to ask how you are."

Will flinched. Ma didn't ask who Molly was, but the question hung there.

Will let it hang. "I'll write a note for Pa to send. Will you excuse me so I can go to do it now, please?"

Pa waved him away from the table and Will went to his room to find pen and paper.

Dear Sirs,

Thank you for your concern about my progress. I am very well and settled here. I now go under the family name of Dixon and have been fully adopted. I would prefer you not to write to me further. Please tell Molly that I am well, but not to contact me. I have left my old life behind.

Your humble servant

William Dixon

He read it over and blotted the ink. Then he placed the letter in an envelope and decided to take it down to Pa at breakfast, to make it less likely that Ma would read it and ask him about Molly. It had been helpful that, on their arrival, the guardian said many of the children had known a lot of pain and preferred not to talk about the past. He was certainly able to use that to keep away anyone who thought of prying. The fact that Daniel had moved on to another place helped too. At the hall, when they were first paraded from the train, his new parents had asked if he was alone or whether they should be bringing any of the other children along with him. He could see Daniel out of the corner of his eye, further down the line, but he assured the Dixons he was quite alone and it had always been that way.

As they had left the hall, William hadn't looked back and it was only later he learned to his relief that Daniel had been taken away elsewhere by train and was now likely to be a very long way away. Distance suited his purposes very well. He felt no guilt in the matter. It was just a question of being practical. He told himself that both Molly and Daniel would want this better life for him and therefore he was justified in whatever actions were needed. He tried not to think what Mammy might have said. She always was too soft and where had that got her? No, Will was just fine on his own, with no past to look back to.

CHAPTER 10

Molly worked her way around the rosary beads in the darkness of her bunk. She'd prayed for Tommy and for Daniel. Then she'd prayed for Mammy's soul and everyone else she could think of, including both Ol' Tinker and Patrick Mahoney senior, and junior come to that. She'd even prayed for the women who ran the children's home she was now in. Somehow, she felt that if she kept praying she would put off the awful inevitability of morning coming and leaving New York.

When she heard she was now considered old enough, and would be taken to find a new family, she had felt a glimmer of hope. "Please, will it be to the same place my brothers have gone?"

"I'm sorry, child, I don't suppose it will." At least the matron had seemed to care, as she'd answered the question.

"Is there word from Tommy, in answer to my note?"

It was then Matron had sat her down and looked grim in reply. "There is, child."

"Is he ill? Can I see him?"

Matron put her hand on Molly's and said, "He's well and happy."

Molly breathed a sigh of relief. "Then I can see him?"

"No, child. He's in a family a long way from here..." She hesitated. "... And he asks that you don't write again."

Molly was confused. How could Tom not want to hear

from her? She was his sister. She was family. "And Daniel?" she asked quietly.

Matron shook her head sadly. "We've heard nothing about your other brother."

"But if I leave here, how will I find them?"

"You can write, child. I'm sure the Children's Aid Society will tell you when they have news."

Molly hung her head. She didn't want to leave New York. Here she felt closer to all she loved; to Mammy, to Daniel and Tommy, even to Ireland itself. Besides which, she'd made friends in the home, though, thank God, at least some of them would be travelling with her.

The months had passed slowly at first. There were chores to do and lessons, but Molly was unused to having time on her hands. Before, all her time was working or taking care of the others, finding rags, making food, from morning to night. Now there was time to think, and the thoughts were dark and frightening. She'd felt more alone in those months, surrounded by people, than she ever had on the streets with Tommy and Daniel. Now she had time to realise she was unhappy. She tried to remember the songs that Daniel had sung to her, but with not hearing them for so long, even they seemed to be drifting away and she was afraid everything else dear to her would float away with them. She clung to the rosary. The wooden beads had taken on such significance to her. It was all that was left of her old life, of her family. She hadn't even been allowed to visit where Mammy was laid. She'd almost laughed when Matron, in all seriousness, answered that it wasn't safe for a young girl to walk the streets of New York alone. Whatever did Matron think she'd been doing before? Even when Mammy was alive, it had been a long time since any adult watched over her.

She lay in the silence, wondering if Sarah was awake, but not daring to call out to her, even in a whisper. Matron might be kindly at times, but the punishments were still real enough. Finally, she pushed the rosary into the pocket she'd sewn in the lining of her underskirt and lay waiting for sleep to take over.

When she woke, although it was still early, there were no chores to do because they were leaving. She was glad, at least, that Sarah was going too, and the two girls washed and dressed, whispering as they did so.

"What do you think it'll be like?" Sarah asked as she started to put on the clean clothes she'd been given to wear.

Molly smiled a wry smile. "Oh, I think it will have green fields and valleys and maybe some cows." She couldn't really remember Ireland; she was too young when she left, but she remembered the stories that Mammy told her and a few of the lines that Daniel sang. In her heart she had created a beautiful haven where it was always summer and where everyone was happy. She knew about the hunger and the famines, but she'd put those in the same box as all the other pain she'd gone through and clung only to the brightness of the sun and the goodness of all that went with it.

"Do you think we might go to the same home?" Sarah asked, putting her hand into Molly's.

"Oh, I hope so," said Molly. "More than anything, I hope so. We could share a room and take care of each other…"

"Come along now, girls. Make sure you're ready to leave." Matron bustled from room to room, checking on progress.

There were eight going from their home and they'd be meeting children from other parts of New York for the journey. More than that, Molly had no idea. Despite the apprehension and fear, it was hard not to be a little bit excited by the new experiences the day offered. They were taken first to the Pennsylvania Railroad's ticketing office and then, by the horse-drawn vehicle, to the railroad's wharf on the banks of the Hudson River.

"Oh, Sarah, have you seen the horse? He's a mighty fine animal and so strong. I feel real grand travelling like this when all I've ever done is walk."

"Mister, can we pat the horse?" Sarah asked the driver, who nodded with a resigned look on his face.

"Come on now, get along there." The attendant escorting them ushered them away and up into the carriage behind.

Molly wanted to put her head out of the window to see what was going on, but there were boys in the group who were bigger than she was and they pushed her away so that they could have the best places. In the end, she and Sarah stayed close together, away from the doors and windows, until they reached the boat that was to take them across the river.

Once they were on the western shore of the Hudson River, Molly looked back across the water to the life she was leaving behind. She pressed her hand against her skirt to feel the comfort of the wooden rosary beads and for a moment closed her eyes in prayer.

"Move along."

She tripped as she was ushered forward and opened her eyes quickly to right herself. Evening had already fallen as they boarded the train at Exchange Place and began the long night of being rocked to and fro as the train rolled its rhythmical journey west. She and Sarah huddled together, trying to sleep. It was hardly less comfortable than their bunks had been and the regular motion of the train quickly brought on slumber.

As the sunlight streamed into the carriage next morning, the girls were roused by the brightness and looked out on the ever changing and alien landscape.

"Where are we?" Sarah whispered.

Molly shrugged and searched the view for anything she could identify. Eventually the train pulled in to the station in Pittsburgh and she mouthed the word to Sarah, reading now coming fairly easily to her. Molly brushed her skirt down and took a deep breath, readying herself for what lay ahead. A whistle was blown further along the platform and the children were corralled together, but this was not their destination and instead of leaving the station as Molly had imagined, they were directed to another train.

Molly's shoulders slumped as they settled themselves once again. There was little else to do but watch the fields go by, at speeds she would not have thought possible. She wondered if it was the same journey that Daniel and Tommy had travelled, and for a moment her heart leaped as she imagined them being at the same final destination. If only that could happen and they could be together once again. She reached for the beads, holding them tightly through the linings of her skirt. Was it ok to pray for something like that to happen? When she eventually released them from her hot, sweaty hand she realised that her skirts had become particularly creased around their shape. She did her best to smooth it out, desperate that no one should know of her one hidden possession. The rosary had taken on a deeper meaning, far beyond its Catholicism. It felt to Molly as though it were a direct link to Mammy and the only one she had. She was terrified lest someone should take it from her.

The afternoon was moving on by the time the train pulled into Pierceton and rolled to a stop.

Sarah slid her hand into Molly's and gave it a squeeze. "Are you all right?"

Molly nodded. "Are you?"

Sarah's brow was furrowed and she was biting her lip. Molly tightened her hold on Sarah's hand. "Stay close to me. Let's hope we can be together."

Molly could feel Sarah trembling as she held her hand. The hall was filling fast with people who had come to see the orphans from the city. Molly looked at them carefully. Some people looked as though they were there for an afternoon out, and were not worth focussing her attention on. Then there were the rugged farmers who would settle for nothing less than a boy and who wouldn't believe a girl could have the strength for farm work. Molly smiled, looking at some of the boys. She thought she could probably do the work of two of them and cause a deal less trouble in the process. She wished she could be wearing the breeches she'd worn to sell newspapers, but that wasn't allowed for a girl, though she could not understand why. She did her best to smooth her skirts down neatly and felt the rosary in the lining as she did so. She wondered if praying with her eyes open would work, and tried not to move her lips as she muttered a Hail Mary.

A woman in coarse farm clothes came and stood before her. She ignored the trembling Sarah and addressed herself to Molly. "And what can you do, girl?"

"Please, ma'am, I can do the work of any boy my size and more besides."

"Will you work in the fields?"

"Why yes, ma'am. I'll do most things that need doing..." She hesitated. "... Me and my sister, that is." She gently pushed Sarah forward. Her face was white but she had the sense to make a small curtsey.

"You'll answer for her work too?" The woman was still addressing herself to Molly, but looked Sarah up and down with a raised eyebrow.

"Yes, ma'am. I most certainly will." Molly crossed the fingers of the hand that was not holding Sarah's.

Suddenly the woman broke into a broad smile. "I expect you'll do. The work's hard, but I was a girl myself once and I remember what it was like helping Daddy round the farm. I daresay the two of you will learn the same way I did."

"What you got there, Ellie Cochrane?" One of the spectators shouted across the room to the woman.

"Never you mind, Jacob Reese. She's capable of more work than you or your brothers – and it's Miss Cochrane to you!"

For all her sternness, Molly could see the corner of her mouth twitch and began to think she might rather like Miss Cochrane.

"Now, you two, take no notice of those boys. They wouldn't know a day's work if it sat down at the next stool in the bar. I'm guessing there'll be papers to sign and then I think we'd best get you back for something to eat." Ellie raised an eyebrow. "And a bath and clean clothes wouldn't go amiss."

Sarah was wide eyed as they followed Ellie Cochrane. She looked as though she could not believe that things were going as well as they seemed. Molly felt the rosary again and smiled, mouthing a silent 'thank you' as she did so.

Once they were out of the hall, and in the small cart on the way to the farm, Ellie began to talk. "Well now…" She looked closely at the girls as the horses trotted on. "There's not much you need to know. I've worked out from the papers I signed that you aren't sisters, so don't you be worrying about that. I inherited the farm when my daddy died. It became mine on account of having no brothers. We've one or two labourers about the place, but I wanted me some female company. Take no notice of the likes of Jacob Reese. He thinks no woman is capable of anything more than bearing children. Truth is, I bought some of his daddy's land when he lost it to the bank and he's never forgiven me. You'll live in the house with me and mostly work on the farm. There'll be some schooling, if they'll take you at the Crawford Schoolhouse, but it's not always easy for a girl. If they won't, then I'll help you best I can. On Sundays there's Sunday School. That's part of The First Presbyterian Church. There'll be no work in my house of a Sunday except as the Good Lord calls us to do of a need. The cow still has to be milked, but apart from that there's precious little that can't wait until Monday."

The journey didn't take long, but the girls were both tired from their long travels and Sarah dozed against Molly's shoulder despite the bouncing of the cart.

"I 'spect you girls would like to see your room. While you get washed I'll get some food for you both and then if you want to sleep you can do so with a full stomach. I'll show you round properly tomorrow."

Molly felt grateful for this understanding woman and hoped that life might continue that way, but hardly dared to believe it could. They followed Ellie through the old farm house.

"It's so big," Molly said in what was intended to be a whisper.

"It was my daddy's place. When we were young there were rather more living here than there are now. I'm hoping you girls will bring it to life a little."

"Look," Sarah said as they turned the corner into a large room. "There are two beds. Who else sleeps here?"

Ellie Cochrane let out a chuckle. "There's just the two of you. I'd a hope of bringing two of you back with me today, so I got things ready just in case. You can have a bed each or share one if you prefer."

Molly looked around the room at the clean fresh cotton and linen and her mouth fell open. "Thank you, Miss Cochrane. Oh, thank you."

"Now don't you go getting all sentimental on me. You've a job to do and, make no mistake, it's a hard one. There are some who wouldn't like being out here in the middle of nowhere either. You'll have a long walk to school too, and there's no saying 'no'."

Molly's smile stretched wide. "We lived in the middle of nowhere in Ireland before we came to New York and I've never run away from working." She looked at Sarah but her friend looked too tired to take it all in. She knew Sarah wasn't so strong, but hoped that with the fresh air she'd soon be as fit as Molly was.

"Now, will you find your way back downstairs to the kitchen? I've food prepared ready that you can eat as soon as you want."

"Yes, Miss Cochrane, we most certainly will." Molly took Sarah's hand and led her over to the water stand to take a wash.

The clothes that were left for them were clean and had no extra holes. Molly ran her hand across the fabric; it was strong but soft to the touch. She held the dress against herself and looked in the mirror. If only Tom and Daniel could see her now. She felt for the comfort of the rosary and resolved to sew new pockets in the linings of these clothes just as soon as she could find a needle, thread and enough material to make a patch.

The days passed happily for Molly. She and Sarah took turns to work in the little dairy attached to the farm and the rest of the time was spent between caring for the chickens and helping with the corn crops. Sarah soon developed a little colour to her cheeks and put on some weight, making her look almost healthy. It made Molly happy to see the change in her friend.

She kept the rosary hidden, fearing that the church people might take it away from her. Being a Catholic was one of the taunts at school that she barely understood the reason for, but it was clear that Irish Catholics were somehow viewed apart from the other townsfolk. As though it were a different religion, and while she didn't understand why, Molly knew better than to ask questions or show her treasure.

"And who d'you think you are, Molly Reilly?" Cal Turner said as she pushed Molly hard against the wall.

Molly balled her fists and then tried to put on her sweetest smile. "If you know my name, why are you asking, Cal Turner?" Her stomach was churning and she really wanted to throw a punch, but knew that would only bring more trouble. She wished that Tommy were around.

"Go back to the gutters of New York where you belong. We don't want your kind here. Nor you, Sarah Duggan." Cal spat in Sarah's direction.

"You leave her be." Molly was seething. How dare Cal treat her that way? Cal was no better than the gangs Molly thought she'd left behind.

"And what's happening here?" Miss Ellie's voice boomed as she jumped down from the cart and approached the school house.

Cal Turner stepped back, but muttered as she went, "You'll pay for this, Molly Reilly."

Molly swallowed. "It's nothing, Miss Ellie, Cal here was just asking how we were getting on." She shot a look in Cal's direction and received one back that was pure hatred.

"Didn't look much like nothing to me." Ellie Cochrane raised her eyebrow and looked at Cal Turner in a pointed manner. "I sure hope you're making my girls feel welcome or I 'spect your daddy would like to be hearing about it."

Cal turned on her heel and Ellie smiled at the girls. "Looks like I got here just in time. Now why don't you girls tell me what really happened as I drive you home? I was just passing and thought you might appreciate a change from walking."

That night they sat and told Miss Ellie the story of what life had been like in New York. Molly missed out her brother's pickpocketing and some of the worst of street life, but she told most everything else, except for the keeping of the rosary. Even Sarah didn't know about that.

All Miss Ellie said was, "Oh, you poor dears," as she ladled an extra helping of soup out for each of them, but those words were heavy with more care than Molly'd heard from any adult. Even Mammy had been in the same position that they were and was part of the fight for survival. Miss Ellie was different, and for the first time in her life, Molly felt safe and secure.

CHAPTER 11

Alone, all alone, by the wave washed strand
All alone in a crowded hall
The hall it is gay and the waves they are grand
But my heart is not here at all.
Slievenamon, Charles J Kickham

It was dark when Daniel left the yard. He hoped the night would provide all the cover he needed to flee. The air was still and silent and his ears were sharp for the slightest cause of alarm. He hadn't left the confines of the farm since the day he arrived and knew nothing of direction, except the little he gleaned by listening to the brothers' talk.

The dirt track went both left and right from the driveway. He tried to remember the direction the cart turned when they arrived and seemed to recollect the town was to the left. Instead, he turned to the right. He'd rather walk many more blistering miles than risk being seen by Jed or Rick.

He knew little of the community which now called itself his home and, having been used to life on the streets, was unaware that any child out alone would be cause for query, night or day. He learned the hard way that everyone belonged to someone, more in ownership than care, and he had gone no more than a few miles before he was picked up by a neighbouring farmer. He hadn't answered to the question 'Where are you running from, boy?', but with so few turns off the road, it wasn't hard for his captor to work it out. With no idea where he was going, running from the man was not much of an option and so, broken and defeated, he allowed himself to be bundled into the cart, left tied up overnight, only to be thrown back out into the yard at the feet of Mr Hawksworth the next morning.

If running away was harder than he'd thought, being returned was even worse. His wounds were already deep when Mr Hawksworth took his belt to him again. No one was there to watch this time. Jed and Rick would likely be too hung over to have surfaced and Mrs Hawksworth was nowhere to be seen. Daniel wondered briefly if the same fate had befallen her, but that thought was more unbearable than his own mistreatment, so he pushed it from his mind.

He trembled as the belt lashed, this time against his legs. As he tried to bear the pain, he wished he had died on the boat with Ma and Da, or caught cholera and died in New York with Mammy. He couldn't stop the tears from falling, however much satisfaction it might be giving Mr Hawksworth. He just prayed for the beating to stop or death to come, and whichever it was to happen soon. When the lashes ceased to rain down, the stinging in his legs was so great that it was a few moments before he realised they'd stopped.

When Mr Hawksworth walked away, Daniel stayed where he was, his breathing ragged, barely able to move. He knew Mrs Hawksworth would not be there to tend the wounds this time and that any salving would have to be done for himself, but he had no creams, just the moisture from the few stray plants around the yard, and he had no idea whether they would serve any good purpose.

After those beatings, it took months for his skin to heal and it was likely even then that there were visible scars. Daniel had no mirror to see them with and there was no one he trusted who he could ask, but he could feel raised skin on the parts of his back that his hands could reach. He tried hard to do his work quietly and keep out of the way of the others. When he was alone in the fields, he sang softly to himself and dreamed of better times.

Time passed slowly, though there was no way to mark it but for the changing seasons and the height of the sun in the sky. It was around harvest the following year when Mr Hawksworth came out to find him in the bunkhouse.

"You're to come to the house tomorrow. There'll be no work in the morning. The assessor for you orphans will be coming. You mind you tell him everything is good. You hear?"

"Yes, sir." Daniel's spirits lifted. He wondered if there was chance of news of Molly or Tom. He doubted he'd get time alone to tell this man what life was really like and truth be told, if he did then he doubted the man would believe him. He'd do anything to avoid another beating and if that meant saying life here was good then he'd do it.

Daniel was overawed by the house when he entered the following morning. Despite his year on the farm this was the first time he'd been allowed inside. He sat in the kitchen waiting for the assessor to arrive, but Mrs Hawksworth hardly spoke and he could see the fear in her eyes. The bath had been filled for him so he could scrub himself clean and there were laundered clothes to put on afterwards. It was his first bath since the night before he'd been taken on the train, and that was the previous harvest time. Washing from a pail was the best he could hope for on other days.

He was told he had to be in the kitchen so the man

117

would think he lived in the house. Was it really so easy to fool someone as that? Would the man not ask questions of the Hawksworths that might reveal the truth? But Daniel knew he needed to play along.

When he was taken through to the drawing room, he was amazed at the luxury around him. He gasped at the carpets on the floor and wondered if he should have left his boots in the kitchen. Mr Hawksworth was already there when Daniel was shown in by Mrs Hawksworth and had clearly been talking to the assessor for a while.

Daniel stood quietly at the point indicated in front of the assessor, with his hands awkwardly holding his cap. Even with the cap to hold onto, they were shaking slightly, so he tried to hold the left firmly with the right to still its movement. He had no idea what he was supposed to do. He simply stood quietly and waited.

The assessor was seated at the table, writing. He looked up. "Flynn, although I seem to have you here as Reilly?"

"Yes, sir. I was with my brother and sister, sir, and their name is Reilly."

The man scribbled a note and did not look at Daniel.

Daniel's mouth felt dry and he wished he had a glass of water to sip, but dared not ask. He longed to ask about the others, but feared the response from Mr Hawksworth if he spoke.

Eventually the man peered up at Daniel. "How is your schooling going, boy?"

Daniel thought as quickly as he could. He didn't want to lie, but he knew he must say what was expected of him. "I like learning, sir."

"Can you read and write?"

"I read better than I write, sir." Daniel kept his answers short.

The man nodded and made a note on his paper. "And the farm work, how do you like that?"

"I like being in the fresh air, sir."

"Do you work hard?" He looked across at Mr Hawksworth as he asked.

At last, a question he felt as though he could answer honestly, though it was true he liked the outdoors. "I believe so, sir." Feeling emboldened and certain now it could do no harm, Daniel asked, "Please, sir, do you know if my brother and sister are well?"

The man looked at him and then back to his notes. He flicked through some papers and pulled out another sheet. Daniel's heart missed a beat as he watched.

"Your sister wrote to us asking after you. She is now in Pierceton. I believe she is happy."

Daniel broke into a broad smile to hear that Molly was well. In his head he repeated the name of the place, Pierceton, for fear of forgetting it. "And Tom, sir?"

"I'm afraid I have no details of where he is."

"We left him in Dowagiac, sir." Again, he'd been careful to remember the place name, in hopes of one day finding him.

Mr Hawksworth coughed and looked meaningfully at the assessor. He smiled at Daniel and said, "I'm sorry, Flynn. I know no more."

Then he began to put his papers together and Mrs Hawksworth, who was standing in the background, stepped forward to lead Daniel back to the kitchen, where he waited until the man had gone before being sent back out to the bunkhouse.

There were no niceties as he left the house, but as he walked back he felt happier than he had in a long time. Molly was safe. No longer in New York, but safe nonetheless. He wanted to sing and sit on his own in the sunshine for a while, basking in thoughts of Molly, but he hadn't covered half the distance when Jed came up to him with an empty basket to make a start on harvesting some corn. No matter, he could sing as he worked. It would take more than that to dampen his mood. He knew nothing of where Pierceton was; it might be further away than New York for all he knew, but maybe Mrs Hawksworth would know when he got a chance to ask.

Under his breath he repeated the place name over and over, etching it too deep to lose with forgetfulness.

He worked cheerfully through the afternoon and long into the evening. He was lighthearted and thought that nothing could change how he felt. However, when he returned to the bunkhouse, there on his bunk in a thousand pieces lay *Moby-Dick*, his one and only possession and source of all possible learning. It was too much for Daniel and he sat with his head in his hands while the tears flowed.

Jed and Rick were nowhere about and he knew there would be no point in challenging them if they were. He wondered why they'd picked today of all days, and then supposed Mr Hawksworth must have had a hand in it. Either way, there was nothing he could do.

It was not until the harvest was done and the fields were bare that he next saw Mrs Hawksworth. Once again, the farm was quiet and the menfolk were away for the evening. He was sitting in the bunkhouse in all but darkness when he heard a voice calling gently to him.

"Daniel? Are you there, Daniel?"

His first thought was that it was Ma calling from another place, but then he saw the lamp in the doorway casting a little light into the room. "Yes, ma'am." He jumped down from his bunk, landing softly on the straw-covered floor.

"I've brought you these." Mrs Hawksworth was carrying a tray with the usual pancakes and syrup, but in addition to those welcome offerings, on the side of the tray sat a small parcel wrapped in brown paper.

Daniel looked up at Mrs Hawksworth in question.

"Go on, Daniel. It's for you."

His hands were trembling as he took it from the tray and began to unwrap the paper. He ran his hand over the leather binding of a brand new book and looked up at Mrs Hawksworth, his mouth open. Then he looked down and ran his finger over *Holy Bible*. He went to speak, but could find no words.

"I couldn't get *Moby-Dick*, I'm sorry."

"But it's beautiful. You can't... I mean... I can't accept it. What if the master finds out?"

"Find somewhere to hide it, Daniel, somewhere safe. Only take it out when there's no one around. The pastor of the church is the only one knows I've got it and he won't say a word."

"Thank you." It seemed inadequate. He now knew that she'd known what happened to his copy of *Moby-Dick*, which meant Hawksworth must have been involved. He wanted to rush and wrap his arms around her. He wanted to feel her soothe his brow as Ma had done when he was small. He could do none of that, so he said it again quietly as he looked into her fine face. "Thank you."

Then Mrs Hawksworth laid down the tray and, leaving the lamp with Daniel, went back to the house. He knew by now he was to leave the light and tray in their usual place in plenty of time for her to take it before the drunken revellers returned.

In his haste to start reading the book he almost entirely forgot about the pancakes, but eventually, confused by some of the old language in Genesis, he laid the book aside and ate the pancakes cold.

The seasons continued for Daniel. Jed and Rick stayed at the farm while other hands arrived and left. Daniel preferred when there were more of them in the bunkhouse as the trouble he faced was less, although the times he could remove his Bible from below the loose floorboard were fewer as well. He worked his way through much of the Old Testament, becoming used to the ancient language after a while, but being careful lest he fall into the trap of using it when he spoke. He was not sure what he thought of this avenging God. He sounded so different to the God that Mammy had talked about. There were lines which stayed with him, such as 'an eye for an eye', and he often pondered on how that fitted with the way he was treated by Mr Hawksworth. Would Mammy still have said it was wrong to respond if she'd known what was happening to him? He was almost grown now, and strong with the work. He wondered what he could do with that strength if he put a mind to it.

It was his sixth harvest on the farm before there was any sign of his loneliness abating. The air was balmy with late summer warmth and the corn was standing tall and all but ripe in the fields when an older man came into the bunkhouse, a heavy canvas bag over his shoulder and a flea-bitten hound at his heels. Daniel was only just back from his labours and was washing up in the bucket by the door, ready to eat. The dog stopped to sniff, then wagged his tail furiously and pawed at Daniel's leg.

"Reckon he likes you," the man said, smiling a broad and partially toothless grin. "His name's Duke."

Daniel's only real experience of dogs had been those roaming loose on the streets of New York and he'd never got too close to them, but Duke was insistent and pushed his nose into Daniel's hand. Daniel was hesitant in patting the little fella's head, but as the dog seemed to like it he moved to scratching him behind the ear. At that point Duke rolled onto his back in a moment of pure ecstasy and Daniel began to laugh.

Half an hour later the two of them were still together, with the man keeping a watchful eye from a distance.

After they'd eaten, with Daniel happily sharing some of his food with Duke, he wove some of the loose straw together into a ball and threw it for the dog to chase after. Duke was clearly partial to a game of fetch and very soon was bringing the ball of straw back for another throw. Eventually, Daniel flopped down on his bunk, exhausted but happy.

"It looks like you could use a friend," the man said as he came over to stand near Daniel.

"I certainly could, sir."

"Call me Benjamin, or better still Ben. I'm nobody's 'sir' these days."

"Well, Mister Ben, sir, it's been a mighty lonely place for a boy growing up, though I've got nothing to compare it to. Not for a long time anyways. I had a family once..." Daniel thought wistfully of those he'd lost. His memory was dimmed with time and he struggled to recall their faces. When he thought of them, though, it was always with warmth and a deep longing that one day he'd see them again.

"I knows a bit about loneliness and it ain't a pretty place to be. I had me a wife and child a long time ago… but that was another life and another place. Now it's just me and Duke. Some days we's happy as we is, and others…"

They sat quietly for a while, each in their separate thoughts, and then Daniel found himself telling this man the story of how he came to be on the farm in the first place and how with no pay and nowhere to go, he supposed he'd be there for a long time to come. He'd never told a soul his story, not even Mrs Hawksworth. He reckoned she knew some of it, but he never said a word.

"No pay, you say?"

Daniel nodded.

"That ain't right."

"I get my board and lodging." Daniel was surprised at his own automatic response to defend Mr Hawksworth. He shrugged and looked down.

"We gets our board and lodging and some wages, though they be slim pickings. But it's better than nothing, and I've got a little put by for my old age."

Daniel looked at Mister Benjamin in amazement. To him the man already looked old.

"It's not these parts as is supposed to have slavery." Benjamin snorted. "We's supposed to be the free men here, though I ain't sure what freedom means to the likes of you and me."

For the time that Ben stayed working on the farm, Duke was never far from Daniel's heels. In the evenings the two of them and the dog would sit in companionable silence or sometimes talk of better days. For Daniel, that time was a doubly happy one, as with Ben around, Jed and Rick paid little heed to him and on the Saturdays Jed and Rick went into town Ben shared the secret of Daniel's reading.

Though, with Ben there, Mrs Hawksworth didn't come down to help his learning.

When spring came and Ben's time at the farm was done, it was a hard parting.

"Can I come with you?" Daniel asked.

Ben shook his head. "You knows Hawksworth wouldn't allow it, but I reckon Duke should stay here to keep you company."

"Oh, but he's your dog. You can't do that."

Duke snuffled close to Daniel.

"He can share your food as well as he's shared mine. I think he's made his choice, don't you? Besides, it will give me a reason to come back next harvest. While he carries on catching rats around the place he should be let alone by the others. Keep him safe."

This last comment could have been addressed either to the dog or to himself, Daniel wasn't altogether sure which, but as Benjamin lumbered over to the truck with his heavy bag, dog and boy stayed close to each other, bringing what comfort they could and looking forward to the passing of the months until Ben might be back with them.

Once Ben had gone, the farm returned to much the way it had been before. However, after Duke bit Rick, leaving a full set of teeth marks firmly imprinted in his work pants, an uneasy truce was established. Daniel was mindful to keep Duke in his sights at all times, lest Jed and Rick got ideas about parting them for good.

CHAPTER 12

"Sir, Jude McCaulay's brother says he's going to fight for the Union. He's answering Mr Lincoln's call. Will you have to fight?" William really wanted to ask if he would have to go himself, but he wasn't sure where to start. There was a part of him deep down that wanted to fight, not so much because he'd thought about the cause, but a simple instinctive feeling. Maybe it harked back to his street days, but he thought it was more than that. It was pride in his new life and wanting nothing to stand in its way. William had his future mapped out. He was going to be successful and if he had to fight to protect that opportunity, then fight he would.

"No, son. I'm too old for fighting now. It's younger men they want. Besides, I can serve the Union through the law and I sure am pleased to do that."

"Jude says he may go if they're still fighting when he's older..." Then tentatively he added, "He asked if I'd go too."

Pa paused a long moment before replying and then more quietly said, "I do hope you won't, son. Soldiering is a dangerous business. It's for the like of people who don't think they've anything much else to do with their lives. I'm counting on you to take over the firm when you're old enough and as for Ma, well, let's just say it would send her to an early grave if anything happened to you."

William nodded. "I know, sir."

"Besides, studying is what you're good at and I see no reason why you shouldn't have the very best education before taking up a career."

"Why are they fighting, sir?"

"That's a difficult one. Mr Lincoln says it's because they don't respect the right of man to be free. As long as there's slavery they cannot claim the principles that the Union holds dear."

There had been freed slaves around Five Points, but they were just other people struggling to survive, not a symbol of a way of life. "But is it ever right to give up everything you have for the rights of another man?"

"I think it probably is, William, but that's something you'll have to work out for yourself. Some things in life are more important than self, but that's not something you can learn from someone telling you. You might learn it from the way they live their life and seeing it done, but you'll never learn it from simply being told. Ma and I love you as our own child and would give everything for you. One day you'll have children of your own and you'll know what that feels like." Pa paused and took a deep suck at his pipe. "Why don't we go into town? There's something I'd like to show you."

"Yes, sir." William furrowed his brow as he thought over what Pa had already said and wondered if anyone would ever be that dear to him.

As they walked along the streets of Dowagiac, Pa stopped first before one building and then another. Each time he said to William, "See this, remember it. One day it will be yours." He gave no further explanation and William asked no questions until they arrived outside the lawyer's office and Pa led William through to the back. "Sit yourself down, William."

"Thank you, sir."

Pa went to the cabinet and drew out a sheaf of papers. He proceeded to fold out a plan of the town on the table top. "It's not so very long ago that this town was founded. My daddy, he was one of the first to settle in this area and when he did he laid claim to a lot of land. Since then, we've sold some plots and bought others and this is what we own now." He showed William the shaded areas on the map, which represented a large section of the town. "I'm mighty happy to have a fine son that I can pass it all on to one day. In the meantime, there's enough there to pay for whatever we need, including you going to university, if you want to, and to pay your way out of having to fight if the need arises."

There was a long pause as William took in what Pa had said. Not just the future amount, but the prospect of university and knowing he was unlikely to have to fight unless he chose to. This was everything he'd dreamed of and yet somehow it felt hollow. Oh, he wanted to be a 'somebody' and if being William Dixon was the way to that, then that was exactly who he'd be, but he wasn't sure that it meant anything to him. He could act the part of the loving son, but then he could act the part of streetwise pickpocket. With the pain of his father going and his mother dying, the separation from his friends and family, he'd locked a big part of himself away for safety. What was the point in getting close to anyone when all it ended in was hurt? It was better to rely on himself than open up to any other. Sure, one day he'd take himself a wife. He could see that, with the role he wanted in life, it was an expected part of it. He couldn't imagine feeling about anyone as his new ma and pa seemed to feel about each other and, more strangely, about him too.

The summer slipped by with only passing knowledge of the conflict. Little was heard of the local people involved, and the news which came brought calls for more men to enlist. William spent his days studying and riding. He made up his mind that fighting was a game he had no wish to play.

It was early September and the sun was warm as William cantered across the ridge and back towards home. Bounty was in fine form and as he sighted the house William pressed her to gallop and then go even faster until the breeze in his face was full of exhilaration. Even that wasn't enough and he pressed Bounty harder and harder until finally, just before home, she cleared the fence and landed awkwardly but still upright, letting out a whinny of pain as she struggled to finish the walk to the stables.

William looked around and was thankful to see no one in view as he led the hobbling horse to her stable. He had been told not to jump that fence with the width of the ditch beside it, but he hadn't wanted to hear that. He washed her off, made her as comfortable as he could and then carefully hung up the tack as he had found it, before slipping into the house unnoticed.

By the time dinner was called he was out of his riding breeches and wearing clean clothes, all evidence of his afternoon activity put aside.

Towards the end of dinner, and before he could be excused, there was a knock at the dining room door and Briggs entered. "Excuse me, sir. I'm dreadfully sorry to disturb you, but I thought you should know that Bounty is awful lame."

Pa stood from the table, wiping his mouth with his napkin. "What happened to her?"

"I don't know, sir. I found her that way."

"God dammit, man, I pay you to look after her. What do you mean you don't know?"

"I've been up in the top field this last few hours, sir, and she was like it when I came back."

"I'll be out to her directly, Briggs."

"Very good, sir." Briggs withdrew, leaving the family to finish dinner.

Pa pushed his plate away. "Excuse me, dear, I think I should go out to Bounty." He got up to leave, but before going he turned to Will. "Son, when did you last ride Bounty?"

"That was three days ago, sir."

"And was she all right then?"

"Yes, sir. Very fine indeed, sir."

"And you're not aware of anything happening to her since?"

William shuffled his feet and hesitated.

"Whatever it is, out with it, lad."

"I thought... but I could be wrong... I thought I saw her with Briggs in the top field, sir."

"Well, did you now?" Pa stormed from the room.

"Can I go too, Ma? I want to see how Bounty is."

"Very well, but keep out of Pa's way. He's a little overwrought at the moment and he'll need to talk to Briggs."

William shot out after Pa and hurried to the stables. He didn't go inside, but hung back listening.

"Confound it, man, riding the horse I can forgive, but lying to me..."

"Excuse me, sir, I think you may be mistaken."

"Are you calling my son a liar? He saw you with his own eyes in the top field with Bounty. It's you has made her lame, isn't it?"

William caught sight of movement through the doorway and realised that Briggs had spotted him. His heart raced as he wondered if Briggs had the courage to call him out. He wondered what Pa would say if he knew the truth. It had already dawned on him that whilst he might have been forgiven for riding Bounty and jumping the ditch, the lies he'd now told would be far harder to explain. He closed his eyes, breathing deeply as he waited for what was to happen next.

Briggs turned away from the doorway back to Bounty's stall. In a low voice he said, "I'm sorry, sir. It won't happen again."

William let out the breath he had been holding and leaned back against the wall of the stables.

"I think, sir, with rest she will be fine. I've put a cold compress on the leg and I'll sit up with her through the night to change it."

"That's the least you can do, man. And let me tell you, if this happens again I shall have no choice but to give you notice. I know you've been with us for years, Briggs, but this kind of behaviour is unacceptable, d'you hear?"

"Yes, sir."

As William heard Pa's footsteps coming towards the door of the barn, he quietly moved around the corner to wait for him to pass. He swallowed hard and then, once the coast was clear, he made to go back across the yard towards the house.

Briggs called after him. "Excuse me, Master William."

William missed a step, but then made to continue.

This time Briggs spoke with more force to his voice. "Excuse me, Master William. I'd like a word if I may."

As he turned to go back, William could feel his cheeks colouring and he stood as tall as he could. "What is it,

Briggs?" He spoke in as haughty a tone as he could muster.

"I know your game, Master William, and I won't forget." Briggs turned to go back to the barn.

William, feeling a little disconcerted, turned back toward the house. What trouble could Briggs give him that really mattered? Of course his Pa believed him, why shouldn't he? He'd had little cause to doubt the perfect son that William pretended to be. If it came to a showdown, then surely Pa would believe him over Briggs, there was no question, but his palms were sweating nonetheless and he felt a little uneasy about the day's activities. The most immediate problem was that he wouldn't be able to ride Bounty, but maybe Pa would buy him another horse to fill the time until Bounty was fit.

Recovering some of his spirit, he smiled to himself. After all, why should he suffer for Briggs' wrongful behaviour?

CHAPTER 13

"Oh, please can we, Miss Ellie, please?" Molly had even let herself start thinking about what she might wear to the dance if Miss Ellie said 'yes'. Sarah's dress was already finished in the hope they could go and now they needed to work on Molly's, but their needlework was good and there was still time enough.

Ellie smiled. "I can remember my own first dance in town. I'd have been fifteen myself then, though that was a few years ago now. How could I say 'no' to two such fine young ladies when I'm thinking of going myself? It's only harvest once a year and it will be nice to turn out as a family. Besides, what was the point in my teaching you girls to dance if you're never going to have an opportunity?"

Sarah hugged Miss Ellie and Molly followed suit as soon as Sarah had let go.

"How will we get there?" Sarah asked, a note of worry in her voice.

"Why, we'll take the cart, of course."

Molly looked at the concern etched on Sarah's face.

Miss Ellie laughed. "I've been young myself. I think I know what's troubling you, girl. We can clean it out first, silly. Your dresses will be fine. There'll be no mud on those beautiful lace trimmings when my girls arrive at the dance."

Molly and Sarah broke into joyous laughter. "Do you

133

think the Masters Spencer will be there?" Sarah asked Ellie, with a serious look on her face.

"And why's that, Sarah – are you sweet on one of those boys?" Molly gave her friend a rueful smile. "I reckon they will be, if their daddy lets them."

Sarah blushed. "Oh, Miss Ellie, that Joseph is awful nice, don't you think?"

Ellie smiled. "I sure do. What about you, Molly?"

Molly gently shook her head, and for a moment she felt a hint of sadness cross her face. "I'm not ready for all that just yet." Her hand inadvertently reached down to where the rosary still sat in an inside pocket of her dress. She thought of Mammy and how she'd been left with two young children when their pa had gone off to work the railways. She wondered where he'd ended up; if he were still alive. Then she thought sadly of Daniel and wondered where he might be now. She took a deep breath. It would take a lot of certainty before Molly would give up her life and independence to any man. Sarah, however, had seemed to fall in love with a new boy every week, until she'd seen Joseph Spencer working in his daddy's store. Since then, whenever they weren't working or at school, she would beg Molly to go with her to the store for every imagined need.

The next few days passed in a whirl of excitement, with Molly focussing on making Sarah look as presentable as any farm girl could. She was still a slight figure and with her hair brushed out and neatly dressed she looked pretty enough to turn a few heads, or so Molly thought. For her own part, Molly struggled to tame her rather wayward curly hair and was a more buxom and muscled figure when compared to her friend. She had no pretence of being elegant, and no great wish to be so either, but what she lacked in beauty she made up for in spirit and good humour and she was well enough liked.

By the Saturday of the dance, Molly's dress was complete and, whilst not the height of fashion, it was acceptable and even she thought it didn't look too bad.

"Well, my, what do we have here?" Miss Ellie stood back to take a good look at her charges. "Now don't you just look lovely, girls?" She sighed. "It reminds me of when I was fifteen, but that's enough of that."

For a moment Molly saw her eyes glisten and wondered if there'd been a young man she'd never told them about. Now wasn't the time to ask, but she did wonder at Miss Ellie's being alone all these years.

The cart had been cleaned as promised. When they went to climb up, Molly found that Miss Ellie had laid rugs across the seats and floor to make sure they got as little mud and muck as possible on their finery. There were some spare rugs to wrap around them, as the nights were getting colder, but thankfully the day was dry and the road was clear. Once they were in the cart, Ellie geed up the horses and they trotted into town.

"Now, don't you girls mind me. If any young men ask you to dance you're to say 'yes'... as long as you want to, and not to fuss about leaving me on my own. I'll be right as anything, enjoying seeing you dance the night away."

"And will you dance too, Miss Ellie?" Sarah asked.

"I sure will, if some nice gentleman invites me to. You don't come to a dance just to spectate. Though there's some as do."

"Then I hope there's a nice gentleman there who does ask you," Molly said, and slipped her hand under Miss Ellie's arm. Miss Ellie squeezed it gently before getting back to concentrating on the horses.

The hall was busy with folk from all the surrounding farms as well as the town. Molly felt overawed by all the people and hoped she might see others she knew, to make her feel easier. Miss Ellie led them to the far side of the room and they found seats together where they could watch what was going on while they waited for the dancing to begin.

It wasn't long before Miss Ellie was talking to friends her own age and the girls were left to look out for each other.

"Do you think anyone will want to dance with us?" Sarah asked, fidgeting with her skirt.

"I dare say there'll be someone without a partner who'll come to ask you, but I'm just as happy to watch."

"Oh, Molly, how can you say that? Don't you think anyone will choose to dance with us? What if we were the last ones with no partners?"

"Oh, I don't know, Sarah. You know what it's like being a farm girl and how the local boys never seem to forget where we came from. I'd just as soon watch everyone else as take part. I don't want to get my hopes up."

The music began and talking became more difficult. Molly could hear the giggling of the other girls above the noise and felt a little awkward in the stiff fabric of the dress she was wearing. She looked across the room, only to see Joseph Spencer making a bee-line straight for Sarah. She smiled to herself; perhaps being a farm girl wasn't so bad after all. Maybe much was in her imagining. She gently squeezed Sarah's arm and felt it shaking very slightly.

Joe made a slight bow as he approached and offered his hand for Sarah to join him. She looked across at Molly as she got up, the colour rising high in her cheeks.

Molly shooed them off towards the dance floor, then

watched them in the reel that moved around the room. Although they had started together they were soon separated, as partners were swapped and moved on from set to set. She noticed Joe kept looking to see where Sarah had got to and she reckoned he was feeling much the same as Sarah seemed to be. She lost sight of the two when Miss Ellie sat beside her and pressed a glass of lemonade into her hands.

"She could do worse," Miss Ellie said.

"But…"

"How do I know about things like that?" Ellie laughed. "Because I was young myself once, though you might find it hard to believe now. I had my fair share of courting days. I know what to look for. And as for you, Molly Reilly…" Ellie gave a meaningful glance in the direction of Joe's older brother Henry. "… I think you might be up and dancing yourself before much longer."

Molly felt herself colouring. "I can't… I…" she stammered, but before she could say anything further Henry was in front of her and inviting her to join him in the next dance.

By the time Molly and Sarah sat down next, much of the night had passed. They had from time to time been in the same sets on the dance floor, but at no point had any chance to speak to each other.

"He's asked if he can see me again," Sarah rushed to tell her friend.

"Do you think Miss Ellie will allow it?" Molly wasn't really sure how these things worked, but she was aware there were certain things which were not done, and hadn't they been told in Sunday School they shouldn't be alone with a boy?

"I don't see why not. It's not like we're really her

children, is it? Besides, why can't you chaperone me?"

"Me? Isn't it supposed to be an adult?"

"Maybe I could ask him back to tea. Perhaps Miss Ellie would like him being around."

"Oh, I don't know." Molly had not heard Miss Ellie come up behind her.

"What's that you don't know?" she asked.

Molly looked at Sarah and thought it better to let her do the answering.

"Joe's asked if he might see me again," she said, looking wistful. "I was wondering…"

Ellie smiled. "Go on. You were wondering if I might invite him over to have supper with us."

"Oh, would you, Miss Ellie, would you?" Sarah flung her arms around Miss Ellie's neck and planted a kiss on her cheek.

"Now, less of that, girl. You'll have everyone wanting to know what's going on. I'll talk to his father and see if something can be arranged."

As the months wore on, Joe became a regular visitor to the farm. He could often be found on a Saturday, after the store had closed, helping Sarah with whatever chores she still had to finish, before they all sat down to supper together. Even by the time of the dance the following year, the two were still keeping company.

It was on one such Saturday in the spring of 1863 that Joe arrived rather more flustered than was usual. He said nothing about what was bothering him as they worked the afternoon and Molly couldn't help but wonder if he was waiting for time alone with Sarah. It became clear that Sarah was thinking much the same when she ran into the dairy behind Molly.

"Do you think he's going to ask me to marry him?"

"I don't know. There's certainly something he's thinking about. Maybe he's waiting to talk to Miss Ellie about it. What would you say if he asked you?"

Sarah threw her head back and laughed. "Why, 'yes', of course. It's the first time in my life I've had someone love me for who I am and I'm not about to go throwing that away in a hurry."

"I suppose not," said Molly, smiling to her friend. "Don't you think we're still a little young for all that?"

"You speak for yourself, Molly Reilly. If I'm old enough to work for my living then I'm old enough to come home to my own house of an evening."

"Oh, but, Sarah, what would you do? You couldn't stay on at the farm."

"Why ever not? If Miss Ellie could pay me as she pays the other workers, I could still do a good day's work."

Molly was hesitant to ask her next question. There were times that Sarah still seemed very slow to understand how things might be. "But wouldn't you have children of your own to look after before long?"

Sarah stopped what she was doing and stood looking at Molly, her mouth open. Slowly she put her hand to her mouth and sat down on a churn. "Oh, Molly, I couldn't. What if they grew up orphans as I did? What if I died giving birth to them?" The colour had quite drained from her face. "I don't often think about those days in New York, but every now and then I remember and a shudder runs through me. What will I do, Molly?"

"He hasn't asked you yet." Molly was holding a butter churn in her left hand, but instinctively her right one reached down and patted the rosary. She often thought of those days and longed for news of Daniel and Tom.

"But what should I do?"

Molly gave a start and looked at her friend. She forced a smile. "You'll be fine, you just see if you're not."

When they went in to supper Molly was anxiously watching her friend. Sarah was fidgeting and clearly in a state of some excitement.

As they all sat down, Joe looked as though he was about to burst. "Now we're all here, I must tell you our news."

Sarah looked on eagerly, but Molly realised that Joe wasn't smiling.

"It's Henry. He's received his draft papers. He's to go to fight with Mr Lincoln's men. Pa doesn't know what he shall do without him and Ma is in such a state. I don't know that I shall be able to come over quite as regular as I do now. I'll be needed at home more."

Sarah's disappointment was evident. "Oh, Joe, is that all it is? I thought you were going to…"

"All? All!" Joe's face flushed red. "How can you say, 'Is that all it is?', when my brother has to go away to war?" He got up from his seat and took up his coat. "Excuse me, Miss Ellie, I'm needed elsewhere." And with that, Joe strode toward the door.

Sarah got up and rushed to him. "Oh, Joe, stop. I didn't mean…"

"I've no mind to what you meant, Sarah. Now leave me be. Good day to you." And with that he marched from the room, leaving Ellie and Molly in dumb silence whilst Sarah burst into a flood of tears.

"But I thought he was going to ask me to marry him," she managed to get out through the sobs. "Now he's gone and I don't know when I shall see him again."

Molly wrapped her arms around her friend.

"You weren't to know that's what he'd be saying," Miss Ellie said in a gentle voice. "I'm sure he'll come around."

"Miss Ellie," Molly said, "if it's all the same to you, I could go and talk to him tomorrow and explain."

"That would be very kind of you. I'm sure this will all be sorted in no time. Either that or I could talk to Mrs Spencer, but I think it will be best dealt with by you young people."

Molly set to find Joe after church on the Sunday. Sarah, who had not slept the night before, had stayed home and made Molly promise to return with news just as soon as she could. Molly enjoyed the walk to the store in the spring sunshine, though it seemed strange to be calling there on a day when the store was closed. She knocked at the door to the living quarters and waited.

It was Henry who answered the door. She had seen him a few times since the dance nearly eighteen months previously, but they had not been alone together in that time.

She looked up at the tall young man and blushed. "I'm sorry to trouble you, but it was Joe I was looking for."

Henry smiled at the sight of her and he stood taller. "He's away up at the orchard. I'll walk up there if you don't mind the company."

"Thank you."

They walked in silence for the first part of the walk, then Molly said, "I'm sorry to hear you have to go off to war."

"I don't mind owning I'm not keen to go. I never was much of fighter and I hadn't reckoned on becoming one now. It's Ma I'm worried for."

"That's what Joe said yesterday, before he and Sarah had a misunderstanding. Oh, it was so stupid." Molly suddenly found herself telling Henry the whole story. "... And now I'm to try to make things right for her with Joe. She didn't mean anything by what she said. It was just..."

141

"Molly…" Henry had stopped and was facing her, his face earnest. "Molly, while I'm gone will you write to me and be my sweetheart?"

Molly looked up into his face and had no idea what to say. She hardly knew him, but he was Joe's brother and Joe was a good sort. She could see no real harm in saying 'yes', and if it brought him comfort while he was away then that had to be good. "Yes," she said, "I'll write to you."

He took her hands in his. "Oh, Molly, I'm so pleased. I've been wanting to ask you if I might see you for ever so long, but…" He shrugged in a way that showed he had not yet fully left boyhood behind, and Molly melted.

She'd almost forgotten the purpose of her visit by the time they came to the orchard and, as it was, she was grateful for Henry's presence as he set about the explanation to Joe before Molly could begin.

The colour drained from Joe's face as his brother explained. He sat down heavily on a log and ran his hand through his hair, leaving it part way through as his mouth opened and closed again.

It was the way Henry ended the story which quite sealed the steps Joe decided on taking. "Why, if you did ask her and she were to say 'yes', just think how happy it would make Ma. Sarah could move into the house and help in the store so that Ma would barely notice I was gone."

Joe nodded slowly. "I'd like some time on my own to do some thinking, if it's all the same to the two of you."

Molly nodded and, with her arm linked through his, led Henry back towards the town. She'd done all she could and now needed to await the outcome.

CHAPTER 14

So fare thee well father, and mother adieu.
My sisters and brothers, fare thee well unto you;
I am going to America, my fortune to try,
When I think of Bunclody, sure I'm ready to die.
Bunclody, Traditional

Ben did return the following harvest and the ones after that, and Duke greeted him with pleasure but never strayed far from Daniel's side. Daniel told the older man of all the happenings, including the beatings and the privation, and for those short times it felt good to have a friend. He was too young for the draft and Ben too old, but he reckoned Jed and Rick might be called.

Ben shook his head sadly as he answered the youth. "They's essential labour and won't have to go, unless they volunteer."

Daniel felt his heart sink. He'd kept himself going with the thought that the end of them being around was in sight. With the knowledge that this was not the case, his hope was gone. "I don't reckon I can bide here another season if they won't be away."

"You could always away to fight yourself. The Boss can't stop you going then."

Daniel looked down at the ground, remembering his days on the streets. "I'm no fighter. I'm sure if I had to I could kill a man, but not for Mr Lincoln, who I don't even

143

know. I'd do it for those I loved... but there ain't many of them left as are known to me." He felt a tear escape, and tracked his sleeve across his face. He took a deep breath and shook his head back, his untidy hair falling away from his face. "Would you help me to get away from here, Ben? If I were to run, would you help me to plan it?"

An iron-like resolve had come over Daniel as he'd thought of Molly and his past days. He'd wallowed too long feeling sorry for himself and it was clear there was no one but him could do anything about it. He was nearly eighteen and almost a man – surely Hawksworth would let him go this time. Hawksworth could get himself another young slave, for surely once Daniel came of age he'd have to be paid and have a choice in where he worked. It was only a few months away, but an urgency had entered Daniel and he was desperate to respond.

Ben was studying him carefully. "Are you sure it's what you want?"

Daniel nodded.

"You'll not be able to take Duke. With a dog at your feet you'll be found too soon."

"But Duke can stay with you, now you're back. You need his company too."

"Sure I do, lad, but he chose your company over mine. He'll not take the loss of you well."

Daniel scratched Duke's ear and sighed. "I've got to do it, Ben. My life is slipping away here and there's people I must be looking for."

Ben gave a despairing shake of his head and looked away. "Then I'll help you, but it won't be easy."

Daniel felt a weight lift at the decision made. He would never be truly alive while he lived here. He'd no idea where Pierceton was and no amount of questions to Ben or Mrs

Hawksworth had shed any light on the matter. Dowagiac was on the railroad, he knew that and presumed the same must be true of Pierceton. He'd go in search of Tom and maybe he'd know where Molly was.

As the harvest time wore on, Daniel spent what time he could with Ben, planning for his leaving. He'd agreed he wouldn't go until the work was nearly done and Ben was in a position to follow not long behind. They were sure the old man's life would become harder once Daniel had departed and neither of them wanted the risk of anything being taken out on Duke.

Between them they'd made a rough bag from some sacking left lying in the corner of the barn. It would hold the few things Daniel had to carry with him. Ben had whittled a small bowl from an old piece of wood. It would serve for drinking and food, when he could find anything. Daniel had kept back a small stone jar from a mealtime when a celebration had come their way. He'd hidden it with his Bible under the floorboard which had been the protector of his meagre gains.

"You'll have to head through the town if you're to get anywhere. T'other way goes nowhere of any use. You need to get to the railroad and the town's the only place round here you'll do that. Hide up in a wagon and hope it goes some place useful." Ben gave Daniel all the advice he could, but his own experience was limited and he'd never travelled the distances that Daniel now sought to go. "It won't be safe to buy a ticket. This place has eyes everywhere. Soon as they know you've gone there'll be folks looking for you, and none of 'em good 'uns."

That much Daniel had assumed. He knew not to trust anyone until he was a long way from the farm. As the time drew near, he kept back what biscuits and meal he could do without, though there was precious little to get him through a working day. At this time of year there should be some scraps of harvested produce left back in the fields, so he hoped he wouldn't starve before he could find his way. He thought it best to hide up somewhere for a day or two, rather than risk being seen in the open, but he knew there'd be search parties, so nowhere was safe.

This time he would go before dawn on Sunday, with part of a night's sleep to bolster him and in hopes there'd be no other travellers on the road at that hour. He'd keep to the fields and rest as soon as it was light. With half the town hung-over, he might manage at least a head start before being followed.

It was the chosen Saturday at last. Ben and Daniel were alone and the time was near.

"I want you to take this." Ben thrust a small packet at Daniel. "It's not much, but it will get you a little along the way."

Daniel frowned and looked inside the packet. He let out a gasp. "I can't. You need it."

"You've helped me out and not been paid. By rights, that money's as much yours as mine. It's half of what I've got. I'll be fine with what remains."

Daniel looked deep into the old man's eyes and wrestled with words that wouldn't come. "Thank you. I wish I could take you with me."

Ben smiled. "Then you'd be found before you'd gone half the distance. I'll be all right here. I'll have Duke for company."

The dog snuffled his hand and moved to sit closer to Ben's feet. It was as if he could sense that his relationship with the two men was changing once again and that his future rested with his former master.

"Take care of him," said Daniel. They were needless words, he knew, but he had no idea how to convey the gratitude he was feeling and was lost for something meaningful to say.

"I will," Ben replied. "Now away to sleep, and Daniel... good luck." He clapped Daniel on the shoulder as he got up and moved to his bunk.

Tonight Daniel would sleep with his belongings close and his boots ready to put on.

The sun was far from rising when Daniel swung his legs down from the bunk and landed almost noiselessly on the extra straw he'd spread around that part of the barn floor. He stilled his breathing and listened to the sounds of the night. He'd heard the revellers come home and thought there was little real chance of waking them, but still it was a risk he didn't want to take. He felt a nose snuffle the leg of his trousers and reached down to give Duke's head one last pat. Then he lifted his boots and carried them out to the back of the barn, the side furthest from the house, before stooping to pull them on. He paused for one final check that everything was carefully stowed, then slung his small pack across his shoulder and made for the edge of the fields.

This side had yet to be harvested, which would make it easy to follow the line of the corn and know his direction in the almost complete dark of the moonless night. As his eyes adjusted, the starlight provided some outline to the shapes ahead, but when the clouds passed across the sky, all was black. Once he moved to other land that he didn't know he would need at least a slither of moon, the pre-dawn light or the gloaming to guide him on his way.

He kept close to the corn as he went, waving his stick ahead of him lest he walk into an outgrowing branch and cause injury. His steps were steady and rhythmic as he heard them tread lightly on the packed earth. Ben had rehearsed him carefully on where he needed to go for the disused barn, and he planned to shelter there for a day or two. As he walked, Daniel couldn't help but wonder if he might be better to make straight for the railroad and find some place to hide there until he felt safe enough to move on.

His decision was made for him. As he was nearing the barn he heard more than just the night sounds of the animal world. He stopped and breathed slow and even, quietening his body and freeing his senses. There was no mistaking the sound of human snoring coming from the other side of the wall.

He wondered at his misfortune of another seeking shelter in the same place on the one night that he had planned to use it. From the sounds, he suspected that this man needed shelter from the wrath of a wife, following a drunken night in the town. There was nothing else for it; Daniel would have to make for the railroad. He had perhaps no more than an hour before the day would be all but light, and no time to lose if he were going to conceal himself without risk of being found before his journey had yet begun.

Duke woke Ben as he usually did, a couple of hours after Daniel had left. The old man sighed as he faced the day, knowing it would be a little less safe and a lot less companionable than the day previous. He threw cold water over his sleep-ridden face and prepared for a day's work like any other. He knew better than to expect Jed or Rick to appear at the start of a Sunday and somehow, though it was not his business to know why, this never seemed to trouble

Hawksworth. Ben shook his head at the thought and went to collect his vitals before his work began. His hope was to do the work of two men, to delay the point that Daniel's absence was noticed.

Once out in the fields, Ben worked as hard as his tired bones would allow, stripping cob after cob from the stems as he made his way along the field. He wondered if he could go unnoticed and stay in the field through lunch, but as it was, events ran faster than his planning and a shout went up late morning that summoned all of them back to the yard. Jed and Rick looked barely past sleep as they stood there, apparently as bewildered at the call as Ben. Hawksworth stood before them, belt in hand, a look of menace playing across his mean features.

"And which one of you is the thief?" He glared first at one, then another, his gaze boring through them. His eyes narrowed. "Flynn?"

Ben searched for words to cover for his friend but found none that wouldn't be exposed within minutes. Sadly, he shook his head and answered truthfully, but without proffering information. "I don't know, Mr Hawksworth, sir."

Hawksworth whipped around. "You don't know! Then I guess we've found our thief."

Ben cringed at the prospect of Daniel being searched for as a thief rather than merely a deserter from his post.

Hawksworth stopped in front of him and brought his belt down on the palm of his own hand in a gesture intended to threaten. "And when –"

Hawksworth had not got much of his sentence out when Mrs Hawksworth came running out to them. "It wasn't Daniel." She panted out the words as she caught her breath. "I know it wasn't Daniel."

Hawksworth reeled round and caught her across the cheek with the leather end of the belt. "Silence, woman. You know no such thing."

She put her hand to her cheek and she had tears in her eyes as she answered with a defiance that Ben in that moment admired.

"I do know. I saw him." Her face was red as she pointed at Jed. "He took the money, last night when you all came back."

This time it was the buckle end that caught across Mrs Hawksworth's face, and blood immediately started to flow from the gash it caused. She put her hand to the wound.

"You saw no such thing, woman. You were abed when we came in and if you go on protecting the boy there will be many more where that came from."

She held her apron up to the wound to stem the bleeding and, with a further moment's hesitation and tears dripping from her cheeks, she turned and hurried back to the house.

Hawksworth loomed over Ben. "Where is the boy?"

Ben stood his ground and looked back at the man. He held his gaze as he answered honestly, "I don't know... sir." Sure, he'd suggested Daniel hide in the old barn, but he knew the boy would make his own mind up and besides, he'd no way of knowing how far he'd have got by now.

Hawksworth made as though he were going to strike the old man, but thought better of it and brought his quivering arm back to his side. Ben prayed that Duke would have the good sense to stay hidden in the barn. Now was not the time for the little dog to come to the attention of a man so intense that anything was possible.

"Rick, you come with me in the cart and we'll go look

for him. Jed…" Hawksworth hesitated. "… You stay back here and hold him if he returns. And you…" He snarled, turning back to Ben. "You need to do the work of all four of the men!" He cracked the belt down against the gravel of the yard and then turned on his heel back to the house.

Ben stood a while, listening. He heard a scream that only a woman could make and screwed up his eyes as if he thought that might shut it out. Would that he were a younger man and able to defend those who needed him. He pulled himself together and headed towards the barn. As soon as he was near enough, but away on the field side, he gave a low whistle to call Duke to him. The dog came out limping and Ben flinched, knowing one of the brothers had got to him first. He knew better than to show concern until he was out of sight of the yard, and headed straight to the field he'd been working that morning.

Once he was there he dropped to the ground and ran his hands over Duke's small frame. Duke flinched as Ben felt his side, and he knew it was a boot that had touched it most recently. Thank God, he thought, for Duke's sake as well as his own, the wound would heal and was no more than bruising… this time. He wanted the harvest finished quickly now so they could be away from this place, and this time he had no plans to return.

Daniel walked on towards the town. There was precious little time until the sun would start to rise and already the darkness had lost its hard edge. He'd heard a train away to his right. He would have to cross the main dirt road into town to get there, but it was still early enough, he hoped, for that not to cause a problem. He waited alongside the irrigation ditch at the edge of the field and listened. The sinister chirrups and rustles of the night creatures were all that disturbed the peace. He smiled – chirrups were good, it was silence he needed to fear. Slowly, so as not to raise his heart rate, he made his way over the dirt track and across the ditch on the other side. This was land he was not familiar with and he reached out carefully to feel the line of the crop and check what obstacles confronted him. He was relieved to find more corn. He needed to make his way through the crop toward the far side of the field. He hoped the farm hands here could sow in straight lines. He reached forward into the darkness to feel his way through the high stalks that grew to either side. If the wildlife would forgive his intrusion, at least the corn would give him cover awhile.

Before he'd finished crossing the field, he could see the corn well enough without use of his hands and wove his way onwards, hoping the railroad wasn't much further. It was too light to come out into the open within sight of the town, but maybe if the yard were deserted he'd still be able to break cover and make it to a wagon. He was contemplating this when he felt the earth vibrating slightly and he shuddered with the happy knowledge that he was nearer to the tracks than he'd realised. The thought gave him energy and he walked a little faster.

At the edge of the corn, Daniel looked out from the safety of his cover. He could see the rail tracks ahead of him and guessed the rail yard must be away to the left, but not visible. He began to move through the corn in that direction, keeping to the edge of the crop as best he could. He heard another train and pressed his way back into the corn behind him, waiting as still as possible for the train to pass. Once Daniel reached the corner of the field he could see wagons in the distance and knew the yard was at hand. He could wait for night to fall, hoping that this wasn't a field to be harvested today, or he could try to cross the open ground in daylight. He was impatient to get away and the day was still waking. He reckoned he'd be safe if he took it steady and drew no attention to himself.

He rested a moment to calm his anxiety and then stepped out boldly in the direction of the wagons. His ears were alert to every sound and, whilst he didn't want to draw attention by turning to look around him, his eyes darted left and right, taking in as much as he could see while looking forward. No one disturbed his progress and within a short time the first of the wagons was close at hand. Daniel could feel himself relax slightly as, from the shelter of the wagon, he looked about for a safe hiding place. There was a line of grain trucks, each covered by tarpaulins. He couldn't tell if they were full or empty, but if he could get into one of them, under the tarpaulin, he reckoned it would be as good a place as any. He stayed to the sheltered side of the wagons and made his way to the sanctuary of the nearest of the grain load. When he released the corner of the tarpaulin and found the wagon empty, he sent up a silent prayer of thanks. Then, slipping his pack from his shoulder and throwing it in ahead, he hauled himself up and through the opening he'd created, before pulling the tarpaulin almost completely back across the gap, but leaving just a little light filtering through.

For Daniel, the day was slow in passing. His only clue of how much time had elapsed was the change in light as the sun tracked across the sky and the vibrating of the wagon on the tracks with every approaching train. It wasn't a busy line, but there was freight, as well as the less frequent human cargo. He had hoped that maybe his own wagon would start to move and take him from this place, but he'd heard no one working nearby and, except for the occasional bird, had attracted no company through the morning.

As the afternoon wore on, Daniel's optimism grew and he started to think what he might do that night when darkness fell. He needed to find a train to stow away on that would be leaving Iowa City, but from the number of trains that were only passing through he feared it could be weeks before that was likely to happen. He wondered if he could risk a ride on a regular fare paying train, but he would have to get past the station master unnoticed. Word would be out by now that he'd gone missing and he had no way of knowing how seriously the sheriff would take it. He took out a biscuit and quelled his aching stomach with a couple of mouthfuls. His meagre supply might have to last a while, so satisfying his hunger was not an option. He waited.

At last the light began to fade and he felt the quiet of night descend like a thick blanket shrouding his surroundings, giving him a false sense of calm and safety. He wondered how Ben and Duke were doing without him and hoped that his leaving had not been a burden to them. Then, hearing nothing from outside, he eased himself up from the metal floor and moved each limb in turn to get some life back, ready to venture out. The wagon creaked slightly as he moved and he stopped again, listening for any answering sound. None came. He reached for the lip of the wagon, threw back the tarpaulin and hauled himself up to look out into the night. He could see nothing and that was good.

He dropped silently down again and retrieved his pack. He would make his way further up the tracks in the direction of the station, but staying as far behind the goods wagons as he could. He hoped an idea would come to him somewhere along the way.

His arms were strong from the work and he was able to haul his own weight, then lower himself down the outside of the wagon with ease, onto the gravel below. Even so, there was a crunch as he landed and he strained his ears to hear any returning noise. How far would he have to get before he would feel safe?

In the clouded dark, he walked as a blind man, using his hand to feel his way along the wagons in the yard. As each ended, he groped to feel the next and was relieved when it came. Part way down the line he sensed a change in the shape and wondered what these new wagons held as he continued down the long line. The next gap was a longer one and he thought he might be at their end. He inched to his right, searching for the edge of the track, and in doing so almost walked into the back of an engine's cab that overhung where he was walking. He felt his way around its side and imagined its graceful lines. He knew it would be dirty, but he was no stranger to dirt and a little blacking might help act as camouflage.

He hadn't got past the front of the engine when he saw a lantern in the distance and heard the heavy tread of a boot on the gravel. He flattened himself back against the engine, his heart quickening. He breathed slowly and deeply. Now was not the time to panic. It could be anyone and, likely as not, nothing to do with him. He realised he'd be best out of the way and as he was only a couple of steps past the train's cab he inched his way back as silently as he could and reached out to find the step that would give him access to the footplate.

The lantern was swinging as it was carried and he found it hard to tell the light's direction, but as the beam seemed to be gaining slightly in brightness, Daniel guessed it was coming toward rather than away from him. He felt for the opening of the engine cab and then ran his hands around the edges of the inside to find a corner more suited to hiding him. He dropped down below window level and crouched in the dark. He needed to steady the pounding in his ears, but his body was giving every indication it was ready to run.

The uneven rhythm of the crunching gravel told him there was more than one man, but they were still too far away for him to hear their voices. He cursed himself for staying around the train tracks and not making his way back into the relative safety of the corn, but it was too late for remonstrations now. His only hope was that they weren't looking for him.

CHAPTER 15

William looked down at the paper in his hands. He felt a shudder run through him. He hadn't thought it would come to this, although others he was at school with had been called away to fight and some had signed up willingly. He presumed it was because they could see little else but farm work in their futures, but it was different for him. He was already working alongside his father and doing mighty fine. He'd decided not to go to university. He said it was because he wanted to be no place but at home with his parents and that he thought his pa would teach him as well as any man could. His words had the effect he'd hoped for and the pride that Ma and Pa showed in him proved it.

That wasn't the whole truth, though, and he knew it. At the heart of his choice was a fear that they'd forget him if he weren't there, or worse, that Briggs might find a way to show him for what he really was. He'd got his sights set on owning this town, or as much as wasn't owned by the Round Oak Stove Company, at any rate. At least, he would do so if there were a way to get out of the draft.

"Sir," he said, knocking courteously on the door of his father's office. "May I talk to you, please?" As a clerk, William sat outside the office, although his father included him in meetings whenever he could.

"What is it, William?" His father was poring over a document on the large table in the room. As far as William knew, it related to an Indian land holding which some of the town were disputing. He looked up at William with a distant look of bafflement across his face.

"Sir, I received a letter this morning. I've only just opened it."

His father shook his head, then put his pen down and gave his attention to William. "I'm sorry, William, can this wait until later? I'm expecting Councillor Taylor along shortly and I want to be ready for him."

"I'm sorry, sir, but no, I don't think it can wait." William felt dazed. "It's my draft papers, sir. They want me to present myself to the recruiting office next Monday." He gulped as the closeness of the date sank in. "Sir," he continued, looking down at his shoes, "I don't want to go."

Mr Dixon removed his spectacles and looked closely at William. "I guess you're right, William. This is pretty important." He folded the plans which were on the table, moved them to the side and, indicating to the chair, said, "Sit down, son."

William moved to the table and with a trembling hand pulled the chair out and sat opposite Pa.

"It seems to me there are four lines of possible action."

William thought Pa sounded as though he were addressing a client about a case, but sat quietly. He'd been thinking it through for himself and had thought of only three possibilities.

"Firstly," said Pa, "you could be there at 8 a.m. sharp on Monday." He hesitated before going on. "But that's not something any of us want to see happen, especially not your ma."

William gulped.

"Secondly…"

William looked up sharply. He was relying on one of

the options being better.

"Secondly, we could place you with one of our clients in an essential occupation, such as farming, and ask for you to be excused."

William's eyes widened. He had not thought of that possibility. He looked down on the children who'd ended up with farm work and he certainly didn't want to find himself having to roll up his sleeves and get his own hands dirty. "And the other options, sir?"

"Well, thirdly, we could try to buy your place out and have you excused. I could claim your ma needs you at home or that you are essential to the office."

"Would you, sir? Would you?" William couldn't mask the eagerness in his voice.

"I'm not so sure that one would work, William. You're still learning and it's hard to show I couldn't do without you here. As for Ma..." Pa shrugged.

"You said there were four possibilities, sir... that leaves one other." William was desperate to hear what it was, and hoped it tallied with his own thinking.

"Well..." His father sounded ponderous. "... We could offer to send someone in your place and buy you out that way, but the question would be whom?"

Silence fell between them and William thought better than to fill it.

After a while his father continued. "It would need to be someone who wouldn't be receiving draft papers otherwise. Someone excused for a different reason, whose place you might need to take. It would cost to do it, but that's not an issue."

William closed his eyes for a moment, hoping his father might have the same person in mind as he had.

"To be honest, William, I can't rightly think of anyone

just for the minute."

William's heart sank. Then, taking a deep breath, he proffered his thought. "Sir, what about Briggs?"

"Briggs?" His father sounded surprised. "Well," he said, pursing his lips, "he certainly wouldn't be called with this wave of recruits." His nose rested on his steepled fingers as he considered. "I'd a mind to offer him a pension at some point anyway, so the money wouldn't be an issue, and obviously if anything happened to him I'd see to it his family were well looked after..."

"So you'll do it, sir?" William was finding it hard to contain his enthusiasm. Anyone else coming into the groom's role would afford William the respect he deserved, now he was pretty much an adult within the family.

"I can't be sure he'll say yes, mind." His father smiled. "But I'm sure we can make it worth his while. And he's always had a soft spot for your ma. I'll talk to him tonight. Now, if you'll excuse me..." He picked up his glasses and the plans. "... I've a meeting to prepare for." He gave William a conspiratorial wink.

All William could do was wait for the outcome. He knew his father would tell him as soon as there was news. When the lunch hour came he took up his coat and went out into the fresh air. He would have enough time to walk down to Jeanie's house and break the news to her. Even if Pa managed to send Briggs in his place, it wouldn't hurt for her to think about what might have been and to focus on the fact she could lose him at any minute. He grinned to himself.

Jeanie wasn't the most beautiful girl in Dowagiac, but he'd go a long way to find a better catch. Her father was Congressman Makepeace, re-elected that year for the Republican Party and happy for his daughter to be affianced to the son of the renowned local lawyer, George Dixon. Neither Jeanie nor her father knew much of William's early life, but they were all happy that this respectable young man must be worthy of the life he now led and William wasn't about to tell them otherwise. It would go well for him to have a suitable wife on his arm when his father took him into the partnership, and Ma and Pa's introduction to the Makepeace girl had been a clear signal on their thoughts. Besides, what was marriage, to him? It had hardly served his own parents well. If he could better himself by his choice then so much to the good.

He walked briskly through the town to their house and was there within fifteen minutes, at the grand entrance which made even the Dixons' own home look small. He was shown by the maid into the drawing room, where Mrs Makepeace was embroidering and her daughter was reading to her as she worked. As William entered, they both rose to greet him.

"I had no wish to disturb you both; please don't get up on my account."

"William! We had no idea you were coming today. I'd have had lunch prepared for you if I'd known," said the older lady, putting down her work and bustling across to ring the bell.

"Please, don't trouble anyone. It is only a brief visit. I've had news I thought I ought to share with Jeanie and yourselves immediately."

Jeanie looked concerned and moved to his side.

He was gratified to see the colour rise in her cheeks and watched carefully for the effects his news might bring. "I've…" He hesitated for impact. After his talk with Pa the papers seemed no more real than reading of them in a novel. "I've received my orders to attend the recruiting office… on Monday."

Jeanie gasped and swooned onto the settee. He went to her and put an arm to support her.

"Oh, my poor dear," said Mrs Makepeace, fussing over her daughter. "William, that is a terrible shock to give a young girl. You'd have been better to have told Mr Makepeace and have him break it to her."

William almost smiled. He admired the tough edge in the mother, though her excessive concern for her daughter was probably the cause of the latter's fragile nature. He did feel somewhat irritated that her first concern had not been for himself having to go off to war.

"I presume your father will be appealing against it." Her words were matter of fact rather than in any way emotional. "He will speak to Johnson if he needs any back up." It came out as a statement rather than a question.

"I'm sure he will, ma'am and had Jeanie not fainted when she did, I would have gone on to tell her that I hoped she had nothing to fear."

As he said this, Jeanie started to revive, with a little help from her mother's smelling salts.

"Please say it's not so, William?" She looked up at him with her cornflower blue eyes, and William's soft smile was quite genuine.

"Yes, dearest one, it's true, but I hope Pa can address matters so I don't have to go. How could I leave you, even for a little time?"

That was enough to make Jeanie smile and he gently took her hand and kissed it. He talked another minute or two to the mother and daughter and then took his leave, promising to tell them as soon as he knew if Pa's plan had succeeded. He was satisfied that both the women he was leaving would hold him at least a little dearer for the thought they might have lost him to the war, even if the chance now seemed unlikely.

William had an extra bounce in his step as he walked briskly back to the office. As long as Mr Lincoln didn't have his way, then William Dixon was going to do just fine. If things went in his favour, one day he might even take over the Congressman role from his father-in-law, which would suit him rather well, from what he could see. He was William Dixon and that was all they needed to know, particularly if Briggs were out of the way too.

CHAPTER 16

Molly worried for Henry, still away fighting. Receiving his letters was as much about the relief of knowing he was still alive when they were posted as the tidings the words actually brought.

My dearest Molly,

You cannot know how happy I was to receive your last letter. I'm only sorry I couldn't be there to see what a beautiful bride my new sister-in-law made. I know that mother is delighted to have a daughter in the family and I hope one day to make her happy by bringing her a second. You must both miss Sarah on the farm, but your loss has most definitely been Ma's gain and she is mightily relieved for the help. I'm glad Miss Cochrane has found a boy to work for you and the more glad to know he is too young to take my place in your affections.

So far the war has been kind to me and nothing has been asked of me that I could not give. We have been told to say little of our whereabouts for fear our letters might fall into enemy hands, but needless to say we are some way distant from home and the changing landscape is of great interest to me. I have no way of knowing what tomorrow will bring, but know, my dearest, that my thoughts of you gladden this fearful heart and your letters give it courage to be strong.

Until I'm home with you
I remain your humble servant,
Henry Spencer

Molly read the letter through again and lingered long over the words '… I hope one day to make her happy by bringing her a second.' Was she reading too much into that to think he meant to ask her to marry him? It could still be a while before the war was over, but she'd grown fond of Henry and prayed fervently for his safe return. Seeing how happy Sarah was made her wistful, and now she dared to hope that maybe soon her own time might come. She still thought often of Daniel, but they had been but children and she had no way of knowing where he was, never mind whether they might have been more than childhood friends. Henry was a good man and she hoped she might be happy with him and that, if he knew, Daniel would be pleased for her.

"Now what are you looking all starry-eyed over?" Miss Ellie's voice made Molly jump. "Oh dear, I hope that's not a guilty secret you're harbouring there, young lady."

Molly had grown close to Miss Ellie over the years, and the more so since Sarah had moved to the shop. "Miss Ellie, may I talk to you?"

"Why, of course…" Miss Ellie scrutinised her face. "This is something serious, isn't it? Oh Molly, of course you can talk to me." She dropped the teasing voice, took Molly's arm and led her to sit on the big window seat. "Is it Henry?"

Molly pulled a bit of a face, trying carefully to choose her words. "Well, Miss Ellie, it is and it isn't. Oh, it's no good. It's a letter from Henry that's set me to thinking, but nothing's happened to him, if that's what you mean." Molly felt tears prick the corners of her eyes and reached for her handkerchief.

"What is it, child?"

The softness in Miss Ellie's voice broke down her final barrier and the tears began to flow. "Do you think I should marry Henry?"

"Oh, Lord have mercy, has he asked you?"

Molly shook her head. "Not exactly, it's just that what he's said makes me think he's planning to." She handed the letter to Miss Ellie to read.

Miss Ellie nodded as she got to the end. "You may be reading things that aren't there, but I can see what made you think it." She paused. "You don't have to say yes, you know."

"No, but I don't want to say no either. It's not that I wouldn't want to marry him, it's just..." Her voice trailed off and she gazed out of the window across the farm. "Do you think Tom and Daniel would approve?"

"Oh, child, why ever wouldn't they? Henry is a fine young man and look how happy Sarah is with his brother."

Molly spent many hours thinking what she would say when the time came for Henry to propose marriage. She supposed he might ask Miss Ellie's permission and tried to imagine his words. As the days passed, she became quite certain she would accept him, but on condition she could still work on the farm she loved so much. When she wrote back she made no mention of her suspicions, but instead gave him the best of the news from home, which was what he most liked to hear.

The letters from Henry took on a new significance and she was always eager to hear the horse which signalled the post arriving. She said nothing about it to Sarah, but as she worked, her thoughts turned to what she might sew to wear for her wedding and whether there might be enough material for Sarah to be an attendant for her. She was quite sure as the weeks passed that the fighting would be over soon and Henry would be home safe.

Some weeks later, Molly was working in the dairy when she heard the clattering of hooves across the yard outside. She thought little of it but the thrill that a letter might be waiting for her later, when her hands were clean from work. She continued with the butter until she heard the sound of running feet and Sarah's voice calling, "Molly! Molly, where are you?"

She could tell by Sarah's tone this wasn't going to be good news and quickly covered the butter and wiped her hands while calling back. Her first thought was that Joseph was being called to fight, and she was ready to console and support her friend, but as she went out into the bright light of the yard she could see Sarah waving a letter and stumbling toward her with the darkest of expressions on her face. Sarah doubled over, catching her breath as she thrust the letter toward Molly. "I'm sorry," seemed to be the words she gasped as she handed it over and tried to compose herself.

Molly's hands were shaking as she took the letter, written in an unfamiliar hand. It was addressed to *Mr Henry Spencer, Senior*, Henry's father. Molly looked at the envelope and, suddenly stricken, looked to her friend. "No! Please tell me it isn't so." She could feel herself shaking and needed somewhere to sit.

Sarah screwed up her face as though in pain and nodded slowly. "I'm sorry," she said once again as she took Molly's arm and guided her to a nearby hay bale to sit.

Miss Ellie must have heard the commotion and now came rushing to join them. Molly was sitting stock still, dazed and clutching the unread letter. Sarah gently took the letter from her hand and passed it to Miss Ellie.

"Oh, dear Lord," Miss Ellie said as she read the report

and gave a summarised version to Molly. "It's some blessing he didn't suffer." She took her shawl and wrapped it around the shoulders of the shivering Molly. "Let's get you up to the house."

Between them, Sarah and Miss Ellie half guided and half carried Molly, who felt stunned and confused by the news. Having set her mind to marrying Henry, she had become quite certain the happy event would be soon and he would be home safe before the summer was out.

Miss Ellie brought her the largest brandy she'd ever had and she sipped at it slowly. She was quiet as she sat there and Miss Ellie waited with her, while Sarah had to get back to help the family, where Henry's mother was as distraught as any mother could be.

Molly was withdrawn for days and went about her work in hazy confusion. Miss Ellie had offered to let her take a few days off from the work, but she preferred to keep herself busy. She did take the time to visit Mrs Spencer, but the older woman's outward distress had been hard for Molly to cope with while trying to manage her own emotions, and self-pity was for Molly a dark place and not somewhere she wanted to spend too much time. She found tears came unbidden while she worked, but they were tears that Henry's own dreams would not come to pass, rather than for her own lost hope. When she felt sadness for herself she looked instead to the life Miss Ellie had carved out and knew there was more than marriage that could make her happy.

Molly loved her work on the farm, but it gave her time to think and Henry was rarely far from her thoughts. Neither were those she'd loved and left behind, and it set her to thinking. One evening, sitting with Miss Ellie after they'd eaten, Molly was ready to voice the decision she had made. "Miss Ellie, I need to find Tom and Daniel." She had spoken often of her brother and childhood friend. "Losing Henry has set me to thinking of those I still have in this world, and I've been parted from them long enough."

She had little idea where she would even start in finding them. She knew Tom was in Dowagiac and didn't want to be contacted. She'd managed to find out that Daniel was in Iowa, but had received no word of how he was and had no idea if the message she had sent had ever reached him. As to where those places were and how she might get there, Molly had absolutely no idea. She thought they were away from the areas of fighting and she presumed the railroad would be a good starting point, as that was how they'd all travelled to begin with, but her knowledge went no further.

"Miss Ellie, can I take some time to go and find them? I'd plan on coming back here afterwards, but I need to know they are well."

"Lord have mercy, child. A girl can't go gallivanting around the country on her own. Never mind that there are some as don't think it's proper – it wouldn't be safe. Anything could happen to you. I may not be a worrier at heart, but I'd never get a wink of sleep while you were gone."

Molly looked at Miss Ellie and held her gaze. "And what if I dressed as a boy?"

Miss Ellie threw her head back and laughed. "You might have got away with that as a child in New York to sell papers, but you've got a figure now and it's not so easy to hide it. It got you into trouble then and it sure would get you into trouble now."

Molly felt crestfallen.

"Now don't you go getting all sentimental on me, Molly Reilly, but I've got me an idea and I fancy you're going to like it. The corn's in and for a while there's only the animals and the dairy to think of. I've never seen much of this great country of ours. In fact, if truth be told, I've never been very far at all. What if I were to get help in to run the farm for a month or two and come with you?" Miss Ellie was grinning broadly by this time.

"Oh, Miss Ellie, would you really do that?" Molly flung her arms around the woman and kissed her cheek.

"Now, I said don't go getting sentimental on me, and don't you go telling anyone I'm going soft in my old age. It'll take me a week or two to arrange things, but we can set off soon enough. In the meantime, we'd best be finding out about the trains and how long it takes to get there, wherever 'there' is. I've some money put by and this seems as good a use as any for it."

Molly didn't know what to say. Her heart felt lighter than it had for a very long time and she was utterly overwhelmed by the kindness of this woman. "I guess I'd best speak to Sarah, to tell her I'm going away for a while."

"We'll be needing provisions. You can take the cart into town tomorrow and see her in person. I'd leave it at visiting your brother for now. She's bound to talk at table and the family might see it as too soon to be looking up another young man."

"But, Miss Ellie, I didn't…"

"Now don't you go saying you weren't sweet on Daniel, because I won't believe you for a minute. I know you were young, but there's no one you talk of more fondly than that young man. In the meantime, you'd best be working your hardest to get everything in order for while we're away. That dairy needs to be spick and span and everything needs to be up to date."

Molly jumped up. She'd work every waking hour if it

170

would help, though she knew it wouldn't come to that, with the corn in. Then, realising the lateness of the hour, she decided on an early start the following morning. She wished Miss Ellie goodnight and headed to her room. As she went upstairs the words of one of the songs she had been desperate to remember came back to her and she began to sing:

"As I was a walking one morning in May,
I saw a sweet couple together at play,
O, the one was a fair maid so sweet and so fair,
And the other was a soldier and a brave grenadier..."

For a moment she felt a pang and thought of Henry, and wondered if she were really ready to go away.

"Oh, Molly, what will I do without you while you're gone?" Sarah clasped her friend's hands as they sat together the following afternoon.

"You've got Joe now; he'll be here and it's not as though I shall be away for long. I'll be back before you even notice. And I'll write to you."

"And will I write to you?"

Molly hesitated. "Why yes, but I don't rightly know where you'll send the letters. I guess the Post Office in Dowagiac would be as good a place as any. I can find it there when I arrive."

What she wasn't certain of was what she'd do when they went on in search of Daniel, but maybe the Post Office could forward any mail to her without her having need to tell Sarah.

Sarah smiled at her. "Good luck. I do hope you find Tom and that all goes well. Here..." Sarah removed a locket from around her neck. "Take this with you so that you have something of home while you're gone."

Molly hugged her friend and carefully put the locket around her own neck. "Don't you be worrying about me. Miss Ellie says we'll be just fine travelling together." But she still shed a tear as she hugged her friend goodbye and set off back to the farm to get ready for the trip.

She and Miss Ellie packed a small trunk between them. They had arranged for one of the farm hands to take them to the station in the cart. He would then bring the cart back to the farm so it could be used by Miss Ellie's cousin, James, who would manage the farm while they were gone.

The train line was not direct and the journey was far from straightforward, although, as they had found from their enquiries, the distance was not so great. They had arranged to stay in a couple of guest houses along the way and spread the journey to make it comfortable.

"Whatever shall I do with all this time on my hands and no work to be doing?" Miss Ellie said when they were finally packed and tying their bonnets ready to leave.

Molly knew it was not a question which needed answering, as she'd seen Miss Ellie packing a journal and writing materials, as well as some books to read. She also knew, from the clothing that lay in the trunk, that they would do a lot of walking, so as to see the places they visited. Neither she nor Miss Ellie had given much space to ostentation; if truth be told they had little finery they could have considered packing.

As they boarded the train at Pierceton, Molly was surprised to see Sarah walking briskly along the platform to see them off. She stopped in the train doorway to wait for her friend.

"Oh, Molly, I thought I was going to be too late to see

you." Sarah was a little out of breath, but before Molly had the chance to say anything she carried on. "I just had to come to tell you – Dr Shepherd says I'm expecting a baby. Oh, do tell me you'll be back before my confinement?"

"That's wonderful news. I'll be back just as soon as I can. I promise." Almost before she'd had the chance to finish speaking, the guard was closing the doors and blowing his whistle for departure. "Write to me. Tell me all about it," Molly shouted down the platform as her friend was slowly left behind by the departing train.

She stayed at the window until the station had receded from view, then moved along the carriage until she found her seat with Miss Ellie. With a compartment to themselves, the train seemed a far cry from the one she'd arrived on from New York, and yet suddenly she remembered that journey vividly. How much had changed for both her and Sarah. Who would have thought then that Sarah would be the one settled and happy, while Molly was left searching for the missing piece of her life? She remembered her friend's fear that her own children would grow up as orphans and prayed that Sarah would have courage. She resolved to write to her just as soon as they arrived at their first stop.

Molly sank back into the seat and looked out of the window at the passing scenery. She wondered what she would find at the end of her journey. She tried to think whether she was the same person now as she had been more than ten years earlier, when she'd last seen Tom and Daniel. She had no way of knowing what their lives had been like and only hoped they'd been as happy as she had.

"What are you thinking, child?"

Molly became aware that Miss Ellie was watching her and she sighed. "I guess I'm just worried this might all be for nothing. What if they don't remember me?"

Miss Ellie took her hand. "It could never be for nothing. You'll see places you wouldn't have seen and we'll both enjoy the change. Besides, if it answers your questions, it will have served its purpose."

"Did you never think of marrying, Miss Ellie?"

Miss Ellie looked away, out of the window. She waited a long minute before answering, "Yes, I thought about it, child. I very near went and did it, but..." She swallowed hard. "... It wasn't to be. Just like your Henry, he upped and died before he got chance to make an honest woman of me." She looked back at Ellie and her eyes were shining. "I guess I married the farm after that. We all find solace in different things. You girls filled the gap that was left, the one the farm couldn't fill, and I've been mighty happy that you did."

Molly wanted to say how grateful she was and how much she'd enjoyed living with Miss Ellie, but before she could form the words Miss Ellie went on, "Now, child, we've got ourselves a roof for the night in Wanatah and it won't be long until we're there. There'll be time enough to look around while it's still light, though I don't expect it will be so very different from Pierceton – then tomorrow we go on to Michigan City. It really is quite an adventure."

Miss Ellie's spirits seemed to have revived and she had a childlike anticipation on her face. Her enthusiasm was infectious. In another couple of days, Molly would see her own dear brother, and at that thought her excitement took hold and she felt herself grinning at the very prospect.

CHAPTER 17

But we were known from infancy,
Thy father's hearth was home to me,
No selfish love was mine for thee,
Unholy and unwise.
My Mary of the Curling Hair, Gerald Griffin 1803 - 1840

Daniel pressed himself further into the corner of the engine cab. The dark was his protection, but it felt overpowering. He could feel the sweat gathering across his upper lip. He tried to calm his breathing, fearing he'd be too easily heard. They were closer now and he could tell by the volume of the sound that they were coming his way. He heard a shout – "Over here" – and held his breath, hoping they had found what it was they were looking for. The seconds passed and he heard the boot steps starting again. He let out the breath he'd been holding and tried to regain his composure.

As his eyes became accustomed to the dark, he could make out odd shapes around him. Perhaps the moon was rising and the light increasing. He began to wonder if anything around the cab could be used as a weapon to fight his way out of the situation. He saw a large shovel that must usually be used to help load the fire, but it was on the other side of the cab near the engine itself. He wondered if he should try to move to it, or try to bring it to where he was now, but with any movement there would be a risk. He reckoned he had the advantage, just by knowing it was there, and could reach it in a moment if the need arose. He pushed himself further back into the corner and waited.

Daniel could see the edge of the pool of light cast by the lantern now. They were close and advancing fast. He made ready to move, torn between running or staying to fight. It was still possible that it was not him being looked for, but the chance of his being left alone, whoever it was, would be slim. He thought about how to get away. He had little to carry and was fleet of foot. There were entrances to the cab on either side. He thought he saw a flicker of light to his right and he strained to hear if it was that side the crunch of gravel came from. That would put them on the track side of the train. The shovel was almost straight in front of him, but his first choice would be to head out to the left and run. There was no point heading towards the town; they'd find him too soon and he didn't know the hiding places. He'd head back to the corn field and lose himself deep in the crop. It would take dogs to flush him out and by the time they'd mustered the help he'd have moved on and away, or so he hoped.

He was sitting on his haunches ready to spring, working hard to take slow and regular breaths. He could feel a trickle of sweat run down his back as he listened intently and heard the men stop. There was low muttering and his heart pounded. Now he knew for certain. It was him they were after. He would recognise Rick's voice anywhere. He made ready to run like a wild thing, but the pool of light split and he realised they were coming around from both sides of the engine. He would have no choice but to fight, if ever he was going to get out of this. He had the advantage by only a second or two. If they were searching thoroughly, there'd be no way they would miss where he was. Of course, if he moved he'd blow his cover, but he'd have the shovel and be prepared. The element of surprise would be on his side.

As fast as he could, Daniel moved across the cab and took up the shovel. His eyes scanned from left to right, waiting for his assailants to enter the cab. Whichever one of them came first, he'd fight his way out and then run. He wasn't sure whether he would have to swing the shovel left or right, but held it at the ready.

The steps quickened in response to the noise he'd made inside the cab and it was only a moment before a lantern, followed by the face of Rick, appeared to his right. Daniel brought down the shovel as hard as he could. It was heavier than he'd realised and not so easy to move swiftly.

There was an awful scream, followed by the lantern shattering and the sound of Rick falling back to the gravel. Daniel was paralysed with fear. The true nature of what he'd done hit him almost instantly. He dropped the shovel. So much for running. He felt a hand on his collar, but was almost senseless to what was happening.

Seemingly distantly, he heard Mr Hawksworth call, "Rick."

There was a moan in reply but no words.

Hawksworth took his belt and tied Daniel's arms. Then, leaving him attached to the rail of the cab, he went to where Rick was lying. "You son of a bitch, you've damn near killed him," he heard Hawksworth shout.

Daniel's heart leapt as he registered the word 'near'. Rick was alive, thank God.

Then Hawksworth blew a whistle and Daniel realised there must have been others looking for him too. He heard boots at a distance running toward them and knew all chance of escape was lost. He could only hope that Rick wasn't too badly hurt, but with shouts for a doctor to be fetched he feared things didn't look good. Then, before he could find out any more, a Deputy came and took him from the cab, replaced the belt with handcuffs and led him off along the gravel in the direction of the town.

The cell was as barely furnished as it was possible to be, though ruefully, Daniel thought it little worse than the bunkhouse he'd left behind. It was daylight he missed most, as the small window, set high in the wall, let in precious little of the day. He closed his eyes and tried to imagine the feeling of the sun on his skin, its warmth caressing him as no human had since his own mother died. He thought of the feeling of Duke's rough fur beneath his fingers and determined not to give up on life, if it wasn't ready to give up on him.

What light there was from the outside was his only measure of passing time. His meals came at irregular intervals, when the Deputy remembered he'd company below. A small stone was enough to record the days and he used it to scratch at the wall, a new line apart from others that had scratched before him.

He had no more idea of the workings of the law than he had of most other things. He thought there'd be a trial, but he had no certainty of it, and from the angry voices he'd heard from above he wondered if he might be better being forgotten than tried by a mob. What crime would they try him on? Was it for running away he was being held, or for hitting Rick with the shovel? He didn't know which was worse, but couldn't imagine that his treatment by the folks of the town could be any worse than it had been at the hands of Hawksworth.

It was hard to pass the time when you had all the time in the world and no idea when it would end, but there was one thing he was determined about; if they broke his spirit they would have won and he might as well be dead. He did the one thing he'd always done to get him through the darkest times. He sang. Quietly at first, but when no one seemed to object to the noise, he became bolder. He closed his eyes and remembered the days on the New York streets, singing in the hope of being able to eat. Gone were the days on the harbour-side, mimicking his father's voice. Now his was that voice, grown fuller with age, the lilt of his Irish accent more fully apparent when singing than in speech.

"I've been a wild rover for many's the year,
And I spent all me money on whiskey and beer.
And now I'm returning with gold in great store,
And I never will play the wild rover no more..."

When he first started singing he was doing it for himself, but after a day or two he became aware of shadows blocking the light from the grate above. Then the following day, to his surprise, he found a small package wrapped in paper dropped through the grate, and on unwrapping it found a small hunk of bread. Once again he was singing for his livelihood and his singing became bolder. Each day he was rewarded with small items that brought him great cheer and the hope that one day maybe he'd see the sunlight again and know the touch of another human hand.

By no means were all the people as generous of spirit. He'd heard many shouts of 'Bog-rot' and other slurs on his homeland. Although he'd lived in the United States of America longer than ever he'd lived in Ireland, there was no getting away from Ireland having been the only real home he'd ever known. He wondered if life might have been better if they'd stayed, but he doubted that would have been the case.

The days passed, scored in fives on the wall. He'd tried asking what was happening, but received no more than a shrug. He suspected his captors knew little more than he did. He wondered who it was that made the decisions, or whether a decision had been taken and they'd simply omitted to tell him.

The day was warm when the pastor called to see him. He'd already been in the cell for twenty-three days and it was the first visitor he'd had.

The pleasantries were hardly out of the way before the pale-faced but obviously well-fed man said, "And are you saved?"

Daniel blinked. He had not set foot in a church since he was a small child and had no grasp of what the pastor was asking him. He was all too aware, from responses on the farm, that mentioning his Catholic background was unlikely to be what the pastor was looking for. "Sir?" he said, for want of anything more certain to say.

"Are you saved, Flynn? Have you repented of the errors of your ways and of your parents' ways?"

Daniel had regarded his parents as being good people and could think of little of their ways he should be repenting of. He'd read some of the Bible he'd been given, but that hadn't made what the pastor said any the clearer. "I'm a God-fearing man, sir. Though I know little of the church. And I've never been to confession."

The pastor shook his head, a look of sadness on his face. "Do you want to burn in the fires of hell?"

Daniel was becoming increasingly confused and on uncertain ground. "Sir, do you know how long I'm to be held here?"

"You should seek salvation, Flynn. When the good Lord

calls you, what will you say?"

"Am I to be tried for a crime, sir?"

Before the pastor had any chance to answer – though Daniel doubted he would have got a response to what he'd said – the Deputy called the pastor away and Daniel was left in a confused silence once more. He tried to remember the words of Hail Mary, but suspected that would no more impress the pastor than anything else he'd said. He set to wondering about the sort of God that could abandon him to this life. As far as he knew he'd done no real harm, and for the first time he started to lose hold of the determination that had brought him this far. He sat with his head in his hands and could find no song.

CHAPTER 18

Miss Ellie had been right. Wanatah was very similar in character to Pierceton. Molly felt disappointed that there wasn't more to distract her. Tom's statement that she shouldn't contact him was weighing heavier, the nearer to him they travelled. However, without the farm to focus on, Miss Ellie had been relaxed and talkative about her own life and that was providing Molly with much to interest her as they journeyed on to Michigan City.

She was glad of the safety of company and soon realised her plan would have been almost impossible for a young lady on her own. She hoped that once Tom had seen reason he might choose to travel on with them to find Daniel. Surely, he would be mightily pleased to see her, wouldn't he?

Molly started to imagine the possibility of a life with them all together again and wondered what Tom might think of the farm in Pierceton. Then she stopped. From the response to her note she just couldn't picture it, but she couldn't understand why. Somehow, it was like doing a puzzle and finding an extra piece. She was quiet as she thought about it. Maybe she was even wrong to go in search of them, and in her own grief was being selfish, but she'd started now and she'd never been one to give up easily.

When they alighted from the train at Michigan, Molly felt in awe of the place. Somehow the streets seemed wider and the buildings stood straighter and taller. She remembered back to the wharfs in New York. These buildings weren't that tall, but they looked better kept and less sinister, more respectable somehow.

They walked a while in silence and Molly felt the weight of her quest. What if she couldn't find Tom? What if she didn't recognise him? She laughed at herself. Of course she would recognise her own flesh and blood and if nothing else the unruly red locks would give him away. She had a sudden thought. "Miss Ellie, what if he's gone off to war?"

Ellie Cochrane turned to Molly, her face clouded for a moment. "Well, child, that's a prospect we'll have to face if it comes. From what you've said, it's a possibility. He'd be old enough to be gone."

Molly felt the corners of her eyes prick with tears, as she thought of Henry and the sudden prospect that others she knew might be caught up in the fighting. Despite the fact there was no more to be done on that day, she felt an urgency and stepped out a little faster, leaving Miss Ellie to stride to keep up with her.

Ellie laid a hand on her arm. "Child, it will be fine. Just you see."

The strength and certainty in Miss Ellie's voice was like balm to Molly and she reached her hand down to cover the inner pocket of her skirt, felt the rosary safely in place and slowed her pace to a more normal level.

In their lodgings, Molly was fascinated to see the Singer sewing machine on a small table in their room, and presumed it was used as a work room when there were no guests. She ran her hand over the black and gold of the lettering and wondered if one day she might own such a beautiful and, of course, useful item. She sighed, thinking how much times had changed from the hand-to-mouth life she used to lead, and wondered what Mammy would make of being able to sew clothes so easily.

She slept little that night, tossing and turning as she thought what her first words to Tom might be. In her mind she pictured the boy she'd known and tried to cast him forward into the man he might have become. She saw shoulders strong and muscular from labouring, and hair as wild and untamed as it had always been. She tried to remember what Mammy had looked like and their da, but saw only vague shadows that flitted out of focus on the edge of memory.

Sleep did come eventually, but when it did it was short and lacked the refreshment she longed for. She woke with the dawn light and a thousand thoughts to unravel to make sense of any of them. After all this time, the day had finally arrived. She breathed deeply and tried to steady her shaking hands as she buttoned her boots. Then she prayed quietly for Mammy's soul, before packing up to face what the day might bring.

The journey to Dowagiac was not a long one and the fields passed much as they had done the rest of the trip. Molly spent the time rehearsing in her mind the words she would use to enquire of Tom. She had no idea of the numbers of children who'd stayed here from the train all those years ago. It was obvious from Daniel's whereabouts that not all of them would be here, but she hoped there might be enough that some would know or remember Tom and point her in the right direction. He could be on one of the outlying farms and rarely enter the town itself. Molly's thoughts were distant when she felt a hand rest on hers.

"Stop your sighing, girl," Miss Ellie said. "You'll be fine. I know you will."

The warmth of Miss Ellie's smile gave Molly comfort

and she smiled in return, a strong determination within her.

They alighted from the train in the early afternoon and waited while the porter brought their luggage along. Molly wanted to lose no time in the quest and as he drew the cart toward them she stepped forward, shielding her eyes from the sun that her small hat brim was failing to keep out. "Sir, excuse me, but were you here when the children from New York were brought to the town by train?"

He stopped short, seeming surprised to be addressed on any subject other than the cases. He straightened his hat and scratched his brow as though trying to remember. "Which train would that have been, Miss? There's been several over the years."

Molly looked up sharply. It had not occurred to her there might have been multiple trains stopping there with children. "I... I... I..." she stammered as she thought. "... I think it was the first one, but I'm not so sure. If I remember rightly it was September in the year 1854." She searched his face for the answer.

He shook his head. "I've only worked here since '57, when Old Ted gave up the post."

"And Ted, where can I find him?" Molly's fingers twisted the edge of her shirt.

The porter spoke slowly. "When I say 'gave up', I don't rightly mean he did it voluntarily. He was moving an old trunk when he breathed his last."

Molly nodded her comprehension. "Well, thank you anyway. Maybe I could ask the station master too."

The porter simply lifted the end of the cart and continued to wheel it towards the station entrance.

Molly had no more success in asking the station master, or the lady at the house where they had arranged lodgings.

The next step would be to find the Town Hall and see if there were any official records which could be referred to.

By the time they ventured out, it was too late to make their enquiries so they settled for a stroll to investigate the town. Molly wanted to absorb every detail of the place her brother called home and only wished he could have been there to show them around.

"There'll be time for that soon enough," Miss Ellie said when Molly shared her thoughts.

"I know, but don't you think it would have been nice for this first time?"

Miss Ellie smiled. "Happen it would, child, but I'm guessing it means more to your romantic soul than it would to your brother."

Molly thought those were wise words, but they did nothing to quell the longing that things could have been otherwise.

They were at the Town Hall the following day, as soon as someone was free to see them. Molly was fidgeting with her sleeve as they waited in the reception. She felt as though she were so close to her goal and yet this final step was the most significant.

"Thank you for seeing us," she said when they were shown through. "I'm trying to find my brother. I know he lives here somewhere abouts, but I don't rightly know where to look." She explained the story of his being sent on that first train and asked about the records they might have.

The gentleman shook his head. "I'm sorry, my dear," he said, in what Molly could only presume to be a fatherly tone. Not having a father to compare it to made her uncertain, but he sounded sincere in his concern. "We don't have any specific records of the children who stayed here from the trains. They would have been kept by the Society in New York where they came from. His is not a name I'm aware of." He paused, rubbing at his neat beard. "You might try asking at the schoolhouse. They should have records of the children who joined their classes over the years."

"Why, yes." Molly stood up from her chair, her enthusiasm for asking at the school overcoming her initial disappointment. "He must have gone to school. I believe that was required for all of us." She looked to Miss Ellie for acknowledgement, but Ellie Cochrane gave a small shake of her head.

"I know you were all supposed to receive some schooling, but don't put all your hopes on it. I know plenty of farms where the boys have worked year-round without any sight of a schoolhouse. We'll find him somehow, but it may not be through that."

"Sir," said Molly, "are there many young men here with red hair?" She grinned as she recalled her brother's most striking feature. "It was a wild red, with curls that covered his head and escaped from any hat."

The man scratched his beard once again. "There's the lawyer's son, but he gets it from his mother's side, I believe. There are certainly not many round here. I'll ask around. It's all I can do."

They left details of where they were staying, as well as a forwarding address in case they had to move on, and walked back out into the day. Molly was quiet. Tom couldn't just disappear. Of course, he might have died or gone to war, but he'd been here at some point. She walked slowly, thinking as she went.

Miss Ellie had asked for directions to the schoolhouse and they were on their way when Molly looked up and saw a man ahead of them. Wisps of red hair were escaping from under the brim of his top hat. She quickened her pace. It couldn't be Tom; he'd be in farm clothes. This man looked well-dressed. Molly had soon left Miss Ellie some paces behind and in a halting voice called, "Excuse me, sir." The man continued to walk, so Molly went a little faster and called again, this time with a stronger voice. "Sir, excuse me."

He turned and looked at her and Molly searched his face for anything familiar. She thought she could see the hint of a scar, but hope could play funny tricks.

"Ma'am?" He raised his hat to her in greeting.

Molly faltered – could this be Tom? "Good day, sir. I... I... I'm looking for a gentleman called Thomas Reilly."

For a moment she thought she saw a shadow cross his face, but his composure was regained almost as soon as it had been lost. "I thought you might be him. He has red hair. I haven't seen him for a while."

The man's face was blank. No smile, no nod of recognition. Then, in a strong voice, he said, "I'm sorry, you were mistaken. I know no one of that name in this town."

Molly opened her mouth to question him further, but before she had the chance to get another word out he had bidden her good day and set off again with a brisk stride that made it clear he was not expecting her to follow.

Miss Ellie had hung back waiting for Molly, who now turned to her companion.

"I thought... in his eyes... it was just..." The tears began to fall down Molly's cheeks and Miss Ellie put an arm around her shoulder and led her to a place where they could rest a while.

It was some time before Molly spoke again. She looked into Miss Ellie's face, searching for answers. "If he knew Tom, why wouldn't he say so?"

"Hush, child. You don't know that for sure. Maybe he really doesn't know your brother."

Molly nodded and sat quietly, gathering herself and offering a silent prayer that she was wrong.

Eventually, they arrived at the schoolhouse and waited patiently for the children's next break from lessons, so as not to interrupt. Molly smiled as she watched the children and imagined what it might have been like if she, Tom and Daniel could have stayed together and all played in the little yard outside the schoolhouse. Once the lesson had finished, Molly knocked on the schoolroom door and introduced herself to the teacher, who looked to be in her forties, though Molly found it hard to judge.

"Miss Simpson, I'm looking for my brother," she explained. "I believe he would have been a pupil here a few years ago. I'm hoping you may remember him, Thomas Reilly. He came here from New York with the first of the trains."

"Reilly, you say." Miss Simpson drew out a pile of registers from her desk and selected ones for the years that Molly suggested. "I had no boy called Reilly in my classes. Is there anything more you can tell me about him?"

Molly laughed. "He had the most wonderful and wild red hair. It bounced all over the place and wouldn't stay under control."

"I remember one boy that would fit that description."

Molly's heart leaped.

"One of my brightest students, William Dixon, son of the local attorney. He's still in the town and working with his father."

Molly's shoulders slumped. She assumed that was the young man they'd met in the street, but could not be certain. "And there were no others?"

"Not that I remember, my dear. Of course, it can be hard to remember all of them, but I do pretty well. There were other boys who came in off those trains. One of them might know what became of him."

By the time they left, they had the addresses of two outlying farms where they might find young men who had known Tom, but still no definite lead.

"What if we don't find him, Miss Ellie?" Molly asked as they made their way back to their lodgings.

Miss Ellie seemed to ponder the question a while. "I don't honestly know. I'd like to say 'of course we'll find him', but it's all very odd. It's as though... oh, I don't know. I know his letter said to leave things be, and neither one of us believed that could really be the case, but it does seem as though he doesn't want to be found."

They walked in silence for some time before Molly spoke again. "I guess the people in New York did tell me it was so. I just couldn't believe it was true. Why wouldn't Tom want to see me?"

"I've been thinking about that and I just don't know... unless..." Miss Ellie stopped and turned to face her, taking both of Molly's hands in hers. "Unless there are things about your life in New York he doesn't want people to know about."

Molly could feel her face flushing. "We only did what we had to do." She looked down at the ground. "Life was hard... Mammy was dying..." What more could she say to justify the life they had led?

"I know, child. I wasn't saying anything about it. It's just that there may be people that Thomas doesn't want to know about those times."

Molly nodded slowly, the idea making sense to her. She thought of the Roach Guard and the Bowery Boys, of

Patrick Mahoney and of Tom picking pockets. None of it would seem real to someone who'd lived out here all their life.

"Maybe we should just look for men with red hair. That is much harder to change," Molly said, her eyes following the patterns on the sidewalk where she was staring.

"Even hair can be shaved, but it's harder to hide." Miss Ellie put her arm through Molly's and started to guide her along the road once again. "There's still time to find at least one of those farms. Maybe that will give us a clue."

The afternoon was warm and the farm only a couple of miles out of town. Whilst they could have borrowed a gig, they were both missing their outdoor life and it was a pleasant walk.

"Perhaps we should have sent word on ahead," Ellie said. "Two women turning up unexpected might look awful strange to them."

Molly laughed for what felt like the first time in ages. "I guess it's not so strange, with so many of the men away at war. They'll think we're looking for work."

Miss Ellie looked Molly up and down and broke into a broad grin. "Do you normally go looking for dairy work wearing your Sunday best?"

"I think it might be easier to ask for work than explain why we're really there." Molly sighed and fell to thinking about what to say when they arrived.

As things turned out, they were greeted warmly, with the sort of hospitality only an experienced farmer's wife offers. Molly found herself telling the whole story and receiving a sympathetic hearing. They had brought one of the New York children into the farm and he'd been a good worker. He wasn't close to the other boys, as far as the farmer's wife remembered, but had spent the winter times in the schoolhouse and set to studying pretty well. He'd gone off to war now, of his own choosing, but, God permitting, planned to return to the farm as soon as the war was over.

Molly would have come away disappointed, but the farmer's wife sent them on their way, saying, "I have to go into town tomorrow and will see quite a number of people. I'll see if I can find anything out and send word if I do."

Molly believed that she meant it and it gave her more hope than anything had done so far.

CHAPTER 19

There was just one farm left to visit, but despite the good reception they had received earlier, Molly and Miss Ellie decided to send a note in advance of their arrival. The note said they would call the following morning at around 11 a.m., which they thought would give them ample time for the walk.

At breakfast the next day, Molly received a short note in reply. Mrs Franklin was coming into town for the morning to meet with some of the other women and would be very happy to call on them when she finished. She thought that would be around noon. It gave Molly and Miss Ellie a morning with no commitments, so they settled in the drawing room reserved for guests of the lodging house and waited. Molly tried to read her book, but fidgeted with the jacket and read the same paragraph several times without taking in any of its meaning.

The morning passed slowly and she was painfully aware of the ticking of the grandmother clock sitting in the corner of the room, chiming each quarter and counting off the seconds in between. The house bell rang at 11.45 a.m. and Molly jumped from her chair. "Do you think...?"

There was no need for her to finish the question, as within a very short space of time a woman she assumed to be Mrs Franklin was ushered into the drawing room to join them. Miss Ellie got up from her chair as Molly was introduced to the woman and very soon they were all seated around a small occasional table in the brightly lit room.

"It's so good of you to come," Molly said, wondering where to start.

"My dear," the homely woman said in an affectionate tone, "Mrs Crowther has already explained to me and, well, we might have some information that could help."

Molly drew a sharp intake of breath and opened her mouth to speak, but Mrs Franklin raised a gentle hand for her to wait.

"It's our understanding," she said, sitting a little straighter, "that Mr Dixon, the lawyer, that is… anyway, that his son was one of the ones that came in on the trains." She almost whispered as she said, "We don't think William is his real son, even though he looks quite like his mother, or so they say. I've not actually seen him myself."

Molly's head was spinning. The lawyer's son, the one with red hair, might have come from New York. Was it possible? Her heart raced. She could hear Mrs Franklin babbling on to Miss Ellie about her cousin having worked at the house some years ago, but the sound was washing over her. Surely, the man they'd seen in the street in a top hat, he must have been William Dixon. Was that really recognition she'd seen in his face? How could it have been? Thomas wouldn't pretend not to know her. Would he? She thought of the message that she should not make contact and came back to reality with a jolt. She tuned back into the conversation and found it had moved on to farm matters and that Miss Ellie was talking about her own farm and comparing their approaches.

Molly was thinking of all sorts of questions, but it was unlikely that Mrs Franklin was going to be able to answer them, so instead she tried to be polite and join in the conversation about the farms and in doing so realised how, in a strange way, she really missed her daily work. She wondered how Miss Ellie must be feeling after a lifetime of the farm.

They passed a very enjoyable hour with Mrs Franklin and were invited to go out to the farm for lunch the following day so they might look around.

"We can bide here another day quite happily," Miss Ellie said in accepting, and Molly nodded her agreement. She hoped that they would have found Tom and it would be time spent with him, but if not, then in all likelihood they would still be looking.

They set off in the afternoon to the lawyer's office. Even if Mr Dixon couldn't help them directly, Molly wondered if he might be able to check any other public records on their behalf. Molly was shaking slightly as she reached to open the door of the building.

In the outer office they met the same young man they had approached a couple of days previously. "Good day, ladies. How may we be of service?" Despite his words, the man looked distracted and Molly had an uneasy feeling.

She searched his face again, looking for the boy she'd known. Without the curls that had hidden so much of his face, it was impossible to be certain, but she thought, just for a moment, that she saw a look she knew of old.

"Good afternoon, sir. We'd like to see Mr Dixon, if we may."

He raised an eyebrow. "You're seeing him right now. How can I help?"

Molly felt a shockwave go through her. Was she right? Was this really Tom? Her Tom? Why was he behaving like this? She had been only eight when she last saw him. More than a decade of change had occurred since then. Were those Tom's eyes? She searched his face. She looked for scars gained on the streets, but in the dimly lit office she could see nothing.

Miss Ellie interrupted. "Mr Dixon Senior, if you please."

The young man smiled. "Then I'm afraid I can't help you. My father…"

Molly thought he placed undue emphasis on the word.

"… Is out of the office this afternoon and won't be back. Can I take a message for him?"

Miss Ellie looked at Molly.

She hesitated. "No, thank you." Then she flashed a look at Miss Ellie before turning back to the younger Mr Dixon. "Perhaps we could make an appointment to see him tomorrow morning?"

Mr Dixon Junior ran a finger around his collar. "I'm… I'm not sure what his diary is for tomorrow. Shall I leave him a message and ask him to contact you?"

Even upside down and despite the flowing handwriting, Molly could see that a book open on the desk appeared to be a diary, but said nothing. She was becoming sure that this man in front of her was indeed her brother and that for reasons she could not hope to fully understand he was intent on covering up that fact. She wondered if she should give up or confront him now. What had she to lose, except perhaps her dignity? They could still see his father the following day if need be.

She looked up at him from under her dark lashes. "Thomas, Thomas Reilly, don't you know? It's me, Molly?"

Molly could see his hand shaking as he stared at her. His mouth was opening and closing, but without words. She longed to fill the silence but waited patiently, as she would for a frightened animal, hoping desperately that he might come out into the open and trust her.

Then he stood a little taller and in a clear voice said, "I'm sorry, ma'am, my name is William Dixon. I know no one of the name Reilly. I very much think you are sadly mistaken. Good day to you." Then he walked across to the outer office door and opened it for them to leave.

Molly could feel the tears coming before she had even set foot outside the door. These were not silent tears which trickled down her cheeks, but the beginning of heaving sobs that made her reach out to Miss Ellie for support.

Miss Ellie put her hand out and stayed the door. In a voice as commanding as any she had used in dealing with Jacob Reese or Cal Turner, she said, "It appears my companion has been taken unwell. Please bring me a chair, right away."

Molly was vaguely aware that Miss Ellie left no room for William to dissent and he let go of the door and went for the chair, which Miss Ellie gently guided her into.

Leaving Molly for a moment, Miss Ellie marched up to William and, standing directly in front of him, said, "Now young man, you will stop your nonsense and arrange an appointment for us to see your father." She almost spat the last word at him.

From where Molly was and through the tears she heard the words but could not see how William reacted. She heard him clear his throat and as he did so the door to the inner office opened and they all stopped in their tracks.

"Ma'am, who is it who wishes to speak with me?" Mr Dixon shot a sharp look at his son and approached Ellie Cochrane, his hand outstretched to shake hers. He beamed a smile towards her, in complete contrast to the reception they had received from his son. It was then he noticed Molly and a look of surprise crossed his face. He looked first to Will and then back to Molly, his eyes screwed up in question.

Ellie coughed slightly. "Sir, perhaps I may take a moment of your time to explain?" She came over to Molly, gave her a supportive arm and guided her towards the inner office.

Molly responded in bewilderment to the situation unfolding around her and was more than happy for Miss Ellie to take charge. She heard the office door close behind them, leaving William at his desk, and was guided toward a leather sofa to the side of the room.

Mr Dixon pressed a glass of water into her hands and then turned back to Miss Ellie. "Ma'am?" He indicated that she should sit and then did likewise.

"Sir…"

Molly focussed as best she could on what Miss Ellie was about to say, although it all felt as though it was happening far away and not in the room in which she was sitting.

Miss Ellie appeared to be choosing each word with infinite care. "My companion and I have travelled from Pierceton in search of a young gentleman that she knew many years ago when she lived in New York."

Molly saw Mr Dixon blink at the mention of New York.

"We had reason to believe that your… son… may have himself come from that great city and may be the very gentleman."

Mr Dixon nodded, but did not interrupt the flow. Molly's heart leaped at his not immediately denying that his son had come from New York.

Miss Ellie continued. "The name of the young man, then nothing more than a boy, was Thomas Reilly…"

Molly thought she saw Mr Dixon draw a sharp breath, but it could have been no more than normal.

"… Please, sir, do you know if it might be the same

gentleman?"

Mr Dixon stood up and paced across the room. He was silent for a moment, before speaking very precisely. "And why, might I ask, are you searching for him?"

He looked now to Molly for a response. She wondered how much of the story she should tell. What was most likely to make him cooperate? Would he be more guarded if she declared he was her brother or if she said he was a friend? It was clear that William did not want to own her as a sister. Could what she said now make matters any worse? This man seemed kind but he was, after all, a lawyer. "He was... my friend."

Miss Ellie showed a look of surprise, but Mr Dixon seemed to relax slightly. "Then I'm sorry you've had a wasted journey. I'm sure if William says that he does not know you, then he is the one who would remember. I can only think that the boy you are looking for is another one. I'm sorry that we cannot help." Then in a business-like fashion he said, "Now, if you are fully recovered, I'm afraid I have a meeting to get to, so I must leave you. I'm sure my son can you show you out when you are ready."

Before they could have time to protest he picked up his hat and coat and made for the door. They heard him speak to William as he left. "We'll talk later. I'll be back around four." Then he was gone, leaving William hovering awkwardly in the doorway.

Molly was quiet when they left the lawyer's offices. She felt numb and had no idea how to understand what was happening. Every sense told her this was Tom, but if it was, why was he not welcoming towards his sister? Might it be that he didn't believe it was really Molly? She sighed and gently shook her head as though willing her jumbled mind to fall into order.

Miss Ellie didn't intrude on her thoughts, but instead lent her a steadying arm as they walked and asked no questions. They were back at the guest house before much conversation passed between them.

"What do we do now?" Molly asked, desperate for someone to take charge of the situation, but having no idea what could be done.

"We can stay a few days if you think it will help. Maybe approach the young Mr Dixon again."

Molly shook her head. She remembered the fiery temper and the stubborn will of her brother and knew it would take more than time to change his heart. Falteringly she said, "I see little point in staying... It might be worth finding an address so that perhaps I could write a letter to him... Maybe even that will be hopeless." The tears started to trickle down her face and she dabbed at them with her handkerchief. "We can at the very least leave an address where he can contact us." She looked down at her hands, fidgeting with the small square of cotton. "I think maybe it's time to move on." She closed her eyes and felt the full desolation that had been building since earlier in the day. Her own brother didn't want to know her. She had never thought her quest would end like this.

"Maybe we should still go out to the farm tomorrow and take lunch with Mrs Franklin. She may be useful to us if we tell her a little more of why we're here. It will only delay our journey a day." There was a pause and then Miss Ellie said, "And do you still want to go on to find your friend, after...?"

Molly looked up sharply. "Daniel! Why, of course." She felt herself flush. She couldn't possibly go home without finding Daniel first.

Molly spent the evening trying to compose a letter to her

brother. She chose every word with care, hoping above all that nothing she said would drive him further away, but instead might draw him to trust her.

William Dixon, Esq.

Dear Mr Dixon,

I'm sorry we had little opportunity to talk earlier. I have travelled to Dowagiac from Pierceton in search of my brother, Thomas Reilly, whom I last saw some ten years ago, before he left New York in the hope of a better life. I have thought of him often over the years and wish him nothing but goodwill. For my own part, my life has passed pleasantly, working for Miss Ellie Cochrane on Cochrane's farm just outside Pierceton. I was to have married Mr Henry Spencer, had the good Lord spared him in this dreadful war, but sadly that was not the case. The loss of him has made me ever keener to find those others whom I have held so dear this last ten years. I am now leaving Dowagiac to travel on in search of another good friend, Mr Daniel Flynn, whom I have also not seen since he left New York, but with whom I hope to be reunited.

I would ask that if you become aware of the whereabouts of my brother you would be kind enough to make my address known to him, in the hope he might at the very least be in a position to write, telling me of his fortune.

Yours sincerely,

Molly Reilly (Miss)

CHAPTER 20

"William?"

His father had approached him without his being aware. He folded the letter and dropped it to his side. "It's nothing, sir."

His father nodded, though William was sure that his answer had not been believed. This man was a lawyer, after all, and quite used to working to gain the truth. William wondered if his best option would be to tell his father the whole story, or at least a sanitised version of his life that might pass for the truth without a lantern being turned on it.

"Those two ladies...?"

"Yes, sir?" William looked at his father, avoiding his direct gaze.

"Am I right to guess you do know who they are?"

"Not the older one, sir. I've never seen her or heard her name before this day."

"The younger one?"

William felt his face colouring and he looked down to his shoes. What could he say to stop the enquiry going further? "Yes, sir. I knew of her."

"You knew of her, or you knew her? There is a very particular difference."

William felt as though he were in the courtroom and accused of some crime. He pursed his lips as he thought. "I knew her, sir."

Despite the fact that he was still looking down, he saw his father nod an acknowledgement of his words.

"William, look at me."

Hesitantly, he lifted his gaze. Although his eyes settled on his father's for a moment, he looked away again and toward the window.

"Why did you deny them, William?"

He gulped. Why indeed? His quick thinking had saved him from many situations in the past; now he wondered if it could do so again. "I... I was trying to protect Ma, sir."

His father nodded as though that were a natural thing. "And pray what were you protecting her from?"

William raised his hands in the air and shrugged his shoulders. "Sir, it's hard to explain. I was scared that if she knew of my background, Ma might not love me anymore. Sir..." For the first time he looked Pa in the eye. "I like being your son and being a family. I've never had a real family before and this is my home. What went before is not important to me. I don't want Ma to know how poor we were, or how hard my life was. I want her to think of me only as her son."

Much of what he said was the truth. Sure, he left out the bits about petty thieving, picking pockets, the gangs and the brawls, but they were the very things he didn't want Molly to bring back. Of course, he knew who Molly was. He'd recognised her as soon as he'd seen her. He'd felt a ripple of shock run right through him when he'd turned in the street. He didn't want to be made to think about denying her. If he started developing a conscience now, then he'd be in deeper trouble than simply pretending he didn't know his sister.

Pa came across to him and patted his shoulder. He was smiling a soft, indulgent smile and William knew the angle of protecting Ma had won favour. "We knew something of your past when you came to us…"

William gulped.

"We knew all you boys were poor and orphaned, or you would not have been riding that train. Beyond that… well, we've never needed to know anything more and won't ask now."

William felt the tension going out of his shoulders. It was over. He was safe.

When his father left the room, William went over to the fireplace and dropped the letter into the flames. Prodding it with the poker, he made sure that every corner was burnt before straightening up and going back into the hall. He hoped that might be the last he heard from Molly. He had a new ma now and didn't need to see someone who looked so like the one they'd buried in a pauper's grave.

William could not sleep that night. He was haunted by memories he had long since buried and at one point he awoke convinced that Patrick Mahoney Junior had come to take his new life away. He sat up in the darkness, trembling. The night was quiet. He went to the window and opened it wide, breathing in the fresh air as he looked up to the stars in the clear night sky. He could be a million miles from New York and that was exactly how he wanted to stay. He resolved to make sure that Molly had left the town the following day. If not, he would need to encourage her to do so, by whatever means it took. He wondered if he should offer her money, if only she'd leave him alone, but that would mean going to Pa. He closed the window and returned to the crumpled bed. Sleep did come, although fitfully, and when he woke in the morning he felt little refreshed.

It was lunchtime before he could get away from the office to make enquiries as to whether the ladies had left by the morning train. He passed a group of women who he could have sworn stopped talking as he went by. He wondered if they had heard stories of why Molly had been there, but how could they know? What would it have to do with the likes of the local farmers' wives? He straightened his back slightly and walked more briskly, his chin in the air.

He didn't want to ask directly whether Molly had caught a train away from Dowagiac, or for that matter to ask where they had bought tickets to. It was hard to see how he might work a conversation with the station master around to the subject without asking outright. It was more of a problem as he didn't want a ticket for travel himself. He was sitting on a bench at the end of the platform watching the world go by and wondering what to do, when the station master walked from his office, checking all was in order.

"Many travelling?" William asked, trying to sound as casual as possible.

The station master looked glad of someone to talk to and sat at the other end of the bench. "Just one or two. If it weren't for the wheat we'd never stay in business."

William nodded. "Where do folks go to when they travel from here?"

"Most want a one-way ticket to the fighting. God willing, they'll be needing a return." He looked off into the distance and William felt frustrated, uncertain what to say next.

After a while, the older man looked at him quizzically. "Didn't you travel by the train some while back?"

Will felt himself stiffen. Did everyone in Dowagiac

suddenly think they knew his past or was the man thinking of another time? He was relieved not to have to answer when the man continued. "Take those ladies that came in a couple of days ago. They were looking for someone who'd come in from New York, if you will." He shook his head. "One of those orphans…"

William felt himself relax a little. He spoke slowly and carefully. "And did they find who they were looking for?"

"I don't rightly know, but they bought tickets to move on to Iowa City, so I reckon they're probably still looking."

William tried not to smile as he moved the conversation toward everyday pleasantries. He'd found what he needed to know. They'd gone, but it discomfited him to think they had not gone back to Pierceton but might have travelled on in search of Daniel. He swallowed hard. Maybe Molly would be satisfied if Daniel were pleased to see her, and not bother her brother any further. He closed his eyes and tried to let the stress of the last few days seep away, but like an itch, something niggled, and he had no idea how to stop it bothering him.

CHAPTER 21

The train journey that led Molly away from Dowagiac was not nearly as exciting as the one which had taken her there. Not only was she starting to feel like a seasoned traveller, but the anticipation of seeing the boys she had loved so well was replaced with a sense of foreboding. She wondered if she should give up on the whole idea of finding Daniel, after her experience with Tom. Her mind wandered to those fighting against the South. Maybe it would have been better to find that Tom had died in the war. At least then her treasured memories would not feel as though someone had taken a horse whip to them. She thought of Henry and wondered if she shouldn't just go back to Pierceton and mourn her loss. She had been conscious of Miss Ellie watching her for a while and smiled at her guardian.

"You'll never get another chance if you don't go now."

"I know." She could feel the weight of sadness pressing on her, but was touched by how well Miss Ellie knew her.

"It would be a great shame if you were not able to find Daniel either."

Molly knew from the way Miss Ellie spoke that she was in no doubt that William was her brother. She took a deep breath. "Miss Ellie, I know I've asked before, but why do you think he didn't want to know me?"

"Oh, child, you don't have to answer this, but if you can, please tell me – what was life really like in New York?"

Over the years Molly had told much of her story, but

had left out the worst that Tom had been involved in. She looked up with tears smarting at the corners of her eyes. "Tom was a pickpocket and a petty thief." There, she'd said it. "Daniel would sing and draw a crowd while Tom took what pickings he could. He only did it to survive... we'd have been without a roof a lot longer if he hadn't."

Miss Ellie nodded. "And what did you do, child?"

"I never stole. Oh, I took what was left in the streets, but never what had not been cast away."

"And now, child, what life is your brother leading?"

"Why, he works with his father as a lawyer's clerk."

Miss Ellie nodded. "Then it's not likely he'd want his past well known, is it?"

Molly could see what was being said. "Daniel never stole. He tried to earn money by his singing." Her voice dropped to barely above a whisper. "He had a beautiful voice. It was like listening to an angel."

"We will find him," Miss Ellie said with determination in her voice, "and I will hear him sing."

Molly looked up and smiled. She thanked God for the strength of this woman who had taken such good care of her. Then, as the train rumbled toward Iowa City, she reflected on what Tom might have to lose and began to forgive him. She thought she would write to him again, in the hope that as William Dixon he might get to know her, although maybe, for him, even that would jeopardise too much.

The journey to Iowa City was an arduous one, even though they stopped and rested overnight a couple of times to break the trip. Molly wondered what it must have been like for Daniel and hoped he'd had company on the journey, as she had. Miss Ellie had taken to keeping a journal of their travels and was relishing every detail of the adventure. For Molly, it was the arriving that was more important, rather than the travelling.

For the most part, the women travelled in peace, but one afternoon their contemplation was broken by the arrival of a middle-aged man with a very large curled moustache.

"Good afternoon, ladies," he said upon joining their carriage, and proceeded to light up a large cigar, which soon filled their compartment with smoke.

Molly could see the displeasure written across Miss Ellie's face as she wafted the smoke away from her journal. "Sir, if you please, we'd rather you didn't smoke in this carriage," Miss Ellie said with a steely voice.

The man seemed untroubled by her comment as he puffed out another hazy cloud. "And there was me thinking you fine ladies would appreciate the company of a man to protect you on your travels." He leered at Miss Ellie, then got up and moved across to sit by her.

"Sir..." Miss Ellie's voice came out in a higher pitch than normal. "I would thank you not to be so presumptuous." Miss Ellie shrank back into her seat as the man drew nearer to her.

"Now that's not very welcoming, when a fine gentleman offers you his services."

Molly thought for a moment that the man's speech might be slightly slurred and she wondered what she should do. She knew Miss Ellie was more than capable of handling herself, but the man looked undaunted. Molly looked around the carriage for anything she might use in their defence and her eyes lighted upon a walking cane that had been left in the corner of the carriage.

Miss Ellie was moving to stand up, but the man restrained her with his hand.

"Unhand me, sir. This is most unacceptable." Miss

Ellie's voice quivered as she spoke.

"Come on," he replied, "two women travelling on their own, you're asking for a man's company and don't deny it."

Miss Ellie swatted the man with her pocket book, but made no real impression on him.

His focus remained on Miss Ellie, leaving Molly free to stand quietly and reach for the cane. Then, with the pent-up anguish of the events of a few days previously, Molly raised the cane and in a voice both strong and confident said, "You will unhand my friend now, as she has asked, or I will not be responsible for my actions."

As he saw Molly with the cane raised above him, he drew back, and at the same time the compartment door opened and the guard was there.

"Sir," Miss Ellie said breathlessly, "would you please ask the… gentleman… to leave this carriage and find another place to sit."

"Come along, sir." The guard offered a hand to help the man up. "What's been happening here?"

The man sounded haughty as he spoke to the guard. "Whatever do they expect, travelling on a train without a man accompanying them? Isn't it obvious they must be in want of a gentleman?"

"Ladies," the guard said, tipping his hat to them as he escorted the man to another part of the train. Then he closed the carriage door behind them and left them once again in peace.

"Well, I never did." Miss Ellie looked flushed.

Molly realised she was still holding the cane aloft and, with a shaking hand, gently lowered it. She watched Miss Ellie starting to relax, and then after a few moments the older woman started to laugh.

"Would you actually have hit him, Molly? It would have been no more than he deserved." She was still laughing heartily as she spoke and began to wipe a stray tear away.

"I do believe I would have done," Molly replied, beginning, out of sheer relief, to join in the laughter.

"In all my years… Whatever was the fool of a man thinking? I think it probably just goes to show you the ills of strong liquor, and at this hour of the day!" Miss Ellie stood up and brushed herself down to straighten her dress. Dabbing liberally at her eyes to stem the flow of tears, she took a deep breath and deflated onto the seat. She began to look more composed and a little less shaken. "I've got a good mind to take that cane off down the train and find that fellow and tan his backside. He's no better than the boys back home trying to stop me laying claim to my daddy's farm, reckoning a woman couldn't do the same work and had no place to be doing it. One day, though I don't suppose it will be in my lifetime, women will have just the same rights as those there men, you mark my words." She paused a long pause. "Now, where were we when we were so rudely interrupted?"

Miss Ellie busied herself opening the window to dispel the last of the cigar smoke, as Molly looked on, in awe of her companion. She wondered whether the fact that Miss Ellie had not married was the reason she had maintained so much spirit throughout her life – or maybe it was the other way about. She wanted to stay as strong and empowered as Miss Ellie seemed to be, and she wondered whether marrying Henry would have made that impossible. She doubted he would have been happy about the journey she was on at present, but he wasn't there to say anything and wasn't it a form of equality he'd died fighting for? All the same, she feared married life might have been rather different. She touched the locket which lay at her neck and wondered how Sarah was doing.

They were now a day away from Iowa City and Molly felt tired and dirty from the travelling. Whilst she longed to reach her journey's end and hopefully find Daniel, she jumped at the suggestion by Miss Ellie that they stay another day to rest in Davenport before travelling on. The journey from there would not be far and they would arrive early enough the following day.

They took the day to walk and enjoy the fresh air. Molly could almost feel the colour returning to her cheeks with each step. Travelling was more tiring than she had expected and it brought back very vague memories of the trip from Ireland all those years ago. She'd been barely old enough to remember much of it, but every so often there were glimpses of memories and with them pictures of a family that now seemed unreal.

Iowa City was much larger than either Pierceton or Dowagiac, and Molly began to worry about their chances of finding Daniel as she realised the scale of the place. It was unlikely she'd simply see him walking along the street as she had with Tom, so with little idea of where to begin they headed for the Capitol building.

"I'm sorry, Miss. I don't know of any official records pertaining to the arrival of orphans. I know some came, but I don't think we were an official staging post. I have a feeling there was some sort of special arrangement, but I know little more than that." The gentleman directed them to a local orphanage that might have information on what had happened, though with the passage of time he was less than encouraging.

They walked on through the streets in search of the orphanage. It was a while before they found what they were looking for and were extremely grateful that the principal was both present and willing to the see them. The man had grown plump with time and an apparently good life. He looked to be around sixty.

"And what can I do for you fine ladies?" His greeting was jovial and Molly hoped that if Daniel had spent time here he would at least have been happy.

"Sir, I'm looking for a friend who may have stayed here."

The smile slipped from the man's face and his eyes narrowed. "And when would this have been?"

Molly explained the circumstances and watched as the man fidgeted and looked uncomfortable.

"It's a long time ago. I can't possibly be expected to remember every boy who has passed through the home."

"But you were here then." Molly was keen to pin the man down and she was starting to suspect he remembered rather more than he was saying.

"Well, yes, I was here then, but we've had many boys – many, many boys."

"And were some of them from New York?"

"I really don't remember. We've taken boys from all over the place. I'm sorry, I don't think I can help you."

Molly was starting to feel cross. Why would this man possibly not want to help her? "Sir, this is important to me. Please can you help?"

"I'm sorry, Miss, I really don't think there's anything I can tell you of use."

Molly could see him sweating. What did he know about Daniel?

"I'll ask Matron to show you out."

A stocky lady came rather quickly in response to the principal's bell. She did not look welcoming and Molly thought if she were going to ask a question she would need to word it carefully. To Molly's surprise, as they walked away down the corridor, the woman's demeanour changed and she stopped and turned to them.

"I'm sorry to be impertinent, but I couldn't help overhearing your conversation with Mr Knight."

Molly almost smiled, guessing that Matron had been listening just outside the door, which is how she came to respond so quickly to the bell.

"There were boys brought here from New York. I think some of the situations they were placed in were not desirable. Mr Knight prefers not to discuss them. Was there someone in particular you were looking for?"

"Oh yes." Molly spoke in a low voice to make sure Mr Knight wouldn't hear, but it was hard to control the sudden rush of excitement. "I'm looking for Daniel Flynn; he lived with us in New York. He may have been listed as Daniel Reilly."

Matron nodded. "I can't promise that I can find anything out, but I'm sure I've heard the name. I'll take a look when Mr Knight is out. Where can I leave word for you?"

Molly scribbled down the address of their lodgings on a piece of paper and with shaking hand passed it to Matron. "Anything, please, if you can find out anything…"

Then, as they heard movement further along the corridor, Matron ushered them out of the front door, her wall of efficiency restored without any evidence of the softness that lay beneath.

They had an aimless walk around the city during the afternoon. There was nowhere they could think of trying to search for information until they heard something. The schoolhouse might have been a possibility, but they had no idea if Daniel had stayed close enough to the town to attend. They would follow that up later. Molly hesitated outside the Franklin Printing House on Dubuque Street and wondered if the newspapers might have reported anything over the years that could help them. She decided to wait to see if Matron found out anything first.

When they arrived back at their lodgings, Molly was more than a little impressed to find a note already waiting for them. It was written in a clear hand and the content was perfunctory.

'Daniel Flynn stayed in this home for a short while on arrival. He was placed on a farm outside of the city with Mr Hawksworth as his overseer. He was to stay there until he turned eighteen.'

There were details of the farm's address and little more than a sign-off. Molly clutched the note to her. At last she had a link to Daniel, and her heart missed a beat at the prospect that he might not be lost to her altogether. They would make arrangements and travel out to the farm on the following morning.

CHAPTER 22

Molly's journey out to the farm was a bumpy ride and with every jolt her heart pounded in anticipation of what lay ahead. "Do you think finding Daniel might be as easy as simply turning up at the farm?" she asked Miss Ellie, with all the eagerness of a child. In her heart she knew there were many reasons that might be unlikely, the war being the chief of them, but it didn't stop her from hoping.

Miss Ellie covered Molly's hands with her own, but said nothing.

As Miss Ellie stopped the cart in front of the house, a middle-aged woman came out, wiping her hands on her apron. Molly stepped down in as dignified a manner as she could, then turned to help Miss Ellie. By this time the woman of the farmhouse was close by.

"Well, hello, and to what do we owe the pleasure of a visit to our farm?" The woman smiled broadly.

Molly instantly decided this was a woman she could really like. "Ma'am, good day to you. I'm looking for –" Molly got no further with the sentence when a solid man with a ruddy complexion and a large moustache strode across the yard and interrupted.

"What do you want?"

Molly recoiled at his brusque approach and thought that when manners had been given out to the pair, all had been given to one and none to the other. Her warmth toward the woman's greeting was utterly counterpointed by her discomfort with the man. In his company, she saw the woman's smile fade and her stature markedly diminish.

Molly gulped and addressed the man. "Sir, good day to you. We are looking for Mr Daniel Flynn. I was led to believe..." She saw the woman flinch.

"And what is he to you?" The sentence was snarled by the man rather than spoken.

Molly drew back. "He was a friend of my brother when we lived in New York, sir. I'd like to see him."

The man spat on the ground before addressing them again. "He's not here."

"Was he here, sir?"

The man spat again and turned his back to walk away. He headed toward the house and the woman scurried away faster than the train that had brought Molly to Iowa.

Molly and Miss Ellie were left standing in the yard.

"Well, I'll be," Miss Ellie said, looking around her. "Happen we might ask someone in the bunkhouse, if there's anyone to ask." She had begun to walk across the yard when the man came back out of the farmhouse, a gun in his hands.

"Miss Ellie," Molly called with a quiver in her voice, "I think perhaps we ought to leave."

As Miss Ellie turned and saw the man, her eyes flared. "Is that the sort of hospitality Iowa has to offer? Where I come from, visitors are treated with a little respect."

The man raised the gun. "Then get back to where you come from. No one asked you to come snooping around here. Now I'll give you five minutes to be off my land before I use you good ladies as target practice."

Molly was taking no chances and ushered Miss Ellie back toward the waiting cart. As soon as they had clambered up, Miss Ellie geed up the horse and it was on its way and taking them back to the main road. They were half way down the drive when they heard the man loose off a shot from the gun, Molly presumed as a warning. The horse sped up at the sound, but thankfully didn't rear and continued in a straight line along the drive.

Theirs was a glum journey back to town. Molly had never imagined the search would prove as hard as this. She knew she was tantalisingly close to finding Daniel, but was unsure what steps to take next. The man at the farm had not even introduced himself, though she suspected, from what Matron had said, that he was Mr Hawksworth. As they drove the horses, the words of one of the tunes Daniel used to sing echoed back to her over the years. For the first time in a very long while, she began to sing quietly, understanding how Daniel had drawn comfort from the tunes passed down by his pa.

"And from that time, through wildest woe,
that hope has shone a far light,
nor could love's brightest summer glow
outshine that solemn starlight;
It seemed to watch above my head
in forum, field and fane,
its angel voice sang round my bed,
A Nation once again!"

Molly's spirits soared and her determination was renewed. She would find Daniel, whatever it took, and one day maybe she would be reconciled with her brother too.

"You sing beautifully."

Molly smiled. "If you think that's beautiful, you wait until you hear Daniel sing it for us, for as sure as I know anything, I'm going to find him."

Miss Ellie broke into a broad smile. "I wouldn't expect anything less." They were quiet for a while before Miss Ellie said, "What are we going to try next?"

"I shall write to the lady of the house – Mrs Hawksworth, I presume. She seemed so kind and I'm sure she'd tell us what she knows. Then maybe we should go in search of the school."

Miss Ellie nodded her agreement as the horse trotted on.

Molly set to writing as soon as they got back and found pen and paper. If she could catch the last post of the day, the letter should be delivered by morning.

They waited in the following day, and at every rap on the lodgings' door Molly jumped, hoping to be called to take receipt of a letter, but each time she was disappointed. By evening her hope was fading and the energy she'd felt had dwindled.

The following morning, once breakfast was over and the first post of the day had passed them by, Molly decided to go for a walk alone, to clear her head and try to make sense of the situation. She wandered aimlessly around the town before taking a rest against a wall. She thought back to the New York days, of the times they would find a street corner for Daniel to sing and the way the crowds gathered. Thinking herself alone she began to sing, hoping to recapture the determination she had felt the previous day. As she did so, quiet as she was, a small dog came and sat at her feet, looking up at her. She continued to sing to her canine audience and smiled as he seemed to be listening intently. It was only when she finished and looked up that she became aware of a roughly dressed, older man standing nearby, and she started slightly.

"Pardon, Miss. I didn't mean to intrude. I think Duke here recognised the tune and even if he didn't, I certainly did. He was very fond of our friend who used to sing that song."

Molly felt the colour rising to her face and her heart pounding. "Sir, please tell me, who was the friend who sang the song?" She could barely get the words out for the excitement she was feeling.

"He was a young lad I worked with. Daniel was his name."

Molly let out a loud gasp. She took the man's rough hand in hers. "Daniel Flynn, sir. Please tell me, was it Daniel Flynn?"

Though he looked a little surprised, the man smiled at her and nodded. "It most certainly was, Miss. You know him?"

"Know him! He is the very reason I am here. I am searching for him, sir. Where might I find him?"

The old man sucked at his remaining teeth and shook his head. "I don't rightly know. You see the thing is, he ran away from the master, and me and Duke had to leave soon after, before we got blamed. I hope he got as far away as could be, but I've had no word from him. Not that he could contact me easily, as he didn't know where I'd be. I've been out on a farm just north of here and am only in town until I can get a train to take me south."

Molly's tears came unbidden. For a moment she had thought she was close to finding Daniel and now he was as far away as ever. "Thank you, sir." She stroked the dog's head as she spoke. "I'm sorry."

"No, Miss. It's me who should be sorry; I didn't mean to upset you." He paused and looked at her quizzically. "Excuse my impertinence for asking, but you wouldn't be Molly, would you?"

She looked up from the dog, her mouth open. "He spoke

of me?"

The man gave a rueful smile. "Oh, he spoke of you all right. Sometimes I think it was only the thought of you that kept him going. I sure hope you find him. It would mean the world to him to see you again."

"And to me too. Oh, sir, how can I find him? I went to the farm and was threatened with a gun. I don't know where else to look." Her heart was racing at the thought that she had been in Daniel's mind all these years. It was almost too much to bear, not to be able to find him now.

"I don't know what to suggest. He never came into town and he wasn't likely to stay around here. It wouldn't have been safe, but there's no place he spoke of I can imagine him going, unless in search of you."

A horrible thought struck Molly. What if, all the time she'd been travelling in search of Tom and Daniel, he had been back at Pierceton looking for her? She didn't know now if it made sense to stay or to go back. Would anyone send word if Daniel were there? She resolved to write a letter to Sarah just as soon as she could get back to the lodgings, but with Sarah married to Henry's brother she would need to choose her words carefully. She ached with longing to see Daniel, a feeling she had never held for Henry, and felt deeply sad for the man who had died fighting.

"Miss?"

She'd almost forgotten the old man still standing there.

"I should have introduced myself. I'm Ben. Would you sing that song one last time, to me and Duke before we're on our way?"

How could she deny them that? So Molly began once again to sing:

"A Nation once again,
a Nation once again,
and Ireland, long a province, be
a Nation once again!"

As she came to the end of the chorus, with Duke looking up at her, his head cocked and ears raised in concentration, the man suddenly started. "I've an idea of somewhere we might be able to ask someone."

"Oh, sir, tell me." She took his hands once again and hoped he might be right.

"There's a bar where Jed and Rick took drinks with Hawksworth of a Saturday night. I heard 'em talking about it. Happen we could ask in there. They were not ones to keep their mouths shut when they'd been drinking. If anyone's heard anything I suspect they'll know."

Molly nodded vigorously, struggling to contain her excitement. "We could go now."

Ben laughed. "I don't think a pretty young lady like you should be going into a place like that. Duke and me, we'll go and ask and come back and tell you what we find."

Molly stepped back and her shoulders dropped. Now was not a time she wanted to do nothing, but she saw the sense in what he said. "And shall I wait here?"

Ben nodded and then whistled Duke to his heel. They set off along the street, leaving Molly to walk in circles waiting for their return.

CHAPTER 23

"Oh, Miss Ellie, Miss Ellie…" Molly was panting hard as she ran up the steps of the guest house, calling for her friend. "Oh, you'll never guess what." Her hands were shaking uncontrollably and she was gasping for air.

"Sit down, child, and start from the beginning."

"It's Daniel. Oh, Miss Ellie, he needs our help. I do believe the good Lord has sent us to him in his hour of need."

"Whatever has happened?" Ellie guided Molly to sit upon the settle.

"I was in the town… wondering whatever we should do. Oh, it's dreadful!"

Miss Ellie quietly rose and left the room, returning only a minute or two later with a tray of tea. "I'd just asked for this to be prepared when you came back. It looks to me, girl, as though you're in need of it." She poured the tea and held the cup to Molly's trembling hands.

Molly sipped her drink, sat back, took a deep breath and began again. "Daniel is in prison, Miss Ellie. Whatever are we going to do?"

She told Miss Ellie the tale of how she'd met Ben and then how he'd gone to make enquiries. "Anyway, one of the Deputies was there and he told the man about Daniel."

"Lord have mercy, whatever has he done?"

"He ran away from that dreadful man we met at the farm. Oh, how can one man think he has the right to own another in these times? Ben – that was the old man I met – helped him to run away, but then Ben left shortly afterwards so he didn't know what had happened to Daniel. It was only when the Deputy told him that he found out. Oh, Miss Ellie, we have to go to him."

"We do indeed, child, but first you need to eat and take some rest. You look in no state to be going anywhere."

"How can I eat, when I know he needs us?"

Miss Ellie rang the bell and asked for food to be brought to them.

Molly found she was more hungry than she could have imagined, and was very soon feeling a little stronger and ready to go in search of her beloved Daniel.

A while later, as she and Miss Ellie went to find the sheriff's office, Molly could feel a confusion of thoughts going on in her mind. Mostly she was angry. Angry that someone like Mr Hawksworth could have treated Daniel badly enough for him to run away and angry that once he had found the courage to run, he hadn't been left to make his own way in the world without interference.

They eventually found the sheriff's office and, in her haste, Molly stumbled through the door.

Miss Ellie stepped forward while Molly regained her balance, and addressed the bemused Deputy. "Sir, we are here to see Mr Daniel Flynn."

The man laughed. "I don't think Mr Flynn is rightly in a position to make appointments just now. I'll ask him to call on you fine ladies when he's free."

"Is he here?" Molly stepped forward eagerly as the man chewed on a lump of tobacco.

"Ah, well there you see, that's the better question. He was here, but I reckon he didn't like the food so well. He thought he might be better fed at the jailhouse, though I reckon he might be wrong."

Miss Ellie took Molly's arm before she could say anything further. "Then it looks as though we're wasting our time here. Good day, sir." She turned Molly around and led her out of the building.

Molly could hear the Deputy sniggering behind them.

They set off for the jail behind the court, in the hope that their enquiry would be treated a little better there. The brick-built courthouse was on the corner of Harrison and Clinton. Molly stood in front of it, taking shallow breaths as she worked up the courage to go in.

Miss Ellie guided her into the building and began to look for someone who might be able to help. "Excuse me, sir," she said to the clerk in the outer office, "we wish to visit a prisoner who I believe you are holding here."

The man looked up at her in apparent surprise at the interruption. "And who would that be?"

"Mister Daniel Flynn, sir."

The man sucked his teeth and shook his head. "I'm afraid that's not possible. I have strict instructions that he's to have no visitors this side of his trial, not unless his lawyer shows up."

"His trial?" Molly was shaken out of her state of shock. "You mean he hasn't been tried yet? How long has he been held here?"

"I couldn't rightly say, Miss. It's been a while. He's been here for three months and he was with the Sheriff before that."

"Oh, the poor boy. There must be a way he can have visitors." Miss Ellie restrained Molly's arm and took charge. "When is he to be tried? And on what charge?"

"He's only allowed to see his lawyer, and he hasn't got one of those. I suppose someone from the County will represent him. His trial's in three weeks. You'll see him in court then." He looked back down to his work and it was clear to Molly that their interview was over.

Miss Ellie coughed very loudly, causing the man to look up. "Has a figure been set for bail?"

He waved a hand. "Not as far as I know. They said he should be kept here, on account of his being dangerous."

"Dangerous?" Miss Ellie and Molly exclaimed at the same time.

The man nodded. "Now, if you'll excuse me." He returned to his work in a pointed manner, and made no effort to look up even when Molly tentatively said, "Sir?" to attract his attention once more.

Molly lifted her skirts slightly, gave out a loud huff and walked from the office, her head held high.

Once outside, she turned to Miss Ellie. "Dangerous! I know Daniel. He is not likely to be dangerous."

"People change."

"No." Molly could feel the anger rising. "Oh, they change in little ways, we all do that, but they don't change their underlying nature and I know Daniel. He is not a dangerous man."

Ellie Cochrane looked her in the eye. "Then I believe you and I trust your judgement. I will help in any way I can. Now, where do we start?"

Molly hugged her. "Thank you. You won't be disappointed. We could try the newspaper office. I saw it earlier. They might have a report of what happened." Without waiting for her friend's response, she turned and walked along the street in search of the building they had seen earlier.

They were eventually furnished with reports of the events leading to Daniel's arrest, although the report clearly set out that Daniel had indeed been the aggressor and had near battered a fellow farmhand to death, then fled as a result.

"This cannot be right." Molly could feel a burning sense of injustice. "Ben said that Daniel fled the farm to find freedom and that Mr Hawksworth and the others went after him. We have to find Ben. He will set things straight. It couldn't have happened like this."

Miss Ellie rested her hand on Molly's arm. "It would be Ben's word against Mr Hawksworth and this Rick, presuming he is still alive. Who are they going to believe?"

"But we have to do something. We can't leave him there."

"And we will. We just need a clear plan."

They walked and talked for much of the afternoon, their ideas going from one thing to another, but always coming to a reason why their plans would not work.

"Maybe we could talk to Mrs Hawksworth."

"And set her against her husband? We'll not get far with that, even if she does know what happened."

Miss Ellie was always the voice of reason, and right now Molly wished that were not so.

"Might there be other farm hands we could talk to? Ones who saw what happened? Maybe Ben is not the only one."

"And would they speak out, knowing they might never find work around here again if they did?"

"Oh, Miss Ellie, there must be something we can do. Do you think they would let me see him if I told them he was my brother?"

"It's possible, but they seemed fairly clear that he was to have no visitors."

"Maybe they would take a note to him for me. At least

he would know we are here."

Eventually they returned to the guest house and Molly sat down to write.

She was sitting with paper in front of her and a quill in her hand, but her thoughts were empty and she stared off into the distance. What could she say? Right then, she loved Daniel with all her soul, but she'd not seen him since she was a young child and in reality barely knew him. He was just a fanciful notion and a connection to the past she still held dear. Perhaps she was simply desperate to fill the gap which Henry had left. What could she say?

'My dearest Dan…' She dipped the quill back in the ink, as it had largely dried out whilst she'd been thinking. *'I hope this note finds you well, despite the difficulties of your circumstances. My guardian and I are currently in Iowa City, having come in search first of Thomas and then of you…'* She paused. *'I had not realised the problems you were facing until I arrived and made the acquaintance of Ben, who wishes to be remembered to you. It was, in fact, Duke who introduced him to me.'* She realised she was rambling and tried to come back to the point. *'I would dearly like to visit you, but have been told this is not possible. However, I place myself entirely at your disposal to assist in any way I can and enclose with this letter a gift which I hope will sustain you. It is my earnest wish that I and this gift may be reunited with each other and with you, under better circumstances soon. Your loving sister, Molly Reilly.'*

Molly read over the words she had written and dabbed them with the blotter. She stopped, realising she didn't even know if Daniel could read, though she hoped he could. Then a thought occurred to her and she began another letter.

'William Dixon, Esq. Dear William…' She looked up suddenly, then discarded the paper and began to write

again. *'Mr Dixon, Snr. Dear Sir…'* This time she wrote with more urgency, as far as the quill would permit without scratching through the paper or leaving large blots to cover her words. *'You may recall our visit to your office recently when I was searching for my brother. As he chose to deny me, I do not feel I can call upon him again, but I have urgent need of your services. I am not rich, and do not know how I shall pay you, but the matter is that Daniel Flynn, my brother's close childhood friend, has been wrongly accused of a crime and needs someone to represent him to clear his name. We are currently in Iowa City, which I realise is some distance from you, but if there were someone nearby you could recommend to help us, I should be eternally grateful. Your humble servant, Molly Reilly.'*

As she wrote on the envelope she thought carefully, and in the top corner added *'Private, to be opened by addressee only'*. She hoped that might prevent William from being the one to read it first.

Finally, Molly started to write a third letter. It was one she should have written a while ago, but until now the words would not come.

Dearest Sarah,

I hope this letter finds you well. Miss Ellie and I are both well, although our visit to my brother did not have the happy consequence I had hoped. We are now in Iowa City, where I am…' Molly paused, choosing her words carefully. *'… Looking for my brother's childhood friend. We may be away a little longer than anticipated as we have found him in great difficulties and will stay a while in the hope that we may be of assistance.*

I hope that we will be home in time for your confinement.
Your ever loving
Molly

She went to find Miss Ellie, so they could mail all their letters together as soon as possible. Miss Ellie had been writing back to her cousin James on urgent matters relating to the farm and ensuring that he was happy to continue to work the farm for a longer period than they had originally agreed. The letter to Daniel they would take to the jail in person. Miss Ellie looked at Molly knowingly as she wrapped the letter with the rosary. Molly wondered whether the shrewd older lady had been aware of it all along. Molly said a Hail Mary as she packaged them, in the hope that both letter and wooden beads might get to him without interference.

CHAPTER 24

Let the wind and the rain and the hail blow high
And the snow come shovelling from the sky
She's as nice as apple pie
She'll get her own lad by and by
I'll Tell Me Ma, 1800s Traditional

In his courthouse cell, Daniel had given up counting the days of incarceration. He no longer had much idea of how long he had been there and even less of how long he might remain. He almost wished he'd been returned to the farm. The worst that could have happened would have been Hawksworth finally killing him with his thrashings. He was no closer to liberty now than he had been then. He'd lost weight and muscle and felt much older than his young years. The songs were no longer there to give him hope, but to torment him with a life that might have been. He was left feeling half crazed by the passage of each day, with little to put his mind to and even less to tire his body except despair.

He ran his fingers over the brickwork, just for the feel of a different texture, and then sat back against the wall with his head in his hands. Though his rations of food were meagre, his stomach had become used to them and provided his only idea of time passing by letting him know a meal was due. He was rarely disturbed except at those times. His cell door remained closed and locked, and the outside world could have been a hundred miles away. Now was not a mealtime, so it was with a little surprise that he heard boot steps in the corridor and the creaking of the hatch being slid across as it was opened.

"You've had a delivery." The manner was brusque, but that came as no surprise to Daniel.

He got to his feet unsteadily and made his way to the door. The hatch had already been slammed shut and there was no question of conversation to be had. He took up the small packet. It was clear it had been opened and he could only assume that it had once contained a letter, though that part was missing now. He didn't need the letter to know who had sent it.

As he pulled the rough-hewn wooden rosary from the envelope, he sank to his knees. He brought it to his lips and whispered, "Molly?" He'd know this rosary anywhere, even after all these years. He ran to the wall with the barred windows and reached up to take them in his hands. He tried pulling himself up to get a view out of the small slit to the outside world, but he fell back again. Once, pulling himself up would have been so easy, but not now. Was she here? His Molly? He started to shout her name, desperate she might hear him and come to him. "Molly, MOLLY, MOLLY!"

He sank to the floor, tears streaming down his face. For the first time in weeks he felt a song bubbling within him: *"As I was a walking one morning in May..."* He wondered if the fair maid he thought so much about could hear his words and he sang as loudly as he could.

His moment was broken by the sound of boots and a beating against the door. "None of that, d'you hear?"

Daniel stopped singing, but his heart thumped in his chest and he could feel a smile on his bearded face. Molly knew he needed her.

Daniel was certain Molly would not just leave the rosary. She must be telling him that she was close and would be there for him, but what could he do? How could he tell her he knew she was there? How could he say 'thank you'? He began to pace up and down the cell. He had no idea when they planned his trial for, or even if a trial was planned. They had told him little enough of what he was being charged with, although he could probably guess. He began to wonder if it was only Molly who was somewhere close by, or if Tom might be there. He looked down at the scar on his arm. Even after all these years it still showed clear and white. It would never fade, and to Daniel neither would what it represented. It had been a promise, and if it were in his power to keep it then he most certainly would. He hoped that Tom felt the same, because if ever he needed a brother it was now.

CHAPTER 25

The post in Dowagiac was always prompt and opening it was one of Will's first jobs of the day. He often examined the postmarks, testing himself on whether he knew where the places were. As he went through the post that morning, his hand stopped on one envelope. He knew that writing. Surely, it was the same as the letter he had received not so long ago. He drew the letter out of the pile, ready to open it first, but was stayed by the clearly written instruction that it was for the addressee only. One of the rules his father had laid down at the start of William's career was that anything marked as confidential must go straight to him unopened. In a lawyer's office there could be very good reason why they would only want Mr Dixon Senior to see a letter. William's hand froze. Surely, that could not be applied to a letter from Molly Reilly? He went to put it to the side of the desk and then uncertainly brought it back towards him again.

His hesitation was only for a moment, but in that time his father breezed into the office. "And what's that you've got there?" He was too quick for William and took it out of his fingers before William had time to hide it amongst the pile.

"I was just going to bring it to you, while I went through the others," he said, trying hard to smile at his father.

As the older man continued through to the inner office, William slumped in his chair. His hand was shaking. More than anything, he wanted to know what the letter said, yet the possible content terrified him. His heart pounded and his mouth felt dry as he waited for a response from his father. Time passed and he heard nothing, so slowly he collected himself and tried to focus on the remaining letters of the day.

He was still going through the correspondence when his father walked back out of his own office, coat and briefcase in hand.

"I have a meeting to go to. I'll be back in around an hour."

From the matter-of-fact statement, William deduced the letter must yet be unopened, or, if it had had been attended to, must contain nothing of significance. "Yes, sir. I'll mind things until then."

He felt his shoulders lose their tightness as his father went through the outer door, and after a moment's pause William went over to the window and looked out in both directions. He was confused. His father had already disappeared from view, but as there was no meeting in the diary he had no idea where he might have been heading. He opened the door to get a better view of the street, but still saw no one. Once he sat back down, he set to wondering and then, checking through the window again, he went into his father's office to look on the desk. He was carrying a pile of letters, which was his pretence if he were caught in the act of snooping.

Molly's letter was not immediately evident. Almost before he knew what he was doing, William began opening first one drawer and then the next in his father's office. He did his best not to disturb the contents as he looked, but very carefully lifted the uppermost papers in order to look below. His heart was racing and his ears felt almost pained with the concentration of listening for the faintest sound of his father's return. By the time he concluded there was nothing there, he was sweating profusely and his breathing was shallow.

As he took his leave of the inner office, taking one last look around, he felt exhausted. He went across the reception area and slumped into his own chair. The search had taken him barely twenty minutes, but it felt as though it had been hours.

As he began to breathe more evenly, he realised he'd left the pile of letters which had been his excuse and went back to retrieve them. He was less alert this time and when the outer door opened and his father entered reception, William was just leaving the inner office. He started with such force that he dropped the letters to the floor and could find absolutely no words to say.

"William?"

"I... sir... I"

"I expect you were looking for this."

His father addressed him in such a steady tone that William was completely unnerved and before he knew what he was saying had said, "Yes, sir, I was." Was it really so long since he'd lived on his wits that he'd forgotten how to do it? He looked down and sighed.

"And would you mind telling me why?"

William was thinking as fast as he could. How might he recover from the awkwardness of the situation? For the first time ever, there seemed no way out except the truth. He stared at his shoes as he spoke. "I thought I recognised the handwriting, sir."

"William..."

William trembled at the seriousness of his father's voice.

"... I think it's probably time that you and I sat down

and had a very serious talk."

"Yes, sir." William mumbled the words as he nodded. Then he stood aside as his father went towards the door to his office and, having passed William, held it open for him to follow.

His father sat behind the imposing desk and gestured to William to be seated in the chair opposite. William felt small, sitting as he was in a low-backed chair without arms, while his father's high-backed chair only accentuated the difference.

"Sir?" William gulped and tried to hold his hands steady. He could see his glorious world crumbling and everything he'd dreamed of slipping away.

"Why don't you start at the beginning and tell me what's going on?" His father's tone was professional, but not unkind.

William wished he could know the content of the letter before he began to speak. He wondered how much of the truth he could get away with telling and how far back he needed to go. For the time being, he decided that a limited version of the truth was needed and one which would paint him in as good a light as possible.

He couldn't bring himself to look at his father as he spoke. "You know, sir, that I came from New York. Our life was not good there. My father, the one I was born with, that is, went off in search of work and we could only presume he died. My mother, sir, she was a wonderful woman and did all she could…"

He paused, trying to get his story straight as he told it. Would it be worse to say that he had a half-sister and that his mother had clearly slept with another man, or to have denied a full sister when she visited? "I had a half-sister." He realised that by not saying whether the relationship was with his father or his mother, his mother might appear better than she was. "Her name was Molly."

His father nodded.

"We weren't close, sir." If he could have done so without being seen he would have been crossing his fingers as he continued. "It was she who came looking for me recently. I thought it best that she went away again. You and Ma are my family now and … and I had no wish to cause anguish to Ma. My life is with you and I love Ma deeply." He knew this would carry weight with his father, but checked himself from overdoing the detail.

"And who is Daniel?"

William sat up with a start. He was not expecting to say anything about Daniel and this turn of events shocked him. "Sir…" He tried to look his father in the eye as he spoke. "… My natural mother was a kind woman and she took him in. He was without parents when he arrived in New York." Nothing there was exactly a lie, and William hoped he might get away without saying more.

His father sat with his fingers steepled, his lower lip resting on the fingertips as he pondered. "Was Daniel an honest boy?"

That was a question that William was not expecting. His mind raced. Maybe Daniel was searching for work and wanted to come to them, in which case he needed to head this off. However, whatever he said about Daniel might reflect on himself too, and he'd do anything to keep his father from knowing the truth of his life before.

"Sir?" William stalled for time.

"It's a simple question. Do you believe Daniel to have been an honest child?"

"As far as I know, sir, but I really didn't know him that well."

Mr Dixon got up and walked around the office. He looked out of the window and stood with his back to William for some time. William chose to remain silent, although he could feel the sweat gathering as he waited and he would have been grateful to have a drink to sip.

Suddenly, his father wheeled around to face him. "I knew about Bounty."

"Sir?" William gasped. It felt as though the wind had been knocked from him. How could his father have known it was he and not Briggs who injured Bounty? Why did he threaten to sack Briggs if he knew all along it was William? He gripped the base of the chair to stop the room spinning away from him.

"I knew then that it was you who'd ridden Bounty. More than anything, I wanted you to be honest with me." For the first time, his father was looking angry. "I took you as my son and I'd forgive you almost anything... except hurting your mother. That is something I could not forgive."

"I would do no such thing, sir."

His father raised an eyebrow and then turned away from him. "I would have let Briggs go because you are my son, because your ma could not have borne your dishonesty, or the misplaced trust in you. Thankfully it didn't come to that. We've always done the best we can for you, William. We've brought you up as though you were our own. Can't you see that?"

William nodded, but his father's back was still turned to him.

"Can't you see that?" he said more forcefully, his voice faltering as he spoke.

"Yes, sir," William replied, a sick feeling coming over him. He'd thought he'd been so clever, but Pa had known all along.

"You may go. I shall be going out for the rest of the day and will see you at home this evening."

William got up slowly and as quietly as he could. Head bowed, he headed back to his desk.

When his father left the office shortly afterwards, he did not speak to William. William felt bereft. He sighed heavily and stared at the far wall of the office. Had he thrown everything away because of his stupidity? He hoped not, but he had no idea what he was going to do. For a moment, he wished he'd had the courage to go away to fight, instead of sending Briggs in his place. At least the man was still alive, as far as William knew.

It was a long afternoon. There were few callers to the office, and with his father absent no one came for appointments. It gave William more time to think. More time than he really wanted.

Eventually the afternoon passed and he locked the office. He was supposed to be calling on Jeanie, but he had no heart for that now. The walk home seemed longer than ever and he went straight to his room to change for dinner, having called only a cursory greeting to Ma as he went through the hall. He stood in his room, fumbling with the buttons of his shirt, and as he looked down at his bare arm he saw the scar. William sat down heavily on the edge of the bed and felt the colour draining from his face. He ran his index finger over the scar and felt the still raised line.

He'd denied his friendship with Daniel for so long that he wondered what it meant to him. What it had ever meant to him. He was set on a path to wealth and success. That was what really mattered to him, wasn't it? But as he sat there, unbidden tears began to roll down his face. He couldn't remember the last time he'd shed a tear. He hadn't even done that when Mammy had died. As he sat there he wondered if he were crying for Mammy now, crying for a life lived at a distance. For all he'd done, his father, Mr Dixon, had overlooked his behaviour, but William found it hard to understand why he would do that. Did they really care about him enough to forgive him?

He went to the basin and used the warm water left for him. He washed his face and tried to remove any trace of the tears. The only thing he could do was to speak with his father; maybe then he would begin to understand. He finished dressing and, having checked that he was as smart as he could be, he went back down to the hall. Taking a deep breath, he knocked on his father's study door.

"Enter." His father sounded distracted.

William took a deep breath and turned the door handle to go in.

CHAPTER 26

Molly had been to the courthouse every day in the two weeks since she'd sent the letter to Daniel. Every day she asked to see him and every day she was refused. She had tried standing outside, in case she heard him singing, and spent much time trying to work out exactly where in the building he was being held. Eventually a day came when her enquiries met a different response.

"You can see him on Monday... in court." The man smirked at Molly, making her uneasy.

"Why so sudden? He doesn't have a lawyer yet." Molly's thoughts were racing; there was little time for any plan to be put together.

"He'll have who the court gives him, same as the other wretches. After all, who would bother to pay for his representation?" The sneer made Molly angry.

"I would, sir. In fact, I have already written to a lawyer asking for someone to help." Of course, she knew that without a reply from Mr Dixon there was no hope of any progress, but she hoped that perhaps a little more time might bring a response. She wondered if there were any other way to find someone to defend Daniel.

"The judge will be sitting on Monday and your Mr Flynn will be in front of him. Now good day, Miss." He turned away from Molly and, as she could think of no more worth saying, she rushed out in search of Miss Ellie.

It was already Thursday and there was not time enough

to send another letter to Mr Dixon and receive a reply. She wished now that she had gone in person, but it was too late for thoughts like that. All she could do was pray. She felt in her pocket for the rosary, as she had done so many times, before remembering she had sent it to Daniel and wondering if the good Lord would watch over him. Then she thought of the years of trouble that Daniel had lived through and wondered how many other of her prayers had not been answered.

The weekend passed slowly. Although she and Miss Ellie went to the little church, it held no comfort for Molly. As the pastor preached on the works of the Lord, Molly could only think of the poor lost boy who had arrived alone in New York and who God seemed to have abandoned. Despite her own losses, she was grateful for how her life had turned out. She did not feel hard done by, but even from the little she knew, the thought of what Daniel had been through all his life was impossible to bear.

Monday dawned bright, but Molly had been awake longer than the sun and had lain in the darkness, silently crying. Today she would see Daniel for the first time in many years and the thought terrified her. What if he didn't even know she was there? She had no way to tell him. She could only hope he would turn and see her. If he did turn, how would he recognise her, unless the note had been delivered to him?

Molly dressed in the best clothes she had and was ready long before she and Miss Ellie needed to leave for the court.

"Are you all right, child?" Miss Ellie asked, straightening Molly's bonnet and wiping away the remnant of a tear.

"Yes, ma'am," were the only words Molly could find, and then they set off to walk slowly through the town, with

243

Miss Ellie's arm linked through hers, a solidarity that Molly appreciated and needed that morning.

The public gallery of the courtroom had plenty of space and Molly chose seats towards the front, to be certain she could see properly when Daniel was brought in. She could not have faced eating that morning but her stomach was churning nonetheless. Being inside a courtroom was a new experience for her. Looking around, she shuddered. Then she sat with her eyes closed for a moment, taking regular deep breaths. Below them there were one or two men carrying papers to different tables. She thought they might be court officials, but she could not be certain. Only a few others came to join the public gallery, all of them men. Molly had the uncomfortable feeling of being looked up and down, and in catching Miss Ellie's eye could only surmise that her guardian was feeling much the same.

When the court was called to rise, Molly held her breath. The judge came in and sat at the bench. Molly's heart raced as she looked first to one door and then another, expecting to see Daniel being led in. Once they were all seated a more plainly dressed gentleman called the details of the first case and Molly looked at Miss Ellie, her brow furrowed.

"He isn't the first case," Miss Ellie whispered to her.

The possibility of having to sit through other cases before Daniel was called, had not occurred to Molly and as comprehension dawned she felt suddenly tired.

She watched in horror as a dishevelled prisoner, shackled at both arms and legs, was almost dragged to the dock. The truth hit her of just how bad Daniel might look and the thought was unbearable. She covered her mouth with her hands to stop herself from crying out, and Miss Ellie very gently put an arm around her waist as she sat upright and rigid on the bench seat.

She heard few of the details of the case. It was impossible to focus on anything, save what Daniel might be going through. She fervently wished she had the comfort of the rosary to reach for, whether the good Lord had forsaken Daniel or not.

As the jury were sworn in for the first case, it occurred to Molly that these men were more likely to be the peers of Mr Hawksworth than of Daniel, and she felt as though a weight had been added to her shoulders.

The morning passed slowly and with each of the three cases that came before the judge, Molly felt her anxiety increase. She was longing to be outdoors in the fresh air, back in the fields of the farm in Pierceton, or in the cool of the dairy. The courtroom was hot and Molly felt uncomfortable in her starched smart collar and dress. She longed for her farm clothes. She'd seen enough of towns to know they weren't for her and she wondered if her roots in rural Ireland were imprinted too deeply to ever change. As she sat, focussing on the meadows in her mind rather than the waste of human life before her, she barely heard the names called for the next case, but Miss Ellie suddenly straightened. Molly looked at Miss Ellie's face and read all she needed to know. Daniel's case had been called.

Molly moved closer to the edge of her seat and watched the door through which the other prisoners had been brought. As she waited, she was aware that two men had approached the judge. He nodded before moving back, as the clerk called that a break for lunch would be taken and that the court would resume at two o'clock. Molly's shoulders dropped and she exhaled sharply. Whilst thankful for the opportunity of a little fresh air, she had steeled herself for the sight of Daniel and now that would have to wait.

Miss Ellie was clearly glad to be outside for a while and turned her face to the sunshine, smiling. "You could forget just how lucky you are, sitting in that room for very long. Whatever it must be like to be locked up, I can't begin to imagine. Now let's get some food inside you, girl, you're going to need your strength."

They were comfortable enough in each other's presence that Molly didn't need to reply. As they ate, she thought of the men brought before the court that morning and wondered what their lives must be like. One had not been found guilty and that gave her a glimmer of hope that the court might be a fair one, but with no one to put Daniel's side of things it was almost certain that Mr Hawksworth would carry sway. Much as she was anxious to get back inside, the time in the freedom of the air passed all too quickly. Even through the layers of her dress and skirts she could feel the discomfort of the bench seat, before she even sat on it again.

They took the same positions as before. This time there were a few more onlookers and Molly fidgeted slightly as she felt their gazes fall on her and Miss Ellie. She sat as straight as she could and looked forwards into the body of the court.

"All rise."

Once again they stood as the judge resumed his seat and the clerk called the case to be heard: 'The State versus Daniel Flynn'. Molly's head was swimming as she heard his name and saw movement below. She turned quickly to see the sheriff's men escorting a man, bearded and bent, shackled as the others had been at wrists and ankles, who shuffled forwards into the court. As the thought dawned on Molly that this shadow of a man was Daniel she gasped and swayed, but thankfully Miss Ellie was quick to catch her before she fell. She swallowed hard and tried to pull herself together. She despised weak women who feigned swoons at the slightest thing and she had no wish to be taken for one of them. She breathed deeply as she felt the tears coming hot and fast down her cheeks. Never in all their days on the streets of New York could she remember Daniel looking as broken as he did in that court. She fervently wished there were some way he could know her presence, but thought it unlikely he would have the opportunity to look around him.

Molly could hear background noises. She was so focussed on looking at Daniel that they could have been coming from anywhere. She'd heard a door open and close and was vaguely aware of mumblings, but none of it meant anything to her, as she looked at the boy she had loved and cared for and whose name meant so much to her.

The judge used his gavel to call the court back to order and the murmuring stopped. In a clear voice he asked, "And who represents this man?"

CHAPTER 27

Will had no clear idea what he was going to say to his father as he entered the study.

"S-sir." He ran his finger over the scar under his jacket sleeve. He tried to look up at his father, but was scared to meet his gaze. Somehow, in the recent days, a chink had developed in the wall he'd built around himself and brick by brick it was crashing down. For the first time, he had started to understand that there were people around him who loved him. They cared about him, not because of what they could get for themselves, but because of what they could give him. They had not left him at the first sign of trouble. They had not died when he needed them. They did not love him for his pride or because they believed him to be perfect. They could see his imperfections and still put him first. He wondered if that had been how Daniel had felt about their friendship when they were children. He felt a stab of pain as he thought how Molly must have felt when he feigned that he did not know her. Suddenly, William saw himself through the eyes of other people, and for the first time in his life he was ashamed.

"Sir, I did know Daniel. I knew him well. He was…" He struggled to find a word strong enough to express what they had been. "… He was like a brother to me, sir." He looked up at his father, who said nothing, looking pensive and without judgement. William felt the need to carry on. "When we came here, he was one of the party, but when you chose me..." His mouth was dry and he coughed slightly. "... I was scared you would change your mind. You seemed so kind and the thought of a good home was too much for me, sir. When you asked if anyone was with me, I said 'no' for fear of you choosing someone else instead. He was a far better child than I, sir and I own he was a better friend to me than I ever was to him."

William felt the damp of tears starting in his eyes and quickly dabbed them with his hand. "And sir, I'm sorry about Briggs. You were right, it was I who rode Bounty. It was my fault she was lame." He gulped down a sob before trying to phrase the next sentence. "If you think it best, I'll leave, sir. I'll go off to war and take my place as I should have done. I will ask for Briggs to be sent back to his family, sir, where rightly he should be."

His father simply nodded and William's heart pounded at the thought he might really have to leave. Never had he hoped so fervently for the forgiveness he did not deserve. Still his father did not speak, but instead pushed a letter across the desk and indicated for him to read. It was the letter from Molly.

He took it up and read carefully. '... Wrongly accused of a crime.' He looked up suddenly. "Sir, can we do anything?" For a moment William forgot his own situation and remembered all he owed Daniel. "Is there someone there we could write to? Could we help to pay? If I have any money, it can be used for this." Then, suddenly remembering all that had gone before, he added, "Though I realise you might still cast me out and that would be nothing more than I deserve, but even so, sir, is there any way we can help him?"

"William..." His father stood and paced across the room. At the far side, he turned. "Had the situation been reversed, would Daniel have deserted you?"

"No, sir. He would not. Daniel was the truest friend to me and to Molly and would have made a better son than I."

At last William had the courage to look up and meet his father's gaze. To his surprise the man was smiling.

"William, do you know the Bible story of the prodigal son?"

"Yes, sir."

"Then know that you are more my son now than you have ever been and I am proud to call you such."

William blinked. Surely, after all he'd confessed to, that could not be so, and yet there his father was before him, with his arm outstretched ready to shake William's hand and forgive him.

"Shall we go to dinner? We can talk later about what can be done to help this young man. We can also talk about how you can make amends to Briggs's family, as I'm sure you'll want to do." William's father went across and opened the door, ushering William to go ahead of him out of the study to the hall. "Take a moment to compose yourself before Ma sees you've been upset." Then he continued to the dining room, leaving William to take a few deep breaths and check his appearance in the hall mirror before following.

He ran his finger over the scar once more and remembered his words to Daniel from all those years ago. 'You an' me, we ain't got much, but we got each other,' and he hoped he might not be too late for Daniel to forgive him, just as his father seemed prepared to do.

CHAPTER 28

The courtroom was silent as the judge repeated his question. "Who represents this man?" This time his voice held a little annoyance. He looked around the room as the silence ensued.

During the lunch break, Molly had passed the man who had been sitting at the defence bench. She'd have sworn he smelled of whiskey and a bolt of panic shot through her. She looked around and saw him by the door, holding a whispered conversation.

Then the door opened and closed and a tall man strode forward. "I do, Your Honour."

There was a quiet intake of breath that ran around the court as everyone looked toward the speaker. From where she was sitting, it was hard for Molly to see the man who had entered and she did not recognise his voice.

He spoke loud and clear. "I am here to represent Mr Flynn." The man walked confidently forward, as the judge summoned him to the bench.

Miss Ellie took hold of Molly's arm to get her attention and whispered to her, "It's them. They're here. Isn't that Mr Dixon?"

Molly nodded vigorously, struggling for words. "I... I... do believe it is." She swallowed hard and tried to hear more of what was happening.

For a few hushed moments there was near silence in the courtroom, apart from the low muttering between the judge, a clerk and the man who had entered. Molly could see papers being passed across and returned as the judge nodded his assent. Her heart was beating fast as she watched all the movements that went on with the utmost intent, trying to glean anything she could from the shrugs and nods that accompanied the whispers.

Suddenly, the conversation wrapped up and the judge brought his gavel down. "This case is adjourned until first thing on Wednesday."

There was a gasp around the court and then movement below as Daniel was led out of the courtroom and the newcomer left again through the door by which he had entered. Once the judge had left, an excited murmur ran around the court. Miss Ellie gently shook Molly's arm to bring her back to her senses, and for her to realise they could leave the courtroom for the day as nothing further was going to happen.

Molly was dazed as she went out into the sunshine, with little idea of what had just occurred. A gentleman stopped her. To her surprise, despite the obvious quality of the cloth of his suit, he got down on his knees in the dust of the road. Then, taking off his hat to reveal his short red hair, the gentleman, as he bowed his head, said, "Molly, I'm... I'm sorry."

Molly gently lifted Tom's chin and looked into his face, searching every inch to see the authenticity of his words, and she found it in the damp of the eyes and the furrow of the brow, which looked back for her forgiveness. Then she smiled more widely and with greater happiness than she had felt for a very long time and reached down to gently kiss him on the cheek.

Taking his hand, she helped him to his feet. "I'm more glad that you are here than you will ever know. Did you see…? Tell me, it was your father, wasn't it? Please tell me there is hope?"

His eyes were alight and dancing with pride, and he stood taller as he said, "Yes, indeed. That was my father. Mr George Dixon. My adoptive father, that is."

"Oh, Tom…" She threw her arms around him and hugged him, caring nothing for what those around might think. As she drew back, she took both his hands. "Now let me introduce you properly to Miss Ellie Cochrane."

William seemed almost shy as she led him forward and he bowed deeply to Miss Ellie. "Ma'am. William Dixon at your service."

In a faraway voice, Molly said, "He came, your father came. Oh, Tom, how kind of him. And will they let him see Daniel?"

William smiled broadly and said, "I'm William now, not Tom… although I am your brother and will always remain so. My father has gone now to see his client. He has the judge's blessing to do so and we just need to wait."

They walked together and slowly the silences were filled with questions and answers about the years that had passed. Miss Ellie had left them and returned to their guest house to book rooms for William and his father. Little by little, Molly and William each began to find out who the other was in this time and place.

The heavy door creaked open and Daniel looked up from his bench to see a tall, well-dressed man enter his cell. He thought this was the same man who had been in the court, but could not be certain. He rose to his feet, diffident as to what he should do next.

The man held an outstretched hand to him and smiled broadly. Daniel blinked, as though by doing so this mirage might disappear. Slowly he moved forward and took the man's hand. "Sir?" he said, angling his head in question.

"Please sit down, Mr Flynn, and let me introduce myself. I am your lawyer and I am totally at your service."

Daniel shook his head slowly. "I have no money, sir. I have no way to pay you."

"That, my good man, is not a problem. My services are at no cost to you. I should perhaps explain. Your friend William…er, let me go back a stage… Thomas Reilly… is my son by adoption."

"Tom!" Daniel sank to his knees, clutching the rosary tight in his hands. "Sir, thank you, thank you."

"We've done nothing yet. Our work is just beginning."

He smiled the most benevolent smile Daniel had ever seen.

"Now get yourself up and let's start to go over what actually happened."

Daniel sat back down on the bench.

First, Mr Dixon gave a brief background to how he came to be there. "… And so it was Molly who called on us for help."

"Molly!" Daniel jumped up and went toward the cell door. "So she is here." He went back to Mr Dixon and held out the rosary. "She sent me this. It has been all the hope I had until now. Sir, can I see her? Please say she is well."

Mr Dixon smiled. "I believe she is very well and you will see her, but first we must get to business." He indicated that Daniel should sit.

Once he had had time to compose himself, Daniel poured out the whole tale of his life since the train took him onwards from Dowagiac.

Later, when Mr Dixon joined the others back at the guest

house for dinner, he said, "It's a sorry tale and one no young man should have to tell. You'll hear it yourselves in the courtroom, so it's probably best that I tell you the worst of it now. Hopefully, it then won't be too much of a shock."

It was a long night as William and Molly listened to all that Mr Dixon had to say, and they by turn questioned Mr Dixon and grieved for their friend. By ten o'clock, they were still talking, but having looked to his pocket watch, Mr Dixon broke off. "Come on now, William, we'd best turn in. We've a lot of work to do tomorrow if we're going to have young Daniel out of that cell come Wednesday."

They both rose and said their goodnights. Molly dared not ask what needed to be done, but Miss Ellie followed them out to speak with Mr Dixon, before returning to comfort Molly.

It was a very different Daniel who Molly and Miss Ellie watched shuffle into the courtroom on the Wednesday morning. Now, he was clean shaven and wore clothes which were not rags and all but fitted his shrunken frame. The sight of him was enough for the tears to start to flow for Molly. She looked down at where Mr Dixon was sitting in the courtroom ready to represent Daniel and felt a swell of pride to see her brother sitting alongside his father.

The twelve men of the jury looked much like any of the men around the court, but older than Daniel. Some were relatively well dressed, while others wore working clothes. Molly sent up a silent prayer and waited for the case to begin.

"Your Honour..." Mr Dixon spoke clearly and loud enough for all within the court to hear. "It is important for me to explain to you how Mr Flynn came to be in the employment of Mr Hawksworth." He indicated to where

Hawksworth was sitting along the gallery from Molly, watching proceedings.

Molly bristled as she looked across at the man who had fired a shot in their direction just a short while previously.

"Daniel Flynn was born in Ireland, during the dreadful time of the potato blight. His family were starving..." Angling himself toward the jury, Mr Dixon went on to tell the story that Molly knew so well, of his arrival in New York, already an orphan; how he came to live with them and how when Mammy died they found themselves on the streets.

She fought to hold back the tears, trying to pretend to herself that it was another family he was speaking of and wondering how it might be affecting William. Even thinking of these events as having happened to a stranger, it would have been hard not to be moved, but she guessed that was the intent of telling the background. She saw a man she believed to be with the newspaper, writing as fast as he was able, as Mr Dixon spoke.

"...And so, from the orphanage that Mr Flynn found himself in after the train brought him to Iowa City, he was passed into the 'care'..." He paused for the word to sink in. "... Of Mr Ned Hawksworth."

Molly noticed that one or two more had joined the public gallery. Somehow, word seemed to have got around that a spectacle was ensuing.

Mr Dixon continued. "Your Honour, it was normal practice for these orphans to work on farms. In fact, many did so in Dowagiac, where I am normally based. Those who signed for their care guaranteed that an education would be provided and that –"

The lawyer who was presenting the case for the State was on his feet immediately. "Objection, Your Honour.

This is hardly relevant and how can this man know what basis they were taken on?"

The judge looked at Mr Dixon for a reply. He stood erect, his eyes narrowed as he looked back, not to the judge but to the prosecution lawyer. "I know, sir, because I too signed for one of these boys and have brought him up as my own son."

A small gasp ran around some of the spectators in the gallery.

Molly tried to read the expressions on the jurors' faces. Some sat almost immobile and she wondered if they were listening at all. She feared they may have decided their verdict without listening to a word of evidence.

"Objection overruled; please continue, Mr Dixon."

"These boys were to be given an education and treated with respect."

At that there was a ripple of laughter, which emanated from those seated around Hawksworth. "Your Honour, when this offence occurred, Daniel Flynn was running from Mr Hawksworth's farm. He was running away from mistreatment and effective slavery. In all the years he worked for Mr Hawksworth he received no education, not a penny of recompense, and was given many a beating, on occasion to within an inch of his life."

"Objection, Your Honour."

The judge brought down his gavel as the noise levels in the court began to rise. "Can you substantiate these claims, Mr Dixon?"

"I can, Your Honour. Would you allow me a moment to finish the story before doing so?"

The judge nodded his assent. "But keep it brief."

"Your Honour, the terms of the contract would have left Mr Flynn free to find his own place once he turned eighteen, but he did not know that. He had run away once before and when he was caught he was savagely beaten, as I will prove in just a moment. He was terrified of being caught again, as he believed he would lose his life, and so, Your Honour, his actions were taken in self-defence." Mr Dixon beckoned the clerk over and gave him a note for the judge, who then read it and nodded.

Mr Dixon turned to Daniel. "Mr Flynn, if you are able, would you turn and, having raised your shirt, show your back to the court."

Daniel did as asked, revealing welts and scars which covered the whole surface.

Molly cried out, then covered her mouth with her hands, while Miss Ellie laid a comforting hand upon her arm. She was aware of many noises from around the room, until the judge called, 'Order,' once again.

"Thank you, Mr Flynn." Mr Dixon turned back to the court. "Your Honour, I am sad to say that the rest of his body is similarly covered."

"Objection, Your Honour. He can't prove that this has any connection to the case before you." The prosecution lawyer looked almost apoplectic.

"Your Honour, may I call a witness?"

The judge assented and, as Mr Dixon called his first witness, the noise levels in the courtroom raised to a significant level. Molly looked around and was surprised to see the public gallery was all but full with onlookers. The judge called the court to order, this time with a threat that those who ignored him would be taken to the cells. It had the desired effect and Mr Dixon was able to turn to his witness without further interruption.

Once she had been sworn in, Mr Dixon began. "Mrs Hawksworth…"

Molly turned to see Hawksworth as red with anger and bluster as she could imagine possible. At least now all the members of the jury seemed to be listening, though she wondered whether it was for the right reasons.

"She can't be trusted."

The judge brought his gavel down. "Sir, you will not speak again."

"Ma'am…" Mr Dixon began again. "Please can you confirm how you know the defendant?"

She shot a glance across to her husband and then back to Mr Dixon. She spoke hurriedly. "He came to our farm as a boy, sir, and has been there ever since."

Molly wondered at the courage of the woman as she answered. She thought that surely Mrs Hawksworth was putting herself in danger by doing so, and was grateful for the bravery of the woman.

"And under what conditions did he live with you?"

"From the start, sir, he was made to sleep in the bunkhouse and take his meals with the other men, even though he was just a boy. He only came into the house when the inspector called."

"And what inspector was that?"

"The one from New York, sir. He called once a year."

"And did Mr Flynn receive an education?"

"No, sir… that is to say, just a little, but not in the way you mean."

There were murmurs from the gallery once again.

"In what way did he receive an education, ma'am?"

"I helped him learn to read."

"You did what?" Mr Hawksworth was on his feet.

"This is your last warning, sir. Speak again and you will be taken to the cells." The judge stared at Mr Hawksworth and Molly shivered.

"Please continue, Mrs Hawksworth," Mr Dixon coaxed in a gentle tone.

"Daniel asked if I could help him when Hawksworth and the boys had gone into town of a Saturday night. I did what I could to teach him."

Mr Dixon spoke gently and as though trying not to break the spell. "And which boys were these?"

"Jed and Rick, sir. Hawksworth used them for all his footwork, stealing from the farm owner, sir." Mrs Hawksworth's eyes were cast down and she wrung the corner of her handkerchief as she spoke.

This time Hawksworth would not be stopped. "The woman's mad. She doesn't know what she's saying." He was still shouting as he was dragged from the courtroom and led, Molly presumed, to a cell of his own.

"Please come back to the point, Mr Dixon."

Molly thought the judge sounded weary as he said it and she hoped that would not go against Daniel.

"Yes, Your Honour." Mr Dixon turned back to the now white-faced Mrs Hawksworth and tried to coax her back to the story. "And was he a willing pupil?"

"Oh yes, sir. He worked so hard at his letters and his reading. He was desperate to be able to understand."

"And, Mrs Hawksworth, can you tell us what happened when Mr Flynn tried to run away?"

"The first time, he was found by our neighbour and returned to the farm..." She paused, twisting her handkerchief in her hands.

"Go on, Mrs Hawksworth."

When she looked up, Molly could see the tears staining Mrs Hawksworth's face. She was clearly struggling to get the words out. "Hawksworth beat him. I don't mean he struck him once or twice. He beat him until he lay senseless and broken in the yard…" She seemed reluctant to say more.

"Mrs Hawksworth, can you tell us what happened after that?"

She looked nervously across at where Jed and Rick were still sitting and they glared back at her. Biting her lip, she looked up at Mr Dixon. "I… I had to wait until Hawksworth and the boys had gone into town, 'to celebrate', they said. Then I went to Daniel and tended his wounds and tried to bring him round."

Molly could see even from the gallery how pale Mrs Hawksworth looked, and wondered how much more she had to tell. Surely, after this, it would be impossible for her to go back to the farm, and Molly prayed there might be someone who could take her in.

Mr Dixon must have seen her distress too. "Ma'am, if you feel able to continue, can you tell the court what happened next?"

Her eyes flashed up to where Hawksworth had sat and then back to Mr Dixon. Molly saw her chest rise and fall heavily a couple of times before she began to answer. Her hands were clenched into balls as she spoke. "He caught me…"

"Who caught you, Mrs Hawksworth?" Mr Dixon's voice was gentle.

"Ned, that is, Mr Hawksworth."

"And what happened then?"

"He beat me too."

Suddenly, everything seemed to happen at once. A gasp ran around the women present.

Jed shouted, "And why shouldn't he beat the pair of you? You're his property." The judge called 'Order' and asked for Jed to be removed from the court.

Once calm was restored, Mr Dixon turned to Mrs Hawksworth, who was now weeping openly into her handkerchief, her shoulders heaving with the sobs. "Thank you for your courage, ma'am. I have no further questions for you."

Molly thought the cross-examination of Mrs Hawksworth that followed was nothing short of cruel. She was incensed to hear that the woman should know her place and be supportive of her husband, quite apart from when it was suggested that her disloyalty had brought her beating on herself. For the first time Molly understood how, in the eyes of the law, a married woman was no more than the property of her husband and wondered if there were any man good enough to be worth her marrying. She caught Miss Ellie's eye and knew without words passing that the older woman saw things as she did, and no longer wondered at Miss Ellie keeping her independence after the death of the one man she truly loved. If you had money of your own, then it would have to be a mighty special man, with a kind heart that was worth the marrying of.

Finally, Mrs Hawksworth was left to be, by which time she looked totally wrung out by her ordeal, and yet, Molly thought, she would have so much more to contend with when she saw her husband again.

Daniel's full story had been told, as far as any were going to hear, and both Mr Dixon and the prosecution summed up their sides of the case. Neither disputed that Daniel had in fact struck Rick with a shovel, nor that he had caused serious injury. However, while one saw it as an unprovoked and vicious attack on a defenceless man, the other saw it as self-defence, by an innocent and victimised youth, against those who held him captive and treated him ill. Now only the jury could decide which perspective of

Daniel would be deemed the closer to the truth.

CHAPTER 29

Molly was anxious as the judge prepared to speak. Daniel looked tired and careworn and she dreaded the thought he might have to return to the cells that night. She wondered how long he might have to stay locked up and whether she would ever see him a free man.

The judge's gavel fell once again and the court came to order. The judge addressed the foreman, who stood holding a piece of paper which he moved from hand to hand. "Has the jury reached a verdict?"

The man coughed and shuffled slightly. "Yes, Your Honour, we have."

"Will the foreman please tell the court what that verdict is."

"On the er…" He coughed again. "On the charges laid out, we find Mr Flynn guilty."

"Noooo." Molly couldn't help herself from calling out. Daniel would surely be going back to prison.

The judge brought his gavel down with force and silence fell. "Thank you, that will be all." He dismissed the foreman and turned to his notes.

Molly was shaking as she waited for the judge to speak again.

"It is clear to me that Mr Flynn committed the crime of which he is accused…"

The words echoed over and over in Molly's head. The judge was agreeing that he was guilty. She drifted in and out of what he was saying as he continued.

"However, taking into account the background to this case... full recovery of the victim... enlist in the army without delay..."

Molly's heart sank. There was jeering from the other side of the public gallery and the court was called back to order, but Molly didn't want to hear any more.

"... Alternatively, on condition he has full-time paid employment and a place to live..."

Molly only half heard the words. There was open laughter from Rick and some other young men. Who, in a town like this, would go against Hawksworth and employ him? Molly knew it was hopeless.

Suddenly, Miss Ellie was on her feet and attempting to address the judge. "Your Honour..."

"Sit down, woman." The judge looked angry, while the level of the jeering rose.

Now Mr Dixon was on his feet. "Your Honour, perhaps I may be allowed to speak for Miss Cochrane?"

The judge looked surprised, but nodded his assent. "I believe what Miss Cochrane was about to say was that, as she owns a 2000 acre farm..." The noise around them suddenly dropped and only an odd hushed whisper disturbed the silence. "She will guarantee both Mr Flynn's employment and his accommodation on her farm in Pierceton, Indiana." He looked across to Miss Ellie and she nodded.

The judge looked thoughtful and Molly held her breath. She wanted to hug Miss Ellie, but needed to wait for the judge's decision before any celebrations took place. The pause seemed interminable as they waited in rapt attention.

Finally, the judge nodded his head once. "On condition that you leave the state of Iowa by sundown tomorrow, you are discharged into the custody of Miss Cochrane and must remain with her for a period of two years, or otherwise enlist in the army."

Molly could not believe what she was hearing. Not only was Daniel a free man; he would be coming back with them. As she hugged Miss Ellie, her tears began to fall. How could she ever thank this woman, who had already given her so much?

Miss Ellie took her gently by the shoulders. "Now stop your blubbering, girl. There will be time enough for that later. We've got work to do. There's a man down there in need of a good bath and a square meal, and besides that we need to thank Mr Dixon."

Molly wiped away the tears and looked down to where Daniel's shackles were being removed. She broke into a broad grin and could refrain no longer. "Daniel!" Then she walked briskly to the exit, desperate to see her friend.

William was in high spirits as he came out to join Molly. "We did it. My father did it." He and Molly did a little jig, as they would have done ten years previously.

William's father came out shortly afterwards, leading a hesitant Daniel. Mr Dixon was smiling and stepped across to Miss Ellie as Molly went rushing over to Daniel.

She could contain her feelings no longer and threw her arms around him. She stood back suddenly, shocked at how thin he was. Then she took his hands. "Dan..." Her words choked in her throat.

He put a finger to her lips and squeezed her hands. They stood and looked at each other, and grinned.

Suddenly, Molly broke off and turned to Mr Dixon. "Mrs Hawksworth?" She looked around to see if Mrs Hawksworth was there.

He shook his head. "She's gone."

"Will she be all right?"

Mr Dixon looked serious for a moment. "I hope so." But he said no more. Then he guided the young people towards a carriage, which was waiting to take them back to their lodgings.

When they returned to the guest house, all but Daniel were in the mood for celebration. He felt the full weight of tiredness overwhelm him and wanted nothing more than some clean water and a place to lay his head. William showed him to a room and Daniel stood in awe as they opened the door. This was luxury the like of which he had never known. Another clean fresh set of clothes had been laid out for him. He was touched that Mr Dixon had bought for him not finery, such as he himself and William might wear, but clothes fit for the labouring and farm work he knew, and yet with a softness, strength and newness he had never known. He'd heard much of William's story from Mr Dixon during their time together before the trial and was unsure how to behave around his now gentleman friend.

Once he'd cleaned himself up, he joined the others in the dining room for a little food. Whilst he realised the depths of his hunger, his body was too unused to eating more than a few mouthfuls to take much at a first sitting, but he enjoyed every piece of the food he had.

"I think this rightly belongs to you," he said shyly, handing the rosary back to Molly. "God knows you came to me in my hour of need. I have never been so happy as when I saw it."

Molly gently stroked his weathered face. "I knew you couldn't be truly guilty, Daniel Flynn, and thank God to see you a free man again." She kissed his cheek.

He slept soundly that night. He would happily get used

to having a real mattress instead of board or straw, but he counselled himself not to get too used to the situation, as he had no idea what Miss Cochrane would expect of him and he assumed the bunkhouse on the farm would be much like the one he'd known.

There was nothing to keep them longer in Iowa and Daniel had a deadline to meet. He'd barely had time to thank William or even really get used to that being his friend's name. He felt rough and ungainly next to this gentleman with whom he'd rolled in the dirt as a child, and words were stilted between them.

"I hope we will meet again," he said, shrugging with his discomfiture at the situation. "I owe everything to you. I owed you everything years ago and… well… you know." He looked down at the floor as he spoke.

William looked very formal as he held his hat. "It is I who owe all to you."

Daniel brought his eyebrows together as he looked to William in confusion, but there was no time for further explanation. Daniel's train was alongside the platform and Molly and Miss Ellie's luggage was being hauled aboard. Daniel had no luggage to speak of, except a few things that Mr Dixon and Miss Cochrane had provided him with, but that was more than he'd ever had before.

"Take care of my sister," William said, giving a slight bow and putting his hat back on.

"I will." Daniel smiled. "If she'll let me." He laughed then dipped his head slightly to Mr Dixon and touched his cap as he did. "Sir, I'm not a learned man and I find words hard. All I can think to say is 'thank you', though it don't rightly seem enough. And, sir, if there is any way to get word to Ben, please tell him I'm free and thank him for me too."

The older man rested a hand on his arm. "Think nothing of it. I'm only sorry that you didn't come to us in Dowagiac at the same time as William. You boys could have grown up together if we'd known."

Daniel glanced across at William and saw a cloud briefly cross his face.

"Thank you, sir, that's a nice thought, but I'm sure William has been all the son you've needed." He touched his cap again and moved towards the train, where Miss Cochrane stood by the open window and Molly waited to board after a final goodbye to her brother.

As the train rattled through the countryside, Daniel felt as though he were in a dream. Molly slipped her hand into his and they sat a long while in silence. Daniel was enjoying more human contact than he had known for many a year. Her hand was soft and he worried that his calloused palms would hurt her to the touch. He left his hand loose, with hers resting on it, but every so often she would squeeze his and as gently as he could he would squeeze right back.

As the days of travelling passed, Daniel started to regain something of his appetite and began to believe that finally he was safe. He took an interest in asking about the farm and the work that would be involved, and looked forward earnestly to time out in the fresh air once more. The journey was indeed a far happier one than Daniel had known before. This time in heading for a new life he had confidence that it would be a better one. Whilst he knew little of Miss Cochrane or her ways of working, the fact that she had accompanied Molly on her journey and been there when they needed her said all he needed to know. His only regret was that he hadn't managed to find where old Ben had gone before they left. Miss Cochrane had said that if they could find him he was welcome to join them on the farm. Daniel had left word to that effect, in the hope it might reach Ben one day and that he would follow them to Pierceton, but he doubted that would happen.

At the station in Pierceton, James was there with the cart to meet them and they were soon bouncing their way down the track to the farm.

"Why look, Miss Ellie!" Molly pointed to the 'Welcome Home' banner strung between the trees and began to wave furiously as she saw Sarah standing outside the farm.

Daniel felt suddenly shy and nervous, unused as he was to social situations, and as they got down from the cart he hung back behind Molly. Sarah, it seemed, had arranged a whole party for their return and he was made as welcome as any.

"Oh, Molly." Sarah greeted her friend with a hug.

"Sarah! Why, look at you…"

"Well, if you will go away for a few months, then what do you expect?" Sarah did a careful twirl, showing the full extent of her figure. "And you must be Daniel. I've heard so much about you over the years." Sarah took his arm and introduced him first to her husband and then to the others present.

James, Miss Ellie's cousin, was delighted to see them back. He was happy to stay on for a couple of weeks, but was then looking forward to going back to his retirement.

"Sir, I'm ready to work as soon as you want me."

James looked over Daniel with an appraising eye. "It looks to me as though a few square meals might be needed before you do anything too heavy. I'll show you over the farm in the morning, first thing."

Cautiously, Daniel asked, "Where am I to sleep? I'd like to put my things down and rest up a while."

"Miss Ellie's got that covered. Don't you fret." James

grinned at him and Daniel wondered what Miss Cochrane had said.

Five minutes later Miss Cochrane gently touched his arm and beckoned for him to follow. She led him not to the bunkhouse as he expected, but across the yard to the house and up the stairs to a small room at the top of the landing.

"Sarah's done a good job of getting this ready," she said as she opened the door to the room. "You're to sleep here."

"In the house?" Daniel had a moment of panic that he had misunderstood, and held back from believing this was real.

"Yes." Miss Cochrane broke into a broad smile. "You're family now, Daniel Flynn, and you deserve a little of the life that goes with it."

Daniel felt a choke as he went to reply and no words would come. He stood noiselessly, opening and closing his mouth and shaking his head. He fought to stop the tear that had begun to form at the corner of his eye.

Miss Cochrane's face took on the softness of a mother and she gently guided him into the room so he could sit down. "You find your way back down to us when you're good and ready." Then she went out and closed the door.

CHAPTER 30

Daniel put his heart and soul into the farm and was soon as well muscled as he had been before his incarceration. Each evening he worked just as hard at his learning, and with Molly and Miss Ellie for teachers he was soon helping Miss Ellie with the farm management, while Molly took charge of all the affairs of the dairy.

He had grown to love the outdoors over the years, but now he could enjoy his work as well. With the war just come to an end, there was no fear of him being called away to fight and he was happy at the prospect of staying right here in Pierceton.

"As I was a walking one morning in May,
I saw a sweet couple together at play…"

Molly sidled up to him. "And what are you so happy about, Daniel Flynn?"

Her smile lit up his world and he caught her round the waist and spun her around as he continued to sing.

"O, the one was a fair maid so sweet and so fair,
And the other was a soldier and a brave grenadier…"

Molly's face fell and she pulled away.

"Oh, Molly, I'm sorry. I never meant to…"

"No, I know you didn't, Daniel. Now don't you mind

me. I'm just being a silly girl. I saw Sarah and little Henry yesterday and it got me to thinking, that's all. She and Joe are expecting again. This time, if it's a boy, Sarah says they plan to call him Lincoln, which seems rather fitting with all that's occurred. Don't let me stop you singing. I love the sound of your voice. When I hear you singing the songs of home I feel as though I belong somewhere."

"You do belong somewhere, Molly. You belong right here in Pierceton…" He hesitated. "You belong right here with me. I may only have lived here a little over a year, but with you by my side it feels like home and the only place I want to be. Molly…" He hesitated, twisting his hat awkwardly in his hands. Then he took a deep breath and looked her full in the face. "Molly…" he started again, then sank onto his knee in the dried mud in front of her. "I know I'm no Henry Spencer. I'm not a brave man and I've little in the way of money or prospects, but…" He thought maybe he was being too bold. Why ever would someone like Molly consider spending their life with a man as scarred as he was and with so little to offer? She could have the best. He carried on quickly before he lost the courage. "Would you do me the very great honour of being my wife?"

Molly gasped and covered her mouth with her hands. "Oh, Daniel, I wasn't hinting that you should say something."

"Oh no," he said, suddenly flustered and scrambling to his feet. "I didn't ask because of what you said." He kicked the dirt, sending a cloud of dust into the air. "I asked because I love you, Molly Reilly. I've loved you since I saw your smile on my first day in New York. Thinking of you was the only thing that got me through all my days in Iowa. I hoped one day I might come to look for you, though I didn't know how I was going to do it. I'm sorry, I shouldn't have supposed…" He looked at her, searching her face. "…But when you sent me the rosary, a part of me hoped that maybe you felt the same."

"Daniel Flynn…" Her voice was the same commanding tone as the young girl he'd first met. "Get back down on your knee and let a girl get a word in edgeways."

Daniel sank back onto the ground. He was grinning now as he looked up at her and then reached to take her hand. Silently he looked into her tear-filled eyes.

"Nothing, nothing in this world would give me greater pleasure."

Then he was on his feet and swinging her round. He held her tightly in his arms and thought that he never wanted to let her go.

Eventually they stopped, breathless. They sank down together, holding hands and grinning widely. He leaned toward her and hesitantly his lips met hers. In that moment, all the pain was gone and nothing in the world mattered to Daniel, except to live his life for this one soul.

Miss Ellie came up beside them. "Now if I didn't know any better I'd say there was something you hadn't told me."

Molly jumped up and went to Miss Ellie. "Oh, indeed there is, ma'am. I hope it will be all right with you, but Daniel here has just asked me to be his wife and I know I should have asked you first, but I've said 'yes'."

The celebrations began immediately. Work was abandoned for the day so they could all sit down together and plan for the wedding to take place.

"Where shall we live?" Molly asked, looking anxious. "The judge said that Daniel was to live here for two years, but we can't expect you to want us to stay here forever."

"Why ever not?" Miss Ellie said, as matter-of-fact as if they'd been discussing the price of cheese. "You stay there, my girl."

With that she got up and left the room, and in answer to Molly's look of enquiry, Daniel simply shrugged. He'd little idea what went on in the heads of women and wasn't about to start guessing.

It was about fifteen minutes later, after some bangs and crashes had been heard from other rooms in the house, that Miss Ellie returned, reverently holding a large parcel wrapped in brown paper. "This is for you, if you'll take it," she said, placing the package on the table next to Molly.

Molly looked to Daniel once again, but he was certainly no wiser than before. As Molly made no move toward the parcel, Miss Ellie began to unwrap the paper and drew out two lengths of beautifully folded fabric – one of the purest white lace and the other of the finest pale blue muslin. As she passed them to Molly she had tears in her eyes. "My mother gave these to me in the hope I might find myself a man, but that's not going to happen now. If you'll take it, I'd like you to have this to make your dress, and maybe we could work on it together."

It was Molly's turn to cry and as she flung her arms around Miss Ellie, Daniel thought it a good time to slip out of the room and leave the women for a while.

He went instead to his own room and taking up pen and paper began a letter to William.

I hope that I might have your blessing to marry your sister Molly. It would be my dearest wish that you could be present at the ceremony, and as soon as the date is fixed I will write to you again with the details.

He hoped that William would be happy for them, though he had no idea what life he could give his bride and did worry that she could do an awful lot better than to tie herself to him.

Work began in earnest on the dress each evening and for those times Daniel was shooed from the room. He was happy to humour the women and spent his evenings studying hard in an effort to better himself for Molly's sake.

The date for the wedding was fixed for some six months hence, which was ample time for the few preparations that were required. It was Miss Ellie who had encouraged them to wait that length of time and Daniel couldn't help feeling she had something in mind.

When the letter of reply from William arrived, Daniel went out into the yard to sit in the sunshine to read it.

I would be delighted for you to marry Molly and become my brother-in-law as well as my brother by blood. I wish you both every happiness and will write separately to my sister.

Maybe one day I will find a love of my own, though I own I'm the more interested in Jeanie since her father forbade her seeing me. The truth is that I never really loved her and it has taken all that has happened to show me that. She has other suitors and I'm sure she will be happy with one of them soon enough. For my own part, I am satisfied to learn the practice of law and may take up a place to study at university later in the year. Ma and Pa Dixon have forgiven me, which is more than I deserve, and I still look forward to taking over the family business in the fullness of time.

William had included other details of life in Dowagiac, but strangely made no mention of whether he would be able to travel to Pierceton for the wedding. Daniel was sad to think that his dearest friend – except Molly, of course – would not be there. He wondered where Ben might be, but had no way to find out.

The days were always busy on the farm in the summer and that seemed reason enough to both Daniel and Molly for their ceremony to be a little later in the year. Their wedding would be a good time to celebrate the harvest as well as their nuptials and everything was ready for the big day.

"You need to be doing the work of four days today," Miss Ellie said as she prepared to go into town on the Thursday before the wedding.

"But we've got tomorrow and the knot won't be tied until the afternoon on Saturday," Molly replied as she cleared the table from breakfast.

"That's as maybe, my girl, but I've an errand for you both to run tomorrow and there'll be no work on this Sabbath after the wedding, with you newly wed, so you had best get moving."

Molly started to ask about the errand, but if there was one thing that Daniel had learned, Miss Ellie would only tell you something when she was good and ready, and from the set of her face he knew nothing further would be forthcoming.

"I could do the work of an army, the way I feel today." He jumped up from the table and went to bring the cart around for Miss Ellie to drive.

The weather was fine and Daniel knew that most of the work was done and ready and a break of a few days wouldn't cause too much of a problem, but he did wonder what Miss Cochrane had in store for them.

She was away at town the whole day and said little upon her return. She had eaten with friends and was tired and would go to her room. She simply said that all was well and that by ten the following morning they were to be ready in their best clothes, though not those saved for the wedding.

"What do you think she's planning?" Molly asked Daniel as she served his supper late that evening.

"There'd be no surprise if I could guess that one," he said, ready to tuck into his food after finishing what had to be done.

"Oh, Daniel, won't you try to guess?"

"Maybe it's some new stock for the farm, though it would be a mighty fine bull that needed us to be in our best clothes to go to meet him." He laughed and Molly soon joined in.

With not needing to be ready until well into the morning, they both got an early start on Friday and had worked half a day before washing and changing to go out.

"If you look this beautiful today, Molly Reilly, how am I going to stand to look at you tomorrow?" Daniel took Molly in his arms and looked into her eyes as she blushed a gentle pink.

"Now you keep your flannel to yourself, Daniel Flynn, and spare a poor maiden's blushes."

Miss Ellie exchanged little but pleasantries as she drove them into town and stopped the horses outside the lawyer's office to tie them up.

"You don't suppose she's selling the farm, do you?" Molly whispered as Daniel handed her down from the cart.

He shrugged in return and set to follow the two women into the office.

At ten thirty sharp, the clerk ushered them toward a large office where several people were already waiting for them.

"William! Mr Dixon! What are you doing here?" Daniel shook hands with the two of them as Molly hugged her brother.

"We're your lawyers, don't you know?" William said,

grinning at him.

Daniel stood back, momentarily frozen. "But I haven't done anything. I've abided by the court's requirements." He could feel the panic rising and the prospect of the happiness he had envisaged slipping away.

Miss Ellie came to his side and laid a hand on his arm. "I think we'd best get on before you lose your mind. There's nothing bad in what's about to happen. It's just that with a transaction like this both parties should have their own lawyer, and as it was all to be a surprise I took the liberty of contacting your lawyers on your behalf. Now sit you both down and listen to what I've got to say."

CHAPTER 31

Daniel and Molly took seats at the large round table and looked intently at Miss Ellie, who drew in a deep breath and began.

"As you know, my daddy left the farm to me when he died and I've been very lucky over the years in adding to it. It's good land and we've always done pretty well, but I ain't getting any younger. I've never found myself a man as I'd want to marry, though several have tried over the years, and I'm not likely to have any children of my own at my time of life."

Daniel's mind was racing as he listened. He wondered if she would ask him to be her farm manager. He'd learned a lot in the time he'd been there, but he didn't rightly know if he was ready for that. His studying was coming on well, but he still had problems with some of the mathematical calculations. He felt his mouth going dry as he listened, and reached to take Molly's hand in his.

"I took Molly in to fill a void in my life that a woman feels at a certain age. Sarah was her friend and came with her, but it was Molly who'd caught my eye. I can't rightly tell you why that was." She smiled at Molly. "I think, perhaps, I saw something that reminded me of me at that age. Anyway, taking some time out with Molly to travel to find you boys set me to thinking. I know very little of this homeland of ours and happen I'd like to know a little more. The farm will always be home, but I'd like to be able to take time away from it now and again to see what I've been missing all these years."

Daniel could see that Molly looked anxious.

"Now don't you worry, girl. I'll be safe as can be. Mrs Dixon's invited me to visit Dowagiac..."

Daniel for the first time noticed the lady sitting quietly in the corner of the office and presumed her to be William's mother.

Miss Ellie continued. "And I'll find myself a travelling companion rather than going alone, but that's for the future and doesn't need to be thought of for a while." She paused for breath and sipped at the glass of water the clerk had brought for her.

"Anyways, what I want to say is, I've made a small settlement on Sarah and now, as a wedding gift, on condition I can live out my days in a quiet corner of the farmhouse somewhere, I'm making the farm over into Molly's name."

Molly gasped.

"Married women can hold property in their own right now, and she's the closest thing to family I have. I want it to pass to your children in the future so it stays in the family." Miss Ellie came to the end of her speech and silence fell in the room.

Daniel wondered if he'd heard right and was scared to speak in case he'd misunderstood and made a fool of them both.

Molly was visibly trembling and though she opened her mouth to speak there were no words forthcoming.

It was Mr Dixon who broke the silence. "Madam, I think what my client is trying to say is that she would be delighted to accept." He grinned broadly at Molly and Daniel and suddenly everyone started laughing and talking at once.

There were tears and hugs and questions and answers and by the time the papers were signed and sealed and the farm belonged to Molly, the atmosphere in the normally formal office was as festive as the harvest dance.

"Miss Ellie…" Molly took her by the hands as they eventually left the office. "If the good Lord blesses Daniel and me with children, you'll be the best grandmother a child could have." And she kissed her guardian lightly on the cheek.

The chapel was full to overflowing the following afternoon. There were those who knew Molly well from the years she'd lived in Pierceton and there were others from the town who simply came to watch the happy spectacle. As well as that, there was more family than Daniel and Molly could have dreamed of sharing it with. With Mr and Mrs Dixon, William, Miss Ellie, and Sarah and Joseph, Daniel felt a greater sense of belonging than he'd felt since his days back in Ireland. He almost expected his uncle Patrick to appear with his fiddle, and smiled at the prospect. He stood fidgeting with his cuffs, with William standing beside him as his Best Man, waiting for Miss Ellie to lead his darling Molly to the front of the chapel so they could be joined in matrimony. If there were ever a day when he had a song in his heart, this was it. He was bursting to sing the songs of home, no longer for the comfort of them but for the celebration of overcoming a struggle that was now done.

When he at last saw Molly, he thought his heart would drown out the sound of the music as it drummed the beat of a new beginning. The muslin and lace had been turned into the most beautiful gown and Molly's ruddy complexion from life spent outdoors was radiant above it.

Around her neck she wore Sarah's locket, though she'd returned it to her friend on their arrival home.

Daniel felt William gently punch his arm.

"You're a lucky man, Daniel Flynn, and don't you forget it."

There was no risk of that in Daniel's mind. He knew the measure of the chance he'd been given and the old wooden rosary would be given pride of place in their home.

The harvest dance was a great celebration at any time, particularly when the year had been good and the crops were all safely gathered. The work drew the farms together to help each other, and the success of one was the success of all, and this had been a great year. No one had felt like celebrating the end of the war that spring, followed so closely as it was by Mr Lincoln being shot, but now, six months on, the future looked much brighter for everyone than it had for some years.

"Sing for us, Daniel," Molly said to her new husband.

"No one here will want to hear me sing."

"Don't you believe it," William said. He moved to the front of the crowd and held a hand to the musicians for quiet. He went to the fiddler and whispered a few words that led to a nod.

As the room stilled at the sight of this stranger, William stood up on the platform. "I know most of you don't know me, but would you permit me to say a few words?"

There were general nods and mumbles of assent from around the room.

"It has been my honour to be Best Man for my sister's wedding today. When we were children..." He looked across to Ma and Pa Dixon and Pa smiled encouragement back to him. "... We had nothing. Daniel Flynn and I swore ourselves blood brothers and today I am delighted that he has become my brother-in-law."

There were cheers of assent from the crowds and a little shuffling of feet from those impatient for the entertainment to begin. "Anyway, his singing saved the lives of my sister and me. Without it we'd have starved to death. I call upon him to sing to you now to start the festivities."

Daniel moved to the front, leading Molly forwards, and as the music began he sang with all his heart.

"I've been a wild rover for many's the year,
And I spent all me money on whiskey and beer.
And now I'm returning with gold in great store,
And I never will play the wild rover no more..."

The dancing began as the reel played out, and when Daniel had finished that one, another was called for. After a few more dances he sang a ballad to his love and cheers rang out through the hall. He looked at his beloved Molly and knew that at last he'd found the better life his da had wanted him to have and that, though he'd taken the long road, he'd arrived in that land of opportunity.

As he took a short break from the singing to swig from his glass, he raised it quietly and said, "To Ben and Duke, wherever you may be, and to Mrs Hawksworth, God bless you, ma'am." He sipped, then raised his glass one more time and whispered, "To Mr O'Connor, the landlord in Ireland who made it possible," and then, yet more quietly, he said, "Da, I didn't forget." Then with tears in his eyes he turned back to his audience and sang the song that reminded him most of his fatherland, and though it sang of Ireland it could so easily be sung for the country they now called home.

New York Orphan

"... So, as I grew from boy to man,
I bent me to that bidding
My spirit of each selfish plan
And cruel passion ridding;
For, thus I hoped some day to aid,
Oh, can such hope be vain?
When my dear country shall be made
A Nation once again!"

BOOK GROUPS

Dear book group readers

Rather than include questions within the book for you to consider, I have included special pages within my website. This has the advantage of being easier to update and for you to suggest additions and thoughts which arise out of your discussions.

I am always delighted to have the opportunity to discuss the book with a group and for those groups which are not local to me this can sometimes be arranged as a Skype call or through another internet service. Contact details can be found on the website.

Please visit www. http://rjkind.co.uk/wp/book-groups/

BIBLIOGRAPHY

As this is not an academic work, the bibliography is listed in alphabetical order by title of the book and then is followed by other reference sources and finally websites. There have been other documents and sites along the way, but this should be more than enough for anyone interested in reading further.

American Notes - Charles Dickens – 1842

Carols Ancient and Modern – William Sandys – 1833

The Dangerous Classes of New York – Charles Loring Brace – 1872

Extra Extra – The Orphan Trains and Newsboys of New York – Renèe Wendinger – 2009 Legendary Publications.

First report of a Committee on the Sanitary Condition of the Laboring Classes in the city of New York, with remedial suggestions / Association for Improving the Condition of the Poor – 1853

Five Points – Tyler Anbinder – 2002 Plume Books

The Five Points – The history of New York City's Most Notorious Neighbourhood – Charles River Editors

Folksongs and Ballads Popular in Ireland – volume 1 – edited and arranged by John Loesberg – 1979 Ossian Publications

The Gangs of New York – Herbert Asbury – 1927

Hand-book for friendly visitors among the poor. Compiled and arranged by the Charity Organization Society of the City of New York – 1883

Images of America – Dowagiac – Steven Arseneau and Ann Thompson – Arcadia 2005

Improving health care of the poor: the New York City experience – Eli Ginzberg, Howard Berliner, and Miriam Ostow – 1997

The Irish in America – edited Michael Coffey – 1997 Disney Enterprises

The Irish Famine – a documentary Colm Tóibín and Diarmaid Ferriter – 2001 Thomas Dunne Books

Journeys of Hope: Orphan Train Riders: Their Own Stories – edited by Mary Ellen Johnson

Low Life – Luc Sante – Farrar, Straus & Giroux 1991

The New York Irish – Edited by Ronald H. Bayor and Timothy J. Meagher – 1996 The Johns Hopkins University Press

Orphan Trains & Their Precious Cargo: The Life's Work of Rev. H.D. Clarke –compiled by Clark Kidder – 2012

Orphan Train Riders – A brief history of the Orphan Train Era (1854-1929) – Tom Riley 2005 Heritage books

Orphan Train Riders Their Own Stories compiled by Mary Ellen Johnson – Orphan Train Heritage Society of America 2001

Orphan Trains – researching American history ed Jeanne Munn Bracken – Discovery Enterprises 2002

The Orphan Trains: Placing Out in America – Marilyn Irvin Holt 1992 University of Nebraska Press

Orphan Trains – Stephen O'Connor 2001 Koughton Mifflin Company

The Poor Among Us – Ralph da Costa Nunez – White Tiger Press 2013

The Prendergast Letters – Correspondence from Famine Era Ireland 1840-1850 edited by Shelley Barber University of Massachusetts Press 2006

Tales of Five Points in Nineteenth Century New York vol 11 – an interpretive approach to understanding working class life – John Milner Associates

A twentieth Century History of Cass County, Michigan L H Glover, editor – 1906 Lewis Pub. Co

Vocabulum or The Rogue's Lexicon – George W. Matsell 1859

Cloud County History Museum

Dowagiac Museum

Museum of the City of New York

National Orphan Train Museum and Research Center, Concordia, Kansas.

The Records of the Children's Aid Society, The New York Historical Society.

The Library of Congress

New York City Vital Records by Roger Joslyn
www.ancestry.com/wiki/index.php?title=New_York_Vital_Records

Irish Popular songs with English Metrical Translation – Edward Walsh – Dublin

www.archive.org/details/irishpopularsong00walsuoft

www.civilwar.org/education/history/faq

www.dowagiacmuseum.info

www.history.com/this-day-in-history/congress-passes-civil-war-conscription-act

www.irishmusicforever.com

nineduane.queenitsy.com/fulton.html

www.orphantraindepot.com/OrphanTrainHistory.html

www.pbs.org/wgbh/amex/orphan/

www.spartacus.schoolnet.co.uk

www.swmidirectory.org/History_of_Cass_County.html

en.wikipedia.org/wiki/Orphan_Train

ABOUT THE AUTHOR

Rosemary J Kind writes because she has to. You could take almost anything away from her except her pen and paper. Failing to stop after the book that everyone has in them, she has gone on to publish books in both non-fiction and fiction, the latter including novels, humour, short stories and poetry. She also regularly produces magazine articles in a number of areas and writes regularly for the dog press.

As a child she was desolate when at the age of 10 her then teacher would not believe that her poem based on 'Stig of the Dump' was her own work and she stopped writing poetry for several years as a result. She was persuaded to continue by the invitation to earn a little extra pocket money by 'assisting' others to produce the required poems for English homework!

Always one to spot an opportunity, she started school newspapers and went on to begin providing paid copy to her local newspaper at the age of 16.

For twenty years she followed a traditional business career, before seeing the error of her ways and leaving it all behind to pursue her writing full-time.

She spends her life discussing her plots with the characters in her head and her faithful dogs, who always put the opposing arguments when there are choices to be made.

Always willing to take on challenges that sensible people regard as impossible, she set up the short story download site Alfie Dog Fiction in 2012 and has built it to being one of the largest in the world, representing over 300 authors and carrying over 1600 short stories. Her hobby is developing the Entlebucher Mountain Dog in the UK and when she brought her beloved Alfie back from Belgium he was only the tenth in the country.

She started writing Alfie's Diary as an Internet blog the day Alfie arrived to live with her, intending to continue for a year or two. Eleven years later it goes from strength to strength and has been repeatedly named as one of the top ten dog blogs in the UK.

For more details about the author please visit her website at www.rjkind.co.uk For more details about her dog then you're better visiting www.alfiedog.me.uk.

Alfie Dog Fiction

Taking your imagination for a walk

For hundreds of short stories, collections
and novels visit our website at
www.alfiedog.com

Join us on Facebook
http://www.facebook.com/AlfieDogLimited